EDWARD MARSTON was born and brought up in South Wales. A full-time writer for over forty years, he has worked in radio, film, television and theatre and is a former chairman of the Crime Writers' Association. Prolific and highly successful, he is equally at home writing children's books or literary criticism, plays or biographies.

www.edwardmarston.com

By Edward Marston

THE BRACEWELL MYSTERIES

The Queen's Head • The Merry Devils • The Trip to Jerusalem
The Nine Giants • The Mad Courtesan • The Silent Woman
The Roaring Boy • The Laughing Hangman • The Fair Maid of Bohemia
The Wanton Angel • The Devil's Apprentice • The Bawdy Basket
The Vagabond Clown • The Counterfeit Crank • The Malevolent Comedy
The Princess of Denmark

THE RAILWAY DETECTIVE SERIES

The Railway Detective • The Excursion Train
The Railway Viaduct • The Iron Horse
Murder on the Brighton Express • The Silver Locomotive Mystery
Railway to the Grave • Blood on the Line
The Stationmaster's Farewell • Peril on the Royal Train
A Ticket to Oblivion

Inspector Colbeck's Casebook:
Thirteen Tales from the Railway Detective

The Railway Detective Omnibus:
The Railway Detective, The Excursion Train, The Railway Viaduct

THE CAPTAIN RAWSON SERIES

Soldier of Fortune • Drums of War • Fire and Sword
Under Siege • A Very Murdering Battle

THE RESTORATION SERIES

The King's Evil • The Amorous Nightingale • The Repentant Rake
The Frost Fair • The Parliament House • The Painted Lady

THE HOME FRONT DETECTIVE SERIES

A Bespoke Murder • Instrument of Slaughter
Five Dead Canaries • Deeds of Darkness

The Wanton Angel

An Elizabethan Mystery

EDWARD MARSTON

Allison & Busby Limited
12 Fitzroy Mews
London W1T 6DW
www.allisonandbusby.com

First published in 1999.
This paperback edition published by Allison & Busby in 2014.

Copyright © 1999 by EDWARD MARSTON

A CIP catalogue record for this book is available from
the British Library.

ISBN 978-0-7490-1682-1

10 9 8 7 6 5 4 3 2 1

Typeset in 10.5/16 pt Sabon by
Allison & Busby Ltd.

The paper used for this Allison & Busby publication
has been produced from trees that have been legally sourced
from well-managed and credibly certified forests.

Printed and bound by
CPI Group (UK) Ltd, Croydon, CR0 4YY

*To Tom Foster who first introduced me
to the joys and frustrations of theatre.*

And which stage shall contain in length forty and three
foot of lawful assize and in breadth to extend to the
middle of the yard of the said house. The same stage
to be paled in below with good, strong and sufficient
new oaken boards, and likewise the lower storey of
the said frame withinside; and the same lower storey
to be also laid over with strong iron spikes.

Contract for building of the Fortune theatre,
1600.

Chapter One

Edmund Hoode was shouldering his way through the crowd in Gracechurch Street when it happened. The realisation took him completely by surprise and brought him to a sudden halt. He did not even notice that he was standing in a puddle of water or that his shoes were attracting the sniffing nostrils of a stray dog. Truth hit him like a shaft of sunlight breaking through the dark clouds above. He was happy. Gloriously and seriously happy. For the first time in several years, he was unaccountably filled with a pure contentment. It was a small miracle. On a dull, cold, wind-blown morning, amid the jostling elbows and deafening noise of a bustling London thoroughfare, he experienced a quiet joy which took his breath away.

It was baffling. Hoode was no stranger to the exhilaration of lust, still less to the pulsing delights of love, but here was ecstasy of a wholly different order. It was no brief flame of passion which would burn itself out and leave him in the pit of depression which was his normal abode. Indeed, romantic entanglement was, for once, markedly absent from his life and had no bearing on the feelings which surged within him. What he now basked in was a deep and satisfying inner glow. Edmund Hoode, the loyal, hapless, overworked, teased and tormented playwright with Westfield's Men, was enjoying a peace of mind that blocked out all else.

It took a sharp nudge in the ribs to bring him out of his reverie. The old woman whose basket of fruit had struck him so hard and so carelessly apologised gruffly, but Hoode waved her away with a forgiving smile. Nothing could dent his sense of pleasure. As his legs began to move again in the direction of the Queen's Head, he tried to piece together in his mind the constituent elements of his happiness. How had he managed to stumble into this rare condition?

More to the point, how long would it last?

'Well-met, Edmund!'

'Good morrow, Lucius!'

'You are an early bird today.'

'I could say the same of you, my friend.'

'I take instruction from my master. In this, as in all other things, he sets a good example for me to follow.'

There was no irony in his voice. Lucius Kindell was a model of sincerity. Young, keen and fresh-faced, he openly acknowledged Hoode as his inspiration and was a most willing apprentice. Hoode was at once touched and flattered. Kindell was a talented poet, a University wit whose brilliance at Oxford had earned him a wide reputation and whose fledgling dramas had enormous promise. Under the guidance of a veteran playwright, that promise was already bearing fruit.

When Lucius Kindell was first introduced to him, Hoode had been wary and defensive. Oxford and Cambridge graduates tended to be wilful and arrogant, reluctant to accept criticism of their plays and quick to mock those, like Hoode himself, who lacked a University education. Expecting to build a huge instant reputation, they were not prepared to put in the years of patient toil on the stage as they mastered their craft. Lucius Kindell, by contrast, was a modest, unassuming and conscientious pupil who was anxious to learn all that he could from a superior playwright. He had a streak of mischief in him and was a gifted satirist but he had none of the intellectual bumptiousness which so often marred the characters of self-styled University wits.

Hoode's reservations about him soon fled away. Kindell was not only a skilful dramatist and a congenial collaborator, but he brought the best out of his teacher. Hoode's own work actually improved, partly because he set about it with new enthusiasm and partly because he wanted to impress his young charge even more. Lucius Kindell's arrival on the scene was without doubt a contributory cause of the other's happiness. Though far from old himself, Hoode found himself taking a paternal interest in the latest addition to the company's playwrights. Kindell was the son he seemed doomed never to father.

'I had a sleepless night,' admitted Kindell.

'That is only to be expected,' said Hoode, reassuringly. 'Every true poet is justifiably nervous on the eve of the performance of his play.'

'Our play, Edmund. *Our* play.'

'You conceived the drama. I merely acted as a kind of midwife to bring it squealing into the world.'

'You did far more than that,' said Kindell with a glint of admiration in his eyes. 'You transformed it. What I provided were some clever ideas in a shapeless tragedy. You fashioned it into a real drama. Any virtues it possesses were put there by Edmund Hoode.'

'Thank you, Lucius.'

'You are my mentor.'

'That role has brought me intense pride.'

'I sit at your feet.'

Kindell somehow managed to sound grateful without being obsequious. Hoode was delighted that someone appreciated him but he was also conscious of the debt he owed to his young friend. Kindell had concentrated his mind on subjects which he normally avoided. Known for his rumbustious comedies, Hoode had worked with his collaborator on two dark tragedies, both of which explored the power of religion to save and also to pervert. Their first play had been a modest success, their second joint offering, *The Insatiate Duke*, was due to receive its premiere at the Queen's Head that afternoon.

The young playwright had brought a spiritual dimension into the life of Edmund Hoode which had been woefully missing. Instead of penning yet another rustic farce with

12

romantic subplots, Hoode was responding to the deeper challenge of tragedy and confronting far more serious issues. Significantly, his resort to prayer had been more willing, his attendance at church more regular. Writing about the struggle between Christianity and its detractors had brought him substantially closer to his Maker. Hoode was uplifted. He felt cleansed.

Lucius Kindell was apprehensive about the performance.

'How will *The Insatiate Duke* be received, do you think?' he wondered. 'Will they approve of its theme?'

'They must,' said Hoode. 'It is a fine play.'

'And if they do not?'

'Put that thought out of your mind, Lucius.'

'Master Firethorn speaks well of the piece,' said the other, trying to instil confidence into himself. 'So does Master Gill – since you put in those additional songs for him. And the most reliable judgement of all is that of Nicholas Bracewell. He has nothing but praise for my work.'

'And so do I. Fear not.'

'My whole body trembles.'

'Applause will soon still you.'

'If the play merits applause.'

'It does,' insisted Hoode. 'Trust me, Lucius.'

'I do. Implicitly.'

Hoode put an affectionate arm around him and guided his friend into the inn yard. Hurrying towards them with head down, a buxom figure in a flurry of skirts all but collided with them and forced the couple to break apart. Rose Marwood stopped, looked up, blushed, dropped a vestigial curtsey and stammered an apology.

'The fault is entirely on our side,' said Hoode with beaming gallantry. 'We are sorry to block your path.'

'Thank you, Master Hoode,' she muttered.

'Do not let us detain you.'

'That would be too unmannerly,' added Kindell.

They stepped aside to allow Rose Marwood to scurry on past them and lose herself in the crowd. The landlord's daughter was a pretty wench with a shining face and long dark hair which streamed out beneath her cap. She had a bloom on her which habitually turned the heads of the company and Kindell was not immune to her nubile charms. He gazed after her with the fondness of rising curiosity.

'What a splendid creature she is!' he mused.

'Who?'

'Why, Rose Marwood, of course.'

'A pleasant enough girl, to be sure.'

'She is a young woman in her prime,' said Kindell. 'I never see her but I think what a blessing it is that she does not resemble either of her parents. They are ogres whereas their daughter is a portrait of delight.'

Hoode was surprised. 'Is she?'

'Surely, you must have noticed.'

'Rose Marwood?'

'Who else? Low-born, perhaps, but quite lovely.'

'My God!'

Edmund Hoode had mild convulsions as another revelation hit him. Rose Marwood had been inches away from him yet he had been untroubled either by desire or guilt. Her shapely body usually aroused at least a distant lust in him and he was forever haunted by the memory of a time when he had rashly bestowed his affections on her to the point of writing a sonnet in praise of her. Rose Marwood's inability to read had rescued him from real embarrassment and he never met her without being reminded of his earlier folly.

Until now, that is. Proximity to those deliciously full ruby lips, those gleaming white teeth, those dimpled cheeks, those sparkling eyes and all the other attributes of her urgent femininity no longer unsettled him. Edmund Hoode was impervious to her and, by extension, to the seductive presence of women in general. He had finally conquered his demons. The hideous perils of romantic passion were a thing of the past. That was the insight he now gained. Unencumbered by his disastrous involvement with the fairer sex, his life at last had meaning, direction and dignity.

Happiness was celibacy.

The Insatiate Duke presented a similar argument in dramatic terms. Debauchery was the road to despair. Virtue lay in monastic solitude. The rewards of virginity outweighed all of the temporary pleasures of concupiscence. It was not the most endearing message to thrust upon an audience which had come in search of rousing entertainment and which contained a fair scattering of prostitutes, courtesans, wayward wives and lecherous gallants, but it was offered in such a cunning and persuasive way as to sweep all resistance aside. Dark, powerful and harrowing, *The Insatiate Duke* was nevertheless shot through with moments of wild comedy. Laughter was mixed liberally with sorrow.

New facets of Edmund Hoode's talents were on display. Even his closest friends in the company were astonished.

'What *has* got into him?' asked Lawrence Firethorn.

'He excels himself,' said Nicholas Bracewell.

'I have never seen Edmund attack a part with such verve. The wonder of it is, he all but outshines me, Nick. Me, the appointed star in this particular firmament, the smiling villain, the insatiate and tyrannical Duke of Parma. Humbled by a creeping Cardinal, a pale-faced eunuch in a red robe.'

'Edmund's finest hour.'

'In one of his best pieces.'

'Lucius Kindell must take some credit for that,' Nicholas reminded him. 'They collaborated on the play.'

'True,' agreed Firethorn, 'but Edmund Hoode deserves all the plaudits for Cardinal Boccherini. It is the performance of his lifetime. The part fits him like a glove. Heavens, man, he actually stole a scene from me.'

'He will steal another if you miss your entrance,' warned Nicholas, one ear on the progress of the play. 'Cardinal Boccherini has come to confront you.'

'A worthy adversary, indeed!'

A fanfare sounded and Cosimo, Duke of Parma, strode out onto the stage with his entourage. He and the Cardinal were soon engaged in a long, heated debate about moral responsibility. Lawrence Firethorn was at his best in the leading role, sleek and sinister, unperturbed by the charges levelled at him and justifying his villainy in the most shameless way. Edmund Hoode could not match his raw power but he brought a nobility and sincerity to his role which commanded attention.

The verbal duel between the two actors was a mixture of fury and eloquence. Italian cardinals rarely gained sympathy from a Protestant audience such as the one which filled the yard at the Queen's Head that day but Cardinal Boccherini was an exception to the rule. Spectators were cheering him on. They were accustomed to watching brilliant performances from Lawrence Firethorn, the actor-manager with Westfield's Men, but they had never seen Edmund Hoode, so often confined to a cameo role, reach such heights.

Nicholas Bracewell watched from behind the scenes. Owen Elias stood beside him and shook his head in wonderment. A swaggering actor of great versatility, the Welshman was quick to admire the abilities of his colleagues.

'Has he been drinking, Nick?' he asked.

'Edmund?'

'Is that ale we can hear or canary wine?'

'Neither, Owen. He is as sober as you and I.'

'Then something he has eaten has put that fight into him. Find out what it was and the whole company can dine off it henceforth. Let us all profit from this magical sustenance.'

'Food and drink are not responsible,' said Nicholas.

'Then what?'

'See for yourself.'

'Witchcraft?'

17

'No, Owen.'

'Then he must be in love again.'

'I think not.'

'This shower of sparks is aimed at some pretty face up in the gallery, I wager. Edmund Hoode is ensnared once more.'

'Only by his art.'

'What say you?'

'That is all we are witnessing,' decided Nicholas with a quiet smile. 'Sheer histrionic skill.'

'Why have we never seen it in such abundance before?'

'He lacks your confidence.'

'Not any more, Nick. Listen to him. This cardinal has such a supple tongue that it could make me turn Roman Catholic and swear allegiance to the Pope.'

'Stand by!'

With a wave of his arm, Nicholas motioned two soldiers in armour forward. On their cue, they marched onto the stage and laid violent hands upon Cardinal Boccherini. The audience let out a communal gasp of shock. As the prelate was hauled off to the dungeon, spectators began to hiss and protest at the cruel treatment meted out to him. The Duke of Parma revelled in their disapproval and gloried in his wickedness. He also took full advantage of his finest scene in the play.

In calling Duke Cosimo to account for his sinfulness, the fearless Cardinal had been trying to protect the virtue of the beauteous Emilia, a novice from the convent who had caught the Duke's lascivious eye. Elected to be the

Duke's latest victim, she was now defenceless. What Cosimo did not know, however, was that Emilia was in fact his own daughter, conceived in a moment of lust with a lady-in-waiting at the Milanese Court. When Emilia was summoned to the Duke's bedchamber to serve his pleasure, a groan of horror went around the inn yard. Spectators were aware of the true relationship between the couple. Not only was a helpless virgin about to be defiled, she would be forced unwittingly to commit incest.

Richard Honeydew, the youngest of the apprentices, gave a moving performance as Emilia; brave, honest, devout but hopelessly caught in a web of corruption. His tearful pleas for mercy were heart-rending to all but the cruel Duke, who demanded that Emilia surrender her body to him. The novice took a deep breath before delivering her valedictory speech.

> 'Hold still, dread lord.
> Duty and conscience wrestle in my mind.
> I owe obedience to a royal Duke,
> The voice of death in Parma here,
> A mighty power before whom subjects quake
> And even high-born nobles bend the knee
> In supplication. My duty tells me
> Straight I should comply with your imperious
> Wish, abjure vain protest, set modesty
> Aside, cast off these holy garments now,
> Lie in thy bed and submit me to my
> Grisly fate. But conscience rebels against

This foul, disgusting and debasing act.
I have a higher duty to myself
And God, who made me and who guides me here
In this fell hour. No royal lecher will
Defile me, betray my most sacred vows
And take my virgin purity away.
I am a bride of Christ and will not serve
The carnal lust of man, whate'er his rank.
Away, thou hideous beast that preys on
Innocence! Sooner than live to give thee
Satisfaction, I die upon this bed,
Pure and unsullied to the end as now
I join my God and my salvation.'

Before Cosimo, Duke of Parma could stop her, Emilia put a tiny flask of poison to her lips and drained it in one gulp. The effect was startling. After convulsing with sudden pain, she fell across the bed and swiftly expired. The Duke suspected a ruse and shook her angrily to revive her but the girl was now beyond his reach. In a fit of pique, he flung her down on the bed only to be disturbed by his steward with the news that, under torture, the Cardinal had admitted that Emilia was the Duke's own illegitimate child, a secret he had gleaned in the confessional box from the mother who had begged him to keep it from Emilia herself.

Cosimo was distraught. He had, in effect, murdered his own daughter. Remorse finally entered his heart and he knelt beside the corpse in an attitude of grief, weeping real tears as he blamed himself for the tragedy and repented his wickedness. Lawrence Firethorn was superb. He achieved the impossible. Having outraged the spectators only minutes before with his merciless treatment of Emilia, he now contrived to win their sympathy for his plight. When he announced that he was not fit to live among decent, Christian people, he pulled out his dagger and plunged it deep into his heart before falling at the feet of the daughter whom he had tried to ravish.

The steward summoned servants and both bodies were carried from the stage with great dignity. A stunned silence followed the end of the play and it was only when the actor-manager led his troupe out again to take their bow that the spectators were released from their state of shock. Thunderous applause greeted the company. Lawrence Firethorn beamed, Barnaby Gill glowed, Owen Elias grinned broadly, James Ingram felt his blood pulsing and even George Dart, the tiny assistant stagekeeper, a reluctant actor who was required to play no less than six different supporting roles, all of them beyond his competence, managed a smirk of satisfaction.

Nicholas Bracewell was delighted with the warm reception accorded to *The Insatiate Duke* and he threw a glance up to the gallery where a proud Lucius Kindell, overcome with emotion, was clapping as hard as anyone. The afternoon had been a great personal triumph for him but he was the first to concede that someone else deserved even more praise. Edmund Hoode had been heroic. Not only had he turned a serviceable play into a memorable theatrical experience, he had given a performance that blazed into the minds of the onlookers. Firethorn, Gill and the others might strut and preen and blow elaborate kisses of gratitude but the man who was enjoying the ovation the most was Cardinal Boccherini.

Poised and impassive, a very monument of Christian virtue, he gave no hint of the laughter which bubbled away inside him. Edmund Hoode's happiness slipped into delirium.

The Insatiate Duke was good for business. Spectators who had been alternately excited and harrowed by the play now poured into the taproom of the Queen's Head to slake their thirst, to discuss the wondrous tragedy they had witnessed or to calm their shattered nerves with strong drink. The inn was packed to capacity and its drawers and servingmen were stretched to meet the needs of the seething mass of customers.

Any other landlord would have been thrilled by the sight of so much ale and wine being sold but not Alexander Marwood. Seasoned in misery, wedded to pessimism and lacking the merest spectre of light in the darkness of his existence, he found even the infrequent moments of good fortune occasions for complaint rather than celebration.

'Look at them!' he moaned. 'They will drink us dry. They will eat us out of house and home. They will *consume* us!'

'We will make a tidy profit,' said his wife.

'But at what cost, Sybil?'

'None to you, sir. You simply have to look on.'

'Aye,' said Marwood with a morose leer. 'Look on and suffer. With so large and unruly a crowd as this, I fear for my benches, I worry about my tables, I am desperately concerned for the safety of my furniture. Damage will soon come, mark my words. An affray will soon start. I do not simply look on, dear wife. I quail, I pine, I suffer!'

Sybil Marwood inflated her chest, folded her arms beneath her surging bosom and drew herself up to her full height.

'There will be no trouble while I am here, Alexander.'

The landlord nodded in agreement at the grim boast. Big-boned and brawny, his wife had a basilisk stare which could quell the wildest of revellers and a tongue which could lash with the force of a whip. As one who had suffered both her stare and her stinging rebuke on a regular basis, Marwood could appreciate why she held such sway over their patrons. Even in such a rowdy assembly as the one before them, Sybil loomed large. While she remained, the merriment would always stay good-humoured and never spill over into violence.

'There is one consolation,' sighed Marwood.

'What is that, husband?'

'Rose is not here to get caught up in all this.'

'She should be,' said his wife, irritably. 'To serve this many mouths, we need every pair of hands we can get. Where is the girl? Rose's place is here.'

'Be grateful that she is elsewhere, Sybil.'

'Why?'

'Because of the relief it yields.'

'What relief? You talk in riddles.'

'I would hate any daughter of mine to be pitched into this sea of iniquity,' he said with a shiver. 'Drunken men are dangerous. Let a woman pass through a crowd like this and she would be groped and kissed unmercifully. Rose is spared that.'

'Nonsense!' snorted the other. 'I have pushed my way into the heart of this throng and not a single finger was laid upon my person, womanly though it is. There is no danger.'

'To you, perhaps not. But Rose's case is different. This taproom would be a place of dire peril to her. The girl is still young and innocent, Sybil. She lacks your experience and strength of mind. You are a mature woman. Our daughter has none of your . . . of your . . . of your . . .'

His voice trailed away as the wifely stare transfixed him to the spot and deprived him of coherent speech. Marwood felt the familiar icicles forming once more on his spine.

'Go on,' she urged through gritted teeth. 'My what?'

Marwood mouthed words that refused to be translated into sound. Sweat moistened his brow. He essayed an appeasing smile but it looked more like a bold sneer. A violent twitch broke out on his lower lip, another on his right ear and a third on his left eyebrow. He slapped at his face wildly as if trying to swat a series of troublesome flies but he only succeeded in dispersing the twitches to new locations. Additional activity was soon set off until his whole visage was in a state of frenzied animation. Unprepossessing at the best of times, Marwood was now positively grotesque.

Sybil did not let him off the hook of her displeasure.

'Rose does not have my *what*?' she demanded.

He wanted to say 'authority' but the word was stillborn on the sawdust of his tongue. After experimenting with a dozen other words which might have assuaged her, he finally found one which consented to be spoken aloud.

'Beauty,' he croaked.

It was the most ridiculous and inappropriate word to use of the gargoyle which confronted him and Marwood realised it at once, letting out a death rattle of a laugh at the sheer absurdity of such a description. What he had once ruinously mistaken for beauty in his wife had, on closer acquaintance, revealed itself to be no more than a deceptive willingness to please masking a hard-edged and unlovely countenance.

'Do you mock me, sir?' she snarled.

'No, my love. Of course not, my angel.'

'My beauty?'

'Yes,' he gabbled. 'Your beauty, your beauty.'

'Rose does not have my beauty?'

'True, Sybil. So true, so true!'

'So false, you wretch! she scolded. 'Are you blind? Are you insane? Beauty is the one thing that Rose *has* inherited from me. Everyone has remarked upon it. Everyone but you, that is. Rose may lack my grace but she is as beautiful as her mother.'

'Yes, yes!' He was ready to agree to any illusion.

'A moment ago, you denied it.'

'I was wrong, Sybil.'

'As always.'

'As always,' he echoed gloomily.

Marwood had learnt to take the line of least resistance against his wife. It was the only way to make life under the same roof as her at all tolerable. Since he could never hope for any pleasure in bed with her, he devoted his energies to reducing the pain which she routinely afflicted on him. How was it, he often asked himself, that motherhood seemed to soften most women yet had had the opposite effect on Sybil, turning her instead into a flinty harridan? It was unjust.

'Have you spoken with Master Firethorn yet?' she asked.

'I am on my way to do so even now.'

'Keep him to the terms of the contract.'

'Left to me, there would *be* no contract,' he grumbled. 'We do not need that band of lecherous actors, prancing about on a stage in our yard, performing lewd, ungodly plays and bringing all the dregs of London into our premises.'

'No,' she said with heavy sarcasm, 'and we do not need money to buy food, drink and shelter for ourselves and our daughter. Westfield's Men make the Queen's Head one the most popular inns in the city – as you can well see, Alexander. Look around you, man! These people are not here for the dubious thrill of meeting you. The players brought them in, which is why we must renew the contract with Westfield's Men.'

'On the terms we stipulate.'

'That goes without saying.'

'I will certainly say it to Master Firethorn,' vowed her husband. 'And to Nicholas Bracewell. He will be party to the discussion.'

'Dear Nicholas!' cooed his wife with an almost girlish giggle. 'Such a gentleman in every way! How can you rail at the company when they have someone like Nicholas Bracewell in their ranks. I tell you this, sir. If I could have the choosing of a husband for Rose, I would look no further than him. It would be a joy to have him in the family.'

'Joy?' he repeated dully. 'What is that?'

At that moment, Sybil caught a glimpse of her missing daughter through the window and the frost returned at once to her face and voice. She brushed her husband roughly aside.

'Out of my way, sir. I want to speak to Rose.'

'Keep her out of this bear pit,' he said, gazing in dismay around the taproom. 'Her virtue would be in danger.'

After congratulating the company on its success, and after heaping especial praise upon Edmund Hoode and Lucius Kindell, the joint authors of *The Insatiate Duke*, Lawrence Firethorn fortified himself with a glass of Canary wine in the tiring-house before leading a small deputation to the private room where they had agreed to meet the landlord. Barnaby Gill and Edmund Hoode went off with the actor-manager because they were principal sharers in the company and had a major stake in its future. At Firethorn's insistence, Nicholas Bracewell was also part of the group because his counsel was always wise and because he was the only member of Westfield's Men who could mollify and deal effectively with Marwood. There was the inevitable complaint from Gill that the book holder was merely a hired man and not a sharer but his petulant objections were quashed by Hoode and overridden by Firethorn.

When they reached the room, it was Ezekiel Stonnard who let them in. A big, round, corpulent, unctuous man in his fifties with a permanent smirk, Stonnard was Alexander Marwood's lawyer and an old adversary of Westfield's Men. He became proprietary and waved a flabby hand of welcome.

'Come in, come in, sirs,' he said. 'My client will be here in a moment. Pray, do take a seat.'

'We will stand,' replied Firethorn. 'This business will not take long and we have a triumph to celebrate.'

'What triumph might that be?' asked the lawyer.

'My performance,' said Gill, involuntarily.

'Were you in the play, Barnaby?' teased Firethorn. 'You made such little impression, I quite forgot you were there.'

'My jigs earned an ovation, Lawrence.'

'The audience was so pleased when they ended.'

'Both of you gave superb performances,' said the ever-generous Hoode, intervening in the ritual bickering between the two outstanding talents in the troupe. 'Lucius and I were thrilled that our play provided you both with such ideal roles in which to strut and dazzle.'

'Yes,' agreed Firethorn. 'Barnaby strutted, I dazzled.'

'Did you not see the play, Master Stonnard?' said Nicholas, politely. 'Since you came here to discuss our continued lease on the Queen's Head, I wonder that you did not take the opportunity to watch Westfield's Men at work.'

'I am not fond of such entertainment,' said the lawyer, superciliously. 'Theatre is an unnecessary diversion in my view but my view is irrelevant here. All that concerns me is your agreement to the terms of the new contract.' The door opened. 'Ah, here is our genial host! Good day, sir.'

Anyone less genial than Alexander Marwood was difficult to imagine. He came through the door with a frown which changed into a scowl when he saw the four visitors ranged against him.

'Why did you not bring the whole company?' he taunted.

'We *are* the company,' said Firethorn. 'In essence.'

'And excluding our hired man,' said Gill with a dismissive flick of the hand in the direction of Nicholas.

Hoode leapt to his friend's defence. 'Nick is a vital member of this troupe,' he said, 'and he has proved it time and again. We could well survive without Barnaby Gill but without Nicholas Bracewell, we would be utterly lost.'

'I share those sentiments!' affirmed Firethorn.

'Perhaps you would care to share some interest in this,' said Stonnard, producing some documents from inside a leather satchel he was holding. 'I take it that you have now had time to study the contract in detail?'

'We have,' said Firethorne. 'So has our lawyer.'

'What is his opinion?'

'He found little to cavil at, Master Stonnard.'

'Then let us get it signed and over with,' urged Marwood.

'You know my view of this unfortunate arrangement. I wish I had never encountered Westfield's Men. But other imperatives are involved here,' he continued, thinking of his wife. 'If the contract must be signed, let us do it with all due speed then I can get back to the taproom before it is torn asunder by that rabble.'

'But there has been no negotiation,' argued Firethorn.

'Negotiation?' said Marwood.

'Yes. There are several clauses I wish to amend.'

'Take care, sir,' said Stonnard, stepping smartly forward and sending his double chin into a wobble. 'I will not permit any legal quibbles. My client and I spent many hours drafting this contract. It may not be rewritten to satisfy your whims.'

Firethorn bristled. 'They are demands not whims.'

'And complaints,' added Gill. 'The tiring-house stinks.'

'Only when your players are in there,' said Marwood.

Gill struck a pose. 'The place is never swept from one year's end to another. Cleanliness is next to godliness. If I did not have my pomander beside me, I would die of the stench. Let it be entered in the contract that the landlord undertakes to make his premises more wholesome.'

'They *are* wholesome!' wailed Marwood.

'Barnaby spoke only in jest,' soothed Hoode.

'No, I did not!' said Gill.

'This is getting us nowhere,' said the lawyer, waving the contract in the air. 'We are here to examine an important document, not to worry about some phantom smell.'

'Stink,' said Gill. 'A positive reek of decay.'

'You merely caught a whiff of your own performance,' said Firethorn with a chuckle.

Gill flared up, Firethorn baited him afresh and Hoode did his best to calm them down. It was left to Nicholas Bracewell to introduce a serious note into the proceedings.

'If I may be allowed to say a word,' he began, 'then I would ask you to first to consider the limitation of time in the new contract. Six months is not acceptable to us. It gives us no security of tenure. A year is the least that Westfield's Men deserve, bearing in mind that we do not play at all for some months and are therefore paying rent for premises we are unable to use. But if we know that we have a home for at least one year, it enables Master Firethorn and the other sharers to make decisions about the company in the longer term.'

'Well spoken, Nick!' said Firethorn.

'Why stop at one year when we might nominate two?' said Nicholas, 'Or even three? It would save the expense on a lawyer if the contract no longer comes up for such regular renewal and it would show good faith on both sides. Would you at least consider two years?'

'Three!' boomed Firethorn.

'Never!' said Marwood. 'It is like a life sentence.'

'We could never agree to three years,' said Stonnard. 'Nor could I condone any action impelled by the base motive of avoiding a lawyer's legitimate fees.'

'Yet they are exorbitant,' said his client.

'Ezekiel Stonnard always gives value for money, sir.'

'We believe that Westfield's Men do likewise,' said

Nicholas, persuasively, 'and the Queen's Head has proved an excellent venue for our work. Permit me to explain why.'

Lawyer and landlord were treated to a long but cogent description of the company's achievements and the benefits which they brought to all parties. Firethorn and Hoode were happy to let their book holder act as their advocate and even Gill, a brilliant clown on stage but a carping critic of everyone and everything when off it, came to admire the skill with which Nicholas was marshalling his arguments. Marwood writhed in discomfort throughout and Ezekiel Stonnard made several failed attempts to interrupt but Nicholas had hit his stride and the words flowed in a continuous stream.

Concessions were slowly wrung from Stonnard who, in turn, advised Marwood to accept them. To the agonised landlord, each concession was a tooth being drawn from his mouth by red-hot pincers and he groaned accordingly but the contract was finally agreed upon, signed and witnessed. Marwood fled in terror, Ezekiel Stonnard went after him in pursuit of his fee and the others were left to celebrate. Firethorn threw his arms around Nicholas and hugged him gratefully.

'Well done, dear heart! You are our salvation.'

'I simply reasoned with them,' said Nicholas, modestly.

'But with such skill and passion, Nick,' said Hoode. 'You should have been a lawyer. You could haggle with the best.'

'I was trained as a merchant, remember. Haggling is in my blood. The contract has been amended to suit your demands. I just wish I could have brought them around to the notion of extending it for longer than a year.'

'A year is double what they first offered, Nick,' said Firethorn, rubbing his hands with satisfaction. 'It is such a relief to know that Westfield's Men have a home for another twelve months. The Queen's Head is a verminous inn with an even more verminous landlord but I love the place!'

'So do we all, Lawrence,' said Hoode.

'Yes,' added Gill. 'I have scaled the heights of my art on the stage in that yard and I will do so again and again.'

'Thanks to Nick,' said Firethorn. 'Come, lads. To the taproom. We have so much to celebrate. Marwood has been routed once again. Nothing can shift us from here now. Westfield's Men are safe for another whole year.'

Alexander Marwood's misery was compounded by the sight of the commotion in the taproom. Rowdiness was threatening to tip over into a certain affray and his wife was not there to quell the riotous behaviour. Shaking off the pursuing lawyer, he ran on spindly legs through the entire inn until he eventually found Sybil. She was in her daughter's bedchamber, standing over the tearful girl with an expression that combined sorrow, apprehension and a naked lust for revenge.

When Marwood burst in, his wife silenced him with an icy glare and the landlord became a standing statue.

Sybil closed and locked the door before she spoke.

'Have you signed that contract yet?' she asked.

'Just now.'

'Tear it up!'

'What?'

'Tear the contract to pieces!'

'But it is a legal document.'

'I do not care it is a royal proclamation,' growled his wife, giving full vent to her rage. 'I'll not have Westfield's Men trespassing on our property a moment longer. Destroy the contract, Alexander. Throw them out. They have ruined us.'

'How, Sybil?'

His eye fell on his weeping daughter and his heart missed a beat. Rose looked up at him with a mixture of penitence and despair. Her father's worst fear was finally confirmed. His wife hissed in his ear with the force of the West Wind.

'Get them out of our inn – today!'

Chapter Two

Lucius Kindell was mystified by the amiable clamour in the taproom of the Queen's Head. He shook his head in disbelief.

'It is perverse,' he said.

'What is?' asked Owen Elias.

'This merriment. This unwonted revelry. How can they possibly laugh so after such a dark tragedy?'

'It is the laughter of relief,' said the Welshman before emptying the remains of his ale in one loud gulp. 'Confronted with so much death in *The Insatiate Duke*, they want to remind themselves that they are still alive.'

Kindell was unconvinced. 'Unless it be that our play had no real hold on the audience. It amused them for a couple of hours then they shrugged it off like a garment for which they no longer have any use.'

'It held them, Lucius,' said Elias. 'By the throat.'

'Yes,' added Sylvester Pryde earnestly. 'This jollity is no

criticism of your play but a tribute to it.'

'I would like to think so,' said Kindell.

'You heard that applause,' said Pryde. 'You saw how both play and players were hailed. Our audience recognises quality. That is what *The Insatiate Duke* had in abundance. It is a tragedy with considerable power, is it not, Owen?'

'Indeed, it is, Sylvester.'

'Power and depth of feeling. It provokes thought.'

'And the urge to get drunk,' said a smiling Kindell.

'That is human nature.'

Sylvester Pryde gave him a friendly pat on the back and the young playwright was reassured. The two men had lifted his spirits, which, having soared to such heights during the performance, were bound to plunge somewhat in its wake. Owen Elias was an established member of the company and a sound judge of new plays yet it was Pryde's commendation which Kindell valued most even though the former was a relative newcomer to Westfield's Men. There was a supreme poise and confidence about the man which invested all he said with an instant veracity.

Westfield's Men had taken time to appreciate Sylvester Pryde's good qualities. When he first became a sharer with the company, he aroused both envy and hostility. Actors of far greater talent and experience were jealous of a man who was straightway elevated above them by dint of his financial investment and his fellow sharers resented what they saw as his easy arrogance, but, with a combination of industry and persuasion, Pryde soon brought both parties around to a more favourable view of him. Elias, one of his sternest critics at first, was now his closest friend in the company. The Welshman was cheerfully resigned to the fact that the handsome Pryde enjoyed far more success among the ladies than he himself.

Lucius Kindell was dazzled by the new sharer. It was not just the man's wit and intelligence which appealed to him. He was also impressed by Pryde's aristocratic mien and by the whiff of audacity which hung about him. Tall, slim and elegant, Sylvester Pryde was a traveller and a talker, a free spirit, a roving adventurer. His deficiencies as an actor were offset by a striking appearance which enabled him to decorate the stage superbly and by an irresistible charm. The cost and cut of his apparel suggested private wealth and this had estranged some of his colleagues at the outset until they saw how generous he was with his money. It won him universal acceptance.

Stroking a neatly trimmed beard, Pryde winked at Kindell.

'Are you content, Lucius?'

'Very content.'

'You are crowned with laurels today.'

'The play owes more to Edmund than to me.'

'I doubt that.'

'Yes,' agreed Elias. 'It is Edmund who is beholden to *you*, Lucius. Had you not created the role of Cardinal Boccherini, we would not have known what a brilliant actor Edmund really is. And, fine playwright though he may be, I am not sure that he would have tackled a theme as serious and weighty as this without your collaboration.'

'Enjoy your success,' advised Pryde.

'Savour each second of it, Lucius.'

'That is what I am doing,' said the playwright. 'This is truly the happiest day of my life.'

'Greater triumphs lie ahead,' predicted Elias.

'Far greater,' said Pryde with beaming certainty. 'A glittering career stands before you, my friend. We have chosen well, Lucius, you and I. Westfield's Men is the finest company in London and hence in the whole of Europe. My own poor skills as an actor have improved with each day I have spent in the company and your genius has found a true home.'

'I know, Sylvester,' said Kindell. 'Truly, I have been blessed. Westfield's Men are supreme.'

'Do you really believe that?' asked Elias.

'Yes, Owen!'

'Then buy us more ale and we will toast the company!' He let out a guffaw which rose above the tumult around him. The arrival of a familiar figure jerked him up from his bench. 'At last, Edmund! Where have you been? We have had to fight to keep you a place at the table. Sit here with us, man.'

'I am not sure that I may,' said Hoode nervously.

'May and must,' insisted the Welshman. 'Here is Lucius Kindell, your co-conspirator in brilliant invention, flushed with triumph and anxious to have you beside him to share in his joy. Sit, drink and surrender yourself.'

'I wish that I could.'

'Why, what is there to stop you?'

'A wailing landlord.'

'That maggoty Marwood?'

'Yes,' said Hoode, glancing over his shoulder as if expecting a fearsome blow to fall. 'He has cast a black shadow over our celebrations.'

'From what I hear,' said Pryde, 'that is nothing new. This hangdog landlord is the sworn enemy of pleasure. That hideous face of his was fashioned for Doomsday. Ignore him, Edmund.'

'If only I could.'

'What is his complaint against us now?' asked Kindell.

'I do not know, Lucius but I am sore troubled.'

Elias was baffled. When they left the stage after the performance, Edmund Hoode was glowing with joy and with a sense of fulfilment. They had never seen him so elated. A changed man now stood before them. Gone was the wide grin, the shining face and the sparkling eyes. Hoode was now in the grip of a melancholy of almost Marwoodian depth.

'Did you not renew our contract?' said Elias.

'Yes,' replied Hoode.

'And will we not play here for another six months?'

'A year, Owen.'

'Then why this moon-faced moping?'

'It was the ambush.'

'Ambush?'

'Yes,' said Hoode, flicking another apprehensive glance over his shoulder. 'Our landlord has changed his mind, it seems. No sooner had we bought wine to celebrate our triumph than he jumps out of the crowd and informs us that the contract is void and that we must quit the Queen's Head at once.'

'This does not make sense,' observed Pryde. 'The landlord needs the company here. It adds lustre and draws in custom. How many of these people would be here if they had not just witnessed a play in the yard?'

'Very few,' decided Elias. 'This is some jest, Edmund. Practised on you by that misery-monger, Alexander Marwood.'

'He is incapable of a jest.'

'What, then, does this portend?' said a worried Kindell.

Hoode rolled his eyes in despair and sighed dramatically.

'Disaster,' he concluded. 'It was bound to come sooner or later. I knew that my happiness could not last. I knew that I would have to pay dearly for the folly of imagining that fortune had at last smiled on me. It has happened. I sense disaster in the wind. Brace yourselves, lads. Unless I am greatly mistaken, we are about to be struck by a veritable thunderbolt.'

'Out, out, out!' demanded Alexander Marwood, stamping a foot.

'We will not budge an inch,' said Firethorn defiantly. 'We have every right to be here and here we will remain.'

'Then I will summon officers to have you evicted.'

'On what grounds?' asked Nicholas Bracewell.

'Trespass!'

'This is a public hostelry, Master Marwood.'

'I may turn away interlopers if I choose.'

'Interlopers!' exclaimed Firethorn. 'You dare to call us interlopers when we have filled your coffers and kept your customers entertained all these years without a word of thanks from you or your wife? Interlopers, indeed!'

'Aye,' said Marwood. 'Interlopers and lechers!'

'Silence!'

Lawrence Firethorn's command was like the blast of a cannon and it left Marwood's ears ringing. Nicholas stepped between actor and landlord before the former began to rain blows down on the latter's head. They were in the yard of the Queen's Head and the stage was still being dismantled behind them. The book holder was as befuddled as Firethorn by the unexpected turn of events. Why had Marwood pounced on them so vengefully? Nicholas was grateful that he had brought the argument out into the fresh air. An unseemly row in the middle of the taproom would have advantaged nobody. Even in the yard the raised voices were arousing immense curiosity.

'Let us discuss the matter calmly,' suggested Nicholas.

'How can I be calm in front of this death's head?' said Firethorn, jabbing a finger at the landlord. 'The very sight of him puts me to choler. Away, you walking pestilence!'

'It is you who must leave, sir!' insisted Marwood.

'Make us!'

'Constables will do the office for me.'

'But *why*?' asked Nicholas reasonably.

'Because I want you off my property.'

'For what reason?'

'The worst kind, Master Bracewell.'

'We are still none the wiser.'

'I am too ashamed even to speak the words.'

'Then at least give us some hint of how we have caused you such displeasure. Not ten minutes ago, we were agreeing terms and parting as friends. What killed that friendship so soon?'

'Ask among your fellows,' said Marwood darkly.

'My fellows?'

'One of them will know.'

'Know *what*, you map of woe?' growled Firethorn.

'The cause why I behave thus.'

'Behave how you wish,' said the other tartly, 'it will not shift us from here. The law is the law. We have a contract.'

'I will burn it to cinders.'

'You signed it. In front of witnesses.'

'I repent that now.'

'Too late. The contract protects us.'

'Contracts can be dissolved. And this one has been.'

'On the whim of a lunatic?'

'One moment,' said Nicholas, quickly interrupting before Firethorn's anger exceeded his control. 'Let me ask this of Master Marwood. Have you discussed this with your lawyer?'

'My lawyer?' grunted the landlord.

'Do you act on the advice of Ezekiel Stonnard?'

'He would support me to the hilt!'

'That is not quite true,' said Stonnard, who had been hovering within earshot and who now trotted forward to join in the debate. 'I would need to know all the facts before

42

I made a considered judgement. What I have gleaned so far has left me in a state of some confusion.'

'The law is on our side!' asserted Firethorn.

'Not necessarily,' said Stonnard with a polite snigger. 'Do not try to do our work for us, Master Firethorn, or you will be the loser, sir. Leave the law unto trained lawyers.'

'We have a contract. You witnessed it.'

'Indeed, I did. It is a legal document.'

'Then it cannot be revoked by this twitching idiot.'

'Not unless its terms have been broken.'

'They have!' moaned Marwood. 'Cruelly broken.'

'In what way?' yelled Firethorn.

Nicholas moved in again. 'That is something which Master Marwood would prefer to discuss with his lawyer, I think,' he said tactfully. 'Let us withdraw so that he may do so. When Master Stonnard is in possession of all the facts, I am sure that he will communicate them to us.'

'Rest assured that I will,' said Stonnard.

'I want them off my premises!' howled Marwood.

'We hold our ground!' retorted Firethorn.

'Perhaps not,' said Nicholas, guessing at the cause of this sudden turn in their fortunes. 'Perhaps we should quit the Queen's Head for a while and take our celebrations elsewhere. There are inns enough nearby and the taproom is too full to admit of any real comfort. Let us withdraw,' he said, taking Firethorn by the arm. 'Not in any spirit of retreat but as a favour to Master Marwood so that we do not offend him any more than we obviously have.'

'This is sage advice,' said Stonnard.

Marwood disagreed, crying out for them to be forcibly ejected, and Firethorn's response was even more vehement but Nicholas's guidance was followed. The lawyer placated the landlord and the actor allowed himself to be taken back into the inn by the book holder. Lunging forward, Marwood grabbed Stonnard by both hands.

'Help me!' he pleaded.

'I will do all that I may, sir.'

'Find a means to expel Westfield's Men hence.'

'That will not be easy, I fear.'

'They must go. At whatever costs.'

'Ah,' said Stonnard, smirking at the mention of money. 'While we are on the subject of cost, allow me to present you with my bill for services already rendered today.' Detaching himself from Marwood, he handed him a scroll. 'Now, sir. This is clearly a matter of weight and deserves close attention. Let us find a more private place to talk.' Sensing that a large fee might be in the offing, he rubbed his palms together. 'I long to hear what has prompted this change of heart.'

'Sybil,' murmured the other.

'What is that you say?'

'My wife, sir. She and I have been betrayed.'

'How?'

'Utterly.'

Lord Westfield was perturbed. Though no words were spoken directly to him, and though he overheard nothing which might occasion alarm, he saw the knowing glances, the subtle signals and the telltale nudges which passed between his enemies at Court. Something was afoot and he was deliberately excluded from it. The look which the Earl of Banbury shot him across the Presence Chamber was confirmation enough. A single mocking eyebrow, raised for no more than a few seconds by his deadliest rival, sent quiet tremors through Lord Westfield. Evidently, the earl and his cronies had devised some cunning plan. One thing was clear: Lord Westfield would be its victim rather than its beneficiary.

Visits to the Palace of Whitehall were usually events to relish. Surrounded by his own friends, he preened himself shamelessly, exchanged brittle gossip, paid fulsome compliments to the court ladies in their bright plumage, received, in turn, praise for his theatre company from all objective observers, rubbed shoulders with men of influence and was generally given such a sense of his own importance that he could sneer openly at his detractors. From time to time, he was even favoured with a few words from Her Majesty, Queen Elizabeth. It was an idle but wholly satisfying existence. Lord Westfield luxuriated in it.

Today, however, it was very different. Almost none of his intimate friends were at Court and persons of consequence seemed strangely uninterested in conversing with him. When her Grace made her accustomed flamboyant entrance and swept across to the throne, seizing attention with sovereign assurance, Lord Westfield felt oddly out of place, a foreigner making his first bemused appearance in London, an outsider, a newcomer, an exile. It was a paradox. In the place where he was most at home, he was now an unwanted intruder. It made him furtive.

There was no opportunity to get within five yards of the Queen. Ringed by her favourites, she flirted gaily and indulged in badinage until the Portuguese ambassador was admitted to the Chamber with his train and a less sportive note was introduced. Pleasantries passed between the two countries but Lord Westfield did not even try to listen to them. His gaze was fixed on the hated Earl of Banbury, an unrepentant old sybarite with a goatee beard and such costly apparel that it stood out even in such a glorious wardrobe as the English Court. What was his rival up to this time? It was a question which tormented Lord Westfield for hours.

Only when the Queen departed could he begin to seek an answer to his question. As they streamed out of the Presence Chamber in chattering groups, Lord Westfield tried first to engage the Master of the Revels in conversation but the latter excused himself rather brusquely and strode off. Even more disturbed than before, Lord Westfield now fell in beside Sir Patrick Skelton, a short, stocky man in his forties with the distinctive strut of a seasoned courtier. Skelton had such an affable manner that no rebuff could be feared from him and, though he was a deeply political animal, he also had a rare capacity for honesty in a world where dissembling was the more common currency. When the moment served, Lord Westfield took him by the elbow and guided him into a quiet corner.

'A word, Sir Patrick,' he said.

'As many as you like, my lord,' came the obliging reply.

'Her Majesty was in fine fettle today.'

'When is she not? Even the sprightliest of us is put to shame by her vivacity.' He gave a benign smile. 'But that is not what you drew me aside to talk about, my lord, is it?'

'No, Sir Patrick.'

There was a long pause as Lord Westfield searched for the right words to broach an awkward topic. Skelton tried to help him out of his difficulty.

'You wish to ask me about affairs of state,' he prompted.

'Yes.'

'Then do not be diffident. It does not become you and it sits ill with your reputation for plain speaking.'

Lord Westfield cleared his throat. 'You are trusted and respected,' he began, 'as a man of complete integrity. Though you hear every whisper that flies around inside these ancient walls, you are careful to separate idle speculation from hard fact. You never spread wild rumours or pass on any of the scurrilous tales which daily reach your ears.'

'Spare me this flattery, my lord. It is not needed.'

'I merely wished to show you the high esteem in which I hold you, Sir Patrick.'

'Your praise is gratefully accepted. Now speak out.'

'What is going on?'

'Going on, my lord?'

'Something is in the wind concerning my theatre company and I have a strong feeling that Westfield's Men will suffer as a result. I would like some warning of what exact form the threat takes.'

'How do you know that there *is* a threat?'

'Because of the way the Earl of Banbury looked at me.'

'That is all the evidence you have?'

'It is enough in itself.'

'Hardly.'

'Then add to it the fact that his friends were clearly in on the conspiracy and enjoying themselves at my expense.'

'Conspiracy? Too strong a word, surely?'

'I think not. The Master of the Revels is involved in it.'

'Why,' said the other softly, 'what is Sir Edmund Tilney's crime against you? Has he, too, been guilty of looking at you in a certain way?'

'He ignored me, Sir Patrick.'

'That is unlikely in so courteous a gentleman.'

'When I tried to speak with him, he mumbled an excuse and walked away. That was scarcely an act of courtesy.'

'The Master of the Revels is a busy man with extremely wide responsibilities. It was not rudeness which made him behave thus but pressure of work. I happen to know that, at this very moment, he has a private audience with her Grace. He was no doubt hurrying off to attend her.'

'What is the subject of their discussion?'

Skelton shrugged. 'I can only hazard a guess.'

'My guess is that it touches on Westfield's Men.'

'Perhaps, my lord, but then again, perhaps not. And even if your troupe does come into the conversation, it may not be a cause for apprehension. The only time I heard her Grace mention Westfield's Men by name was to praise the quality of their performances.'

'Is that true?' said the other, snatching up the crumb of

comfort. 'When was this? What were her precise words? Did her Grace mention *me*?'

'You and your company earned favourable comment. That is all I can remember, my lord. And Sir Edmund Tilney is even more aware of your pre-eminence. The Master of the Revels reads every new play you intend to perform to ensure that it is fit to receive his licence. He knows the high standards to which your players have always adhered.'

'Then why does he ignore me?'

'Her Majesty, the Queen, had prior claims, alas.'

'That still leaves the Earl of Banbury.'

'And, if I may remind you, Viscount Havelock.'

'He has no part in this.'

'But he does, my lord,' said Skelton. 'Banbury's Men are your closest rivals, it is true, but your company also has to compete with Havelock's Men. Viscount Havelock is as much a sworn foe of yours as the good Earl. Did you receive hostile glances from the Viscount?'

'No, I did not.'

'Did he spurn you in any way?'

'Far from it,' admitted the other. 'He smiled civilly at me and exchanged a polite word. Viscount Havelock is a man of true breeding – unlike a certain Earl.'

'Does not one rival cancel out another?'

'I do not follow.'

'Courtesy from one balances conspiracy from the other. Take heart from that, my lord. Viscount Havelock is far closer to the centre of power than the Earl. His uncle sits on the Privy Council. The Viscount would be the first to learn of anything which adversely affected Westfield's Men and, by implication, which advantaged his own company.' Skelton gave another shrug. 'You are chasing moonbeams here. You have invented a conspiracy which may not even exist.'

'I know the Earl of Banbury.'

'He was merely trying to slight you.'

'He was *gloating*, Sir Patrick.'

'Over what?'

'I dread to think.'

'But calm thought is exactly what is required here,' said the other. 'Your imagination has got the better of you, my lord. Apply cool reason. The Earl may have been savouring a personal triumph which has nothing whatsoever to do with his theatre company. A new mistress, perhaps? A banquet he is due to attend? An inheritance which will help to defray the massive debts he faces? Some small sign of favour from her Grace? The possibilities are endless.'

'I am somehow involved.'

'Only if you let yourself be, my lord.'

'What do you mean?'

'This is a mere game. You and the earl have played it for years. There have been many times when you have been able to score off him and you savoured those occasions. I have been in Court to witness them. Might he not simply have been trying to get some small revenge today? Seeking to unsettle you out of sheer mischief. Come, my lord,' he said with a smile. 'It is not like you to be so needlessly upset by your rival. Do not give him the pleasure of ruffling your feathers.'

'Nor will I,' vowed Lord Westfield.

'Hold fast to that resolve.'

'I defy the earl and his ragged band of players.'

'He is envious of the success of Westfield's Men.'

'With justice.'

'Then no more of these phantom fears.'

'They are banished forthwith,' said Lord Westfield firmly but he immediately succumbed to another tremble of fright. 'Just tell me this, Sir Patrick, for I know you will be blunt and candid. It is the last question with which I will plague you, I promise.'

'Then ask it, sir.'

'Have you heard anything from the chambers of power that will be to the detriment of Westfield's Men?'

Sir Patrick Skelton gave an easy smile.

'No, my lord,' he said confidently.

The courtier excused himself and slipped away to join the stragglers. Lord Westfield was glad that he had sought his information from such a dependable source but he was worried that he did not feel more reassured. As he made his way out of the Palace of Westminster, it was the gloating Earl rather than the comforting courtier who stayed uppermost in his mind. When he came out into the early evening sunshine, Lord Westfield was suddenly struck by another thought.

Something did not ring true. Was it conceivable that Sir

Patrick Skelton had deliberately misled him? Could a man who was renowned for his frankness and moral probity have lied to him?

It was the most worrying development of all.

The Cross Keys Inn was less than fifty yards away from the Queen's Head but the distance between the two establishments seemed more like a mile to the discontented refugees from the latter. Westfield's Men wandered up Gracechurch Street in a daze, wondering what they had done to get themselves so swiftly evicted from their own theatre at the very moment when they had secured tenure of it for another year. It was both bewildering and humiliating.

Lawrence Firethorn smouldered, Edmund Hoode puzzled, Lucius Kindell was dismayed, Owen Elias was outraged and Sylvester Pryde was highly annoyed. Predictably, it was Barnaby Gill who led the chorus of protest, rounding on Nicholas Bracewell and wagging an accusing finger at him.

'This is your doing,' he spluttered.

'I simply advised caution, Master Gill.'

'You forced us to quit the premises.'

'That is not true,' said Nicholas.

'At the instigation of the landlord, you threw us out of the Queen's Head as if we were drunk and disorderly.'

Nicholas was patient. 'All I did was to try to take the heat out of this altercation, and that could only be done by getting out of his sight. Alexander Marwood was implacable. Why stay there to enrage him with our presence? It is much more sensible to withdraw awhile in order to allow his lawyer time and space in which to calm him down.'

'*I'll* calm him down!' said Firethorn. 'With my dagger.'

'That would be too quick a death for him,' added Elias. 'I'd rather roast him over a slow fire and cool him down from time to time by dipping him in a barrel of his own beer.'

'You'd contaminate the liquid,' said Firethorn.

'This landlord contaminates us all,' said Gill, throwing a contemptuous glance over his shoulder. 'Instead of hurling me out, he should be grovelling on his knees in gratitude to me for deigning to display my talents on his premises. I'll not endure this, Nicholas. I have left the Queen's Head for ever.'

'We have a contract,' Nicholas reminded him.

'Then why does the rogue not honour it?'

'I do not know.'

'You spoke with him. You must have some idea.'

Nicholas made no reply. He had already guessed the reason for Marwood's rash behaviour but he did not want to voice it abroad until he had confirmation. It was essentially a matter to be discussed in private rather than a subject for ribald comment in the street. Gill continued to press him but the book holder would not be drawn. His immediate concern was to get his company into the taproom of the Cross Keys where fresh wine and ale would assuage their hurt feelings. The mood of celebration would soon return and most of his fellows would quickly forget that Alexander Marwood even existed as they revelled on into the night.

When they reached the inn, Owen Elias led the way through its yard and into its welcoming interior. Like the Queen's Head, it was a regular venue for the performance of plays though no company had been in residence that afternoon. The landlord was delighted to see a large bevy of thirsty patrons surging into his taproom to fill his empty tables. Brisk business was transacted with the servingmen. Westfield's Men still grumbled but their recriminations lost some bitterness when they supped their first drinks.

Firethorn took Nicholas aside for private conference.

'What is happening, Nick?' he said.

'That is what I will endeavour to find out.'

'When?'

'As soon as may be,' said Nicholas. 'When I have seen the company settled in here, I'll return to the Queen's Head to speak with Master Stonnard. He will be able to cast some light on this unfortunate incident.'

'Unfortunate! It is an insult to us!'

'Bear it with dignity.'

'How can I be dignified when we are so disgraced?'

'There is no disgrace in withdrawing of our own volition. The Queen's Head was too crowded for once with little enough room for our fellows to stretch in any comfort. Here they have space and comfort.'

'And a landlord who knows how to smile.'

'That, too. The crisis is over.'

'But what brought it about in the first place?'

'Can you not guess?'

There was a long pause. For the first time since the confrontation with their testy landlord, Firethorn put aside his own anger and applied some thought to the situation. Instead of glowering, his face became a study in wonderment. Eyebrows slowly arched, eyes glinted, jaw dropped. He stepped in close to speak in an undertone.

'Is *that* what this is all about, Nick?'

'I believe so.'

'No wonder he was so furious.'

'That fury will abate in our absence.'

'But he still has no cause to abuse the whole company.'

'I will tax him with that argument.'

'Shall I go with you?'

'Delicate negotiations may be needed,' said Nicholas. 'The less people involved, the better.' Firethorn gave a nod of assent. 'And please do not spread our suspicion freely among the others. We may yet be wrong.'

'And if we are not?'

'Then we take the appropriate action.'

'What is that?'

'I will not know until the full facts are at my disposal.'

'We must retain the Queen's Head,' said Firethorn with an edge of desperation. 'We belong there, Nick. Our tenancy has not been without turmoil but that makeshift stage of ours is still my favourite theatre.'

'And mine.'

'Can this rift be mended?'

Nicholas Bracewell looked across at the members of the company, robbed of their security in the twinkling of an eye and experiencing once more the cruel precariousness of their profession. Good humour was slowly returning and the first jest was cracked by Owen Elias but they were still nursing their wounded pride. Entitled to celebrate the success of their performance, they had instead been ignominiously turned out into the street. On their behalf, Nicholas was profoundly shocked and saddened.

'Can it, Nick?' pressed Firethorn.

'I hope so.'

Ezekiel Stonnard needed all his patience to cope with his garrulous client. Seated in a private room with writing materials before him, he waited for facts which could be recorded but they took time to emerge from the landlord's cloudburst of vituperation. It was only when the storm had blown itself out that he could probe for detail. Alexander Marwood crossed to the window and drooped in front of it, staring out despondently at the yard where the troupe had so recently enthralled yet another audience. Stonnard rose to join him at the window.

'I am hampered by a shortage of information,' he said.

'And I have too much to bear.'

'Then unburden it to me, Master Marwood.'

'I cannot bring myself to do so.'

'You must. I am your lawyer and, I like to believe, your good friend. You may entrust any intelligence to me. A lawyer is a species of priest, taking confession.'

'You are more likely to administer last rites here.'

'But why? That is what I do not yet grasp. Why?'

Marwood was about to answer when his eye alighted on a figure who had just entered the inn yard. The sight of Nicholas Bracewell was like a dagger through the landlord's heart. He let out a cry, grabbed at his chest and fell backwards into the lawyer's arms. Stonnard disentangled himself.

'What ails you, sir?'

'A member of that accursed company has returned.'

'Let me see.'

Stonnard was just in time to catch a glimpse of Nicholas before the latter came into the building. His response was in sharp contrast to that of his client.

'This is an accident that heaven provides,' he said with an oleaginous grin. 'They have sent an emissary. This matter can be resolved before Westfield's Men engage their own lawyer to take the case to litigation.'

'Could they do that, Master Stonnard?'

'All too easily. You signed that contract.'

'Before I knew the ugly truth.'

'That does not matter. You are legally bound to observe the terms of that contract. Now, sir,' he said, leading Marwood to a chair and lowering him into it. 'Acquaint me with the full facts, then I will summon Nicholas Bracewell to discuss the situation in an amicable atmosphere.

'Amicable!'

'Free from harsh language.'

'I am undone,' said Marwood, sagging forward. 'You ask me to make peace with my vilest enemy.'

'I ask you to instruct your attorney, sir.'

The story eventually began to dribble out. Torn between anger and self-pity, the landlord gave a rambling account of the marital interchange in his daughter's bedchamber. Ezekiel Stonnard listened without interruption. When Marwood came to the end of his sorry tale, he put his head in his hands and sobbed bitterly. Stonnard gave him token comfort before urging him to compose himself.

'Their ambassador must be seen,' he insisted. 'Nicholas Bracewell is a sound man, untouched by the vanity of the players and straightforward in his dealings. Did you not tell me that you have always found him so?'

'Yes,' conceded the other.

'I will fetch him.'

'But he is one of *them*.'

'All the more reason to meet with him. Westfield's Men must be appeased or this quarrel will catch fire and we all may be burnt by its flames.' He introduced the argument which would have the most influence on his client. 'This could be costly, sir.'

'Costly?' gasped the other.

'Extremely costly.'

Marwood finally capitulated and Stonnard left the room at once. When he returned, he was towing Nicholas Bracewell in his wake, alternately patronising and apologising to him. They came into the room and closed the door behind them. The landlord refused even to meet the newcomer's eyes. Nicholas addressed him with studied politeness.

'I am sorry that we have caused you such distress,' he said. 'It was not intended.'

Marwood remained silent. Ezekiel Stonnard took over.

'Do you know the cause of that distress, sir?'

'I think so,' said Nicholas.

'Well?'

'Mistress Rose is with child.'

Her father went off into a paroxysm of coughing. They waited until the fit had passed before continuing.

'Who told you?' asked Stonnard.

'It is the only explanation,' said Nicholas, 'and it was hinted at by Master Marwood when he assailed us as lechers.' He turned to the landlord. 'Name the man responsible for this and he will be roundly chastised before being made to honour his obligations.'

Marwood looked up. 'Name him?'

'We hoped that *you* might do that,' said Stonnard to Nicholas. 'Identify the villain.'

'Has he not boasted to you of his conquest?' sneered the landlord. 'My daughter would not yield up his loathsome name. All she would admit was that he was one of the players. Rose described him as a tall, handsome, loving man.'

'Did she say no more than that?' asked Nicholas.

Stonnard shook his head. 'By all accounts, it was a trial to get that much out of the girl. She is deeply confused. Two facts, however, are certain. The poor creature is, alas, with child. And the father is a member of your company. We look to you to root him out so that he can be held to account.'

'I will help in any way I can,' volunteered Nicholas, 'but the faults of one man must not be allowed to poison your view of the entire company. Westfield's Men have signed a contract and we expect Master Marwood to abide by it.'

'He will do so,' soothed Stonnard. 'In time.'

'When the rogue has been unmasked,' croaked Marwood. He glared at Nicholas. 'I daresay that you may already guess at his name. A tall, handsome, loving man! Which is another way of saying that he is a vile seducer who takes advantage of a virtuous and God-fearing maid behind her father's back. Who is he?' he demanded querulously. 'You have an insatiate duke among your fellows, sir. Tell me his foul name.'

'When I learn it,' promised Nicholas, 'I will.'

Nobody saw him leave. Sylvester Pryde was roistering with his fellows at the Crossed Keys for an hour or more before he slid quietly off into the shadows. They would not miss him. Drink and exhilaration were powerful allies. They would soon obliterate all memory of Sylvester Pryde as Westfield's Men lurched happily on towards the stupor which would bring an end to their madcap celebrations.

The actor flitted swiftly through a maze of streets until he came to a large house on a corner. Unlike its timber-framed neighbours, which were all thatched, the house was tiled and had recently been given a fresh coat of paint. It was patently owned by someone with moderate wealth and a pride in his home. The visitor was grateful that the householder was travelling to Norwich on business, blithely unaware of the fact that his beautiful young wife might entertain a guest in his absence.

Sylvester Pryde lurked in a doorway and watched the window of the bedchamber at the front of the house. It was only a matter of minutes before a candle was lit to signal that the coast was clear. He allowed himself a smile of anticipation before letting himself in through the unlocked front door. She was ready for him and it was an article of faith with him that he never kept a lady waiting.

Chapter Three

Nicholas Bracewell rose early next morning at the house where he lodged in Bankside. Anne Hendrik, his landlady, had already been up an hour and she had breakfast waiting for him. As they sat on either side of the table, it was their first opportunity to discuss the events of the previous day.

'You arrived home late last night,' she observed.

'I was delayed at the Cross Keys Inn.'

'The Cross Keys? Why not the Queen's Head?'

'That is a tale of some length, Anne,' he sighed.

'Am I to be told it?'

Nicholas grinned. 'In detail.'

When he recounted what had happened, Anne was delighted to hear of the success of *The Insatiate Duke* but alarmed at what occurred after it. She could imagine all too readily the state of hysteria into which their fretful landlord had whipped himself. However, while sympathising with the plight of Westfield's Men, her main concern was for

Rose Marwood whom she knew from her own regular visits to the inn yard theatre.

'What will become of the poor girl?' she asked.

Nicholas shrugged. 'Who knows? She does not, alas, have the most understanding parents. They will reproach her bitterly at a time when she most needs tenderness and reassurance.'

'Rose was such an innocent creature. I used to marvel at her. She was no typical serving wench with a coarse tongue and a roving eye. There was a touching purity about Rose Marwood which somehow kept men at bay.'

'Until now.'

'Yes, Nick,' she said ruefully. 'But I will not believe that the girl yielded herself lightly. Rose would need to be deeply and hopelessly in love before she considered sharing a bed with a man and even then, I suspect, a promise of betrothal would be needed.'

'There is no mention of betrothal now.'

'Has the father deserted her?'

'So it appears.'

'Is he aware of her condition?'

'We will not know until we identify him.'

'Can you not guess who he might be?'

'I believe so, Anne.'

'Well?'

'His was the first name which sprang to my mind.'

'Owen Elias?'

'No,' said Nicholas, 'though Owen obviously had to be taken into account as well. He has always had a special fondness for tavern wenches and loses no chance to prove his virility. But he is not the indifferent father. I questioned him bluntly and Owen swore that this was not his doing.' He gave a half-smile. 'Though he did add that he wished that it had been. The thought of seducing Rose Marwood and enraging her father had a double appeal for him.'

'Rose would not look at a man like Owen Elias.'

'Many women have, Anne.'

'I am sure. He is extremely affable and has a vitality about him which is very attractive.'

'Do *you* find it attractive?'

'I did,' she confessed, 'until I got to know him better. But he poses no threat to me, if that is what you are asking.' She smiled warmly. 'I am already spoken for, Nick.'

He met her gaze and returned her smile. Anne was the English widow of a Dutch hatmaker. When her husband died, she took over his business and ran it with a flair and efficiency that nobody realised she possessed. With its bear-baiting arenas and its brothels, its mean tenements and its populous low-life, Bankside was not the safest part of London in which to live and Anne soon felt the need of a man in the house to lend a sense of security. Nicholas Bracewell turned out to be the ideal lodger and they were gradually drawn into a close friendship. While not letting it dictate their lives, it was something on which both set great value.

'Who *is* the father of Rose's child?' she asked.

'It has yet to be confirmed, Anne.'

'But you have a strong suspicion.'

'Yes,' he said, 'and it was strengthened even more when

I returned to the Cross Keys last night and questioned every man in the company in turn.'

She was surprised. 'Every man?'

'With the exception of George Dart and Barnaby Gill. The one is too shy even to look at a woman and the other spurns the entire sex. No,' continued Nicholas, 'I heard what I expected to hear from all of them. Stout denial.'

'Who, then, is left?'

'Sylvester Pryde.'

'Surely not!'

'He is the only person unaccounted for, Anne. When I got back to the others, Sylvester had left.'

'When you were celebrating a triumph?' she said in astonishment. 'His place was surely with his fellows. What could possibly have lured him away at such a time?'

'The latest Rose Marwood, perhaps?'

'No, Nick. I refuse to believe it.'

'Sylvester is the most handsome man in the company,' he argued, 'and well-used to reaping the fruits of his good looks. Rose would not have been his first conquest.'

'I still think him an unlikely culprit.'

'Why?'

'Sylvester Pryde has moved in high circles, Nick. He has consorted with lords and ladies. My guess is that it is among those same ladies that his conquests have been made, not in the taverns of London.' She pursed her lips as she pondered. 'I mean no disrespect to Rose Marwood. She is a comely enough girl but could she really attract such a worldly individual as Sylvester Pryde?'

'It is not impossible.'

'But is it likely?'

'I fear that it is,' said Nicholas. 'Almost as soon as Sylvester joined the company, Rose was smitten with him. I lost count of the number of times I caught her watching us at rehearsal when Sylvester was on the stage. When she was in the taproom, he was always the first to be served.'

'That does not make them lovers, Nick.'

'No. But it singles the name of Sylvester Pryde out.'

'What will you do?'

'Tax him with the charge,' he said. 'That is why I rose so early this morning. So that I could reach his lodging before he left. It is a conversation I would rather have in private. If Sylvester *is* the father of this child, there will be severe consequences. It would be unseemly to let him rehearse with us at the Queen's Head as if nothing had happened.'

'At least, you *can* rehearse there again.'

'Yes, Anne. I wrenched that concession from our landlord.'

'You have a contractual right to play at the inn.'

'The only contract which Alexander Marwood can talk about is a contract of marriage. Lacking that, his daughter has been locked away and treated as if she were a criminal.'

'My heart goes out to her.'

'And mine.'

They finished their breakfast in thoughtful silence. He put his plate aside and rested his arms on the table, reaching out to take her hands between his.

'Thank you, Anne.'

'It was a simple enough meal.'

'I am grateful for the breakfast as well,' he said, 'but I was really thanking you for hearing me out. I am sorry to burden you with the problems of Westfield's Men when you have plenty of your own.'

'That is certainly true, Nick!'

'Share them with me.'

'Another time,' she said. 'I will not hold you up.'

'But you have not told me what *you* did yesterday.'

'I am not sure that I should.'

'Why?'

'Because it might provoke jealousy.'

'Jealousy?'

'I went on impulse,' she said, defensively. 'It was not planned at all. But I was delivering a hat to Mistress Payne and she suggested that we go together. She would not dare to go on her own and was so pleased with the hat that she was eager to wear it. In a moment of weakness, I agreed.'

'To what?'

'An afternoon at The Rose.'

'Anne!' he said with mock outrage.

'It was a disappointing play but well-acted for all that and Mistress Payne was delighted that we went. My hat won her several compliments.'

'You went to The Rose theatre?' he teased.

'Only to oblige an important customer.'

'Supporting the work of a rival company?'

'They pale in comparison with Westfield's Men,' she said, loyally. 'There is only one player among them who is fit to have his name mentioned alongside that of Lawrence Firethorn.'

'Rupert Kitely.'

'Yes, Nick. He towered above the others.'

'That does not surprise me,' he said. 'Rupert Kitely is the mainstay of Havelock's Men. They have a number of talented actors – including one or two deserters from our company – but it is Kitely who is their principal asset. Such a man would be most welcome in our own ranks.'

'What hope is there of his joining you?'

'None whatsoever. He is a sharer with Havelock's Men and tied by contract to the Viscount's service. Besides,' said Nicholas, rising from the table. 'I am not sure that there is a stage big enough to accommodate both Lawrence Firethorn and Rupert Kitely. Each needs his own arena.'

'Do you forgive me?' she asked.

'For what?'

'Spending time and money on your rivals?'

'You are entitled to go to The Rose theatre,' he said, helping her up from her seat. 'It is almost on your doorstep. And it is good to have a pair of eyes on Havelock's Men so that we keep our rivals under surveillance. When I return this evening, I would like to hear more about the performance.'

'Not if you come back at the same hour as yesternight.'

'My apologies for that, Anne. You were already abed.'

'Fast asleep.'

'I know. I peeped into your bedchamber.'

'Then why did you not join me?' she scolded softly.

'I was afraid that I might wake you.'

Anne stood on tiptoe to kiss him gently on the lips.

'I was afraid that you would not.'

A night of passion which would have exhausted most men only served to invigorate Sylvester Pryde. When he dressed next morning, he felt a fresh energy pulsing through him and giving his whole body an agreeable tingle. His lover had fared less well. Hair tousled and limbs pleasantly fatigued, she lay amid the scattered bed linen and fought to open her eyes.

'Must you leave so soon?' she said drowsily.

'Yes, my love.'

'Stay another hour.'

'Nothing would delight me more,' said Pryde, crossing to bestow a kiss on her forehead. 'But I am expected elsewhere.'

'By whom, sir?'

'A very special lady.'

'You swore last night that I was a very special lady,' she complained, sitting up and pouting. 'Was that a wicked lie?'

'No, my sweet.'

'Then why will you not linger?'

'Truly, I may not. I have another assignation.'

She bristled. 'You cast me aside for another?'

'Only during the day. I will return again tonight.'

'Not if you have been cavorting with a rival,' she said tartly. 'My door will be closed to you, Sylvester. I will not share you with anyone.'

'Not even with the Queen of England?'

'Her Majesty?' she said, blinking in wonderment.

'Yes,' he explained with a grin. 'I will pay homage to her Grace when I pass beneath her portrait on the inn sign. There is my assignation. At the Queen's Head with the other players. Be ruled by me,' he said, giving her another peck. 'You have no flesh and blood rival. Only a painted monarch who swings to and fro in the wind in Gracechurch Street.'

'I wronged you,' she admitted.

'Only because I misled you. But I must away.'

Pryde took a last, long, searching kiss before slipping out through the door. To avoid the prying eyes of neighbours, he left discreetly by the rear exit and came out into a narrow lane. Striding purposefully along into a stiff breeze, he reflected on his nocturnal pleasures and wondered how long he would sustain this particular romance. The lady was a willing but very inexperienced lover and he was not sure whether her husband's occasional departures from London would give him enough time to teach her all the refinements she needed to master in order to hold his interest.

When he swung into Gracechurch Street, he dismissed her from his mind and turned his attention to Westfield's Men, recalling their embarrassing departure from the Queen's Head and speculating on the possibility that they might henceforth be banished from their place of work. This eventuality was far more worrying than the fumbling caresses and lunging urgency of his latest conquest. Being a privileged member of such an illustrious troupe as Westfield's Men gave Sylvester Pryde immense satisfaction.

On the stage in the inn yard, he enjoyed a sense of fulfilment such as he had never known before and the notion that it might be taken away from him by a volatile landlord produced a severe jolt.

The crowd was thick but he threaded his way through it with ease until he reached the Queen's Head. His worst fears were confirmed by the sight of Nicholas Bracewell, standing outside the inn, presumably to turn the players away. He closed quickly on the book holder.

'Good morrow, Nick!'

'I have been waiting for you,' said Nicholas. 'When I called at your lodging, they told me you had spent the night elsewhere.'

'That is so. I was called away.'

'It must have been a pressing summons if you left in the middle of our celebrations at the Cross Keys Inn. But that is your business and does not concern me here.' He was having difficulty being heard above the noise. 'This street is too busy. Let us seek a quieter place to talk.'

Taking Pryde by the arm, he guided him down the first turning then swung into an alleyway which gave them a modicum of privacy and a respite from the continual din.

'Are we barred from the Queen's Head?' said Pryde.

'The company is not but one member of it may be.'

'One member?'

'Let me explain, Sylvester,' said Nicholas, taking care to adopt a neutral tone. 'Thus it stands. The landlord's daughter is with child. Suspecting one of us to be the father, he rails against the whole company and would have cast us out into the wilderness had we not just signed a contract with him.'

'Suspecting one of us?' echoed Pryde. 'Does he have no proof? Has the girl not volunteered his name?'

Nicholas shook his head. 'No. Whether out of loyalty or folly, I cannot say, but Rose will not part with it. This argues much for her strength of feeling about the man. Her parents have been stern interrogators but they failed to prise a name out of her. All that she will concede is that he was an actor. And she offered the briefest description of him.'

'Rose Marwood is a pretty piece of flesh,' said Pryde with a smile. 'He was a fortunate man, whoever he might be.'

'His good fortune has been our misfortune.'

'Alas, yes.'

'And it has left the girl in a parlous state.'

'The price of pleasure can sometimes be very high.'

'Let us talk about that price,' said Nicholas discreetly. 'This is a question I have had to put to each and every member of the company, Sylvester, so do not be offended when I direct it at you. The description which Rose gave could fit two or three of our players. Chief among them is you.'

'Me?' said Pryde indignantly.

'Were you the girl's lover?'

'No, Nick. I was not nor would I be. Heavens, man, when I said she was a pretty piece of flesh, it was not because I had designs on her. I am not involved in any way here.'

'Is that the truth, Sylvester?'

'On my honour!'

'I need to know.'

'You have just been told, Nick. Ask the same question of yourself and you will understand how I feel. Are *you* the father of this child?'

Nicholas almost blushed. 'Of course not.'

'Do you find Rose Marwood repulsive?'

'Not at all. She is a most pleasant girl.'

'Why, then, did you not bed her?'

'Because my affections are placed elsewhere, Sylvester, as well you know. And that is only one of many reasons.'

'I can offer even more why I would not even dream of embracing Rose Marwood or her kind. Suffice it to say, that I, too, have placed my affections elsewhere.' He gave a lazy smile. 'Those affections may shift from time to time but they would never alight on the daughter of an innkeeper. We talk of quality here, Nick. With a lady such as Anne in your life, you would not stoop to a dalliance with a serving wench. It would be beneath you.'

'That is true.'

'It is so with me.'

'Yet Rose Marwood was so entranced by you.'

'That does not make me her lover.'

'No,' agreed Nicholas, 'and the vehemence of your denial makes me believe you. I am sorry to have to examine you on the subject but it is in all our interests to discover who the father of this child really is.'

'One of our fellows deceived you.'

'I find that hard to accept.'

'Haply, the father does not even remember the coupling,'

said Pryde. 'If it happened in a drunken moment, it might have no purchase on his mind.'

'Rose Marwood would not give herself to a drunkard.'

'Stranger things have happened.'

Nicholas's mind was racing. Having decided that Sylvester Pryde was the most likely father, he was perplexed to learn that the latter was innocent of the charge. Had one of the others deliberately lied to him? Owen Elias? James Ingram? Edmund Hoode? Lucius Kindell? Could it even have been – his blood congealed at the thought – Lawrence Firethorn himself? Gifted actor though he may be, he was also, when he could escape the vigilance of his wife, a compulsive lecher who would not scruple to show an interest in any attractive woman. If the actor-manager were the culprit, then the fate of Westfield's Men really did hang in the balance.

Sylvester Pryde came to his aid.

'Ask the girl,' he suggested.

'Who?'

'Rose Marwood. She knows the name. Elicit it from her.'

'How?' said Nicholas. 'I would not be allowed anywhere near her. The landlord and his wife have used every means at their disposal to force the name out of her. Why would she tell me what she would never divulge to her parents?'

'Because you would be gentle with her.'

Rupert Kitely was a theatrical phenomenon. Short, slight and pleasantly ugly, he somehow transformed himself on stage into a tall, muscular individual with a dashing handsomeness that earned him a huge female following. The illusion was achieved by a subtle combination of a clarion voice, piercing eyes which reached every part of the theatre, graceful movement, vivid gesture and an inner dynamism which seemed visibly to increase his height and bulk. Kitely was the leading player with Havelock's Men and the prime cause of its continued success. He made every role he played his own, stamping it with his authority and his trademark brilliance, taking it beyond the reach of lesser mortals in the company.

The French Doctor, a light comedy with an undertow of political satire, allowed him to display his comic gifts to the full. As the eponymous hero, Rupert Kitely gave a performance that was full of fire, pathos and hilarious mime. His timing was faultless. Even in rehearsal, he gave of his very best. Unbeknown to him, he had an appreciative audience. A pair of gloved hands applauded him from the lower gallery. Kitely looked up to see their patron, Viscount Havelock, beating his palms enthusiastically together. The French doctor replied with a low bow.

'Thank you, my lord,' he said, 'but the real performance will take place this afternoon.'

'I will be there, Rupert.'

'You honour us.'

'And you honour the name of Havelock's Men.'

Kitely bowed again. 'Your humble servant, my lord.'

'I crave a word with you.'

'I will join you presently.'

Dismissing the company, Kitely quickly made his way to

the steps which led to the gallery. Viscount Havelock was a rare visitor at a rehearsal. Only a matter of some importance could have brought him there and Kitely was eager to know what it was. The patron's broad smile heralded good news.

Charles, Viscount Havelock was an elegant man of medium height in his thirties with a long, shining, open face which gave him an almost boyish appearance, an impression reinforced by the youthful vigour which he exuded. He was completely free from the signs of dissipation which betrayed Lord Westfield and, to a much larger extent, the Earl of Banbury, his two major rivals as patrons of the theatrical arts. The Viscount rose from his seat when the actor came up the steps.

'This French doctor will have the whole audience laughing until they weep with joy,' he said approvingly.

'That is our intention, my lord.'

'It is one of your finest roles.'

'I strive to make it so.'

'Strive but give no sense of having striven.'

'True art consists in concealing the huge efforts which lie behind it,' said Kitely. 'With a poor player, all that you see are the panting preliminaries.'

'This morning I witnessed genuine talent.'

'Above all else, my lord, we aim to please our patron.'

'You do, Rupert.' He waved an arm to take in the whole theatre. 'Do you like The Rose?'

'I adore the place.'

'You are happy that the company took up residence here?'

'Extremely happy, my lord.'

'Have you no regrets?'

'None of consequence.'

'Good. It is a worthy venue for your art.'

The two of them gazed around the theatre with a pride which was buttressed by possessiveness. The Rose was their chosen home. In the time they had been there, Havelock's Men had earned a considerable reputation for themselves and they almost always played before full audiences. Constructed on the site of a rose garden to the east of Rose Alley in the Liberty of the Clink, it was a striking new playhouse which brought spectators from all over London to Bankside. It was built around a timber frame on a brick foundation with outer walls of lath and plaster, and a thatched roof. Over the stage was a decorated canopy, supported by high pillars and surmounted by a hut, containing the winching apparatus which made possible all manner of spectacular effects.

Viscount Havelock inhaled deeply and beamed.

'I never come here without feeling inspired.'

'We are eternally grateful to you,' said Kitely.

'Would you not rather be treading the boards in one of the Shoreditch playhouses? The Curtain, perhaps?'

'No, my lord.'

'The Theatre?'

'It is no match for The Rose.'

'What of the inn yard venues?' asked the other, turning to face him. 'I first saw you at the Bel Savage Inn. And your company was at the Cross Keys for a while.'

'Those days are past. This is perfection.'

'Is it, Rupert?'

'My lord?'

'Even perfection can be improved a little.'

'In what way?'

'I was hoping that you would teach me. Suppose, for the sake of argument, that you could add anything or anybody to The Rose, who or what would it be.'

Kitely did not hesitate. 'Barnaby Gill.'

'The clown with Westfield's Men?'

'He has no equal and his antics would enrich our fare immeasurably. Barnaby Gill is the finest comic talent in the whole of London.'

'After a certain Rupert Kitely.'

'Thank you, my lord,' said the actor with a modest smile, 'but even I could not dance a jig like Master Gill. Put him in Havelock's Men and we would reach new heights.'

'Whom else do you covet?'

'Edmund Hoode.'

'We have plays enough of our own.'

'But they lack the quality of his best work,' returned the other. 'Whether writing a new play or cobbling an old one, he is a virtual master with a sure touch. Even when he turns his hand to tragedy, he does not falter. I hear disturbingly good reports of *The Insatiate Duke*.'

'You were not misled by your informers.'

'The praise has reached your ears, my lord?'

'Ears, eyes and every other part about me, Rupert. I was in the gallery at the Queen's Head yesterday afternoon. It is an extraordinary play, I must concede. A collaboration between Edmund Hoode and a clever young playwright from Oxford. They will go far together.'

'Would that we had them both.'

'Hoode and his apprentice?'

'Do not forget Barnaby Gill.'

'Would you poach anyone else from Westfield's Men?'

'Only their book keeper.'

'Why him?'

'Nicholas Bracewell is their secret weapon,' said Kitely with grudging admiration. 'It is he who holds the company together and raises the standard of what they offer. If I could choose but one of the names I have mentioned, I think I would first take Nicholas Bracewell.'

'Take the others as well,' said the Viscount casually.

'The others?'

'All three of them and this book keeper.'

'That could only happen in the realms of fantasy.'

'We may well enter them before too long.'

Kitely tried to read his enigmatic smile. Unlike other patrons, Viscount Havelock took a direct interest in the affairs of his theatre company, attending every new play without fail and proffering advice on a whole range of matters. Rupert Kitely had come to respect this advice. What he at first took for his patron's unwarranted interference was almost invariably sage counsel. He sensed that the Viscount was there to pass on more valuable advice.

'Do you ever go fishing, Rupert?' asked the patron.

'Fishing?'

'In the river.'

'No, my lord.'

'I think that you should.'

'Why?'

'Because you may catch exactly what you seek,' said the other with a quiet chuckle. 'Bait your hook well, my friend, then cast your line into the Thames and leave it there awhile. Who knows? When you pull it out again, you may have landed all four of the men you value so highly.'

'How, my lord?'

'That is what I have come to tell you.'

Lawrence Firethorn spent the morning brooding on the subject.

'Sylvester is lying,' he decided.

'I think not,' said Nicholas Bracewell.

'He is the obvious candidate here.'

'That is what I rushed to believe at first but I was woefully wrong. Sylvester Pryde is no saint. He is the first to confess that. But I am certain that he did not lay a finger on Rose Marwood.'

'A finger is not the appendage in question, Nick.'

They were standing in the yard at the Queen's Head at the end of an erratic rehearsal of *Mirth and Madness*, a staple comedy from their repertoire and a complete contrast to the tragedy which preceded it. Knowing that they were only allowed in the inn yard on sufferance, the company had been preoccupied and lacklustre, stumbling over their lines, missing their entrances and generally turning a lively romp into something akin to a funeral march. Lawrence Firethorn, surprisingly, had been the chief offender which was why he did not castigate his company, trusting instead that the presence of an audience would serve to unite the players with the play.

'Who, then, was it?' he wondered.

'I do not know,' said Nicholas.

'If not Sylvester, it must be one of our other fellows. Unless we are in the presence of a virgin birth here. Did you see a star in the east, Nick? Are we to expect the imminent arrival of Three Kings, bearing gifts of gold, frankincense and myrrh?' He gave a hollow laugh. 'Forgive my blasphemy, dear heart, but this business has put me on the rack.'

'Mistress Rose is the real victim here,' said Nicholas.

'Indeed, she is, and my wife said the same to me when she heard. I had great difficulty preventing Margery from walking all the way here from Shoreditch to comfort the girl. Women understand these things more than us. It is bad enough to have to face the pangs and perils of childbirth, she told me, but it must be agony to do so without the father at your side. Rose Marwood must be in torment.'

'That was Anne's first reaction as well.'

'I, too, have sympathy for the girl – profound sympathy – but my prime duty is to ensure the safety of the company.'

'That has been done. We have our playhouse back again.'

'But for how long, Nick?' said Firethorn. 'We told the landlord that we would identify the mystery lover and pass the name on to him. I know full well how he will react if we go to him empty-handed. And his fury will be mild compared with that of the fiery she-dragon he is married to. What do we do?'

'Remain patient.'

'That is like telling me to remain dry in the middle of a tempest. How can I be patient when Marwood is yapping at my heels like a terrier? Call him off.'

'I will do my best.'

'He is upsetting the whole company,' said Firethorn irritably. 'He should be more friendly towards us in view of the fact that Westfield's Men contains his future son-in-law.'

'I cannot guarantee that.'

'You think he will disown the girl?'

'Let us find the man first,' said Nicholas cautiously. 'I am distressed at our failure to do so. It can only mean that we have someone among us who adds lies to lechery.'

'There is one sure way to expose him, Nick.'

'Is there?'

'Yes,' said Firethorn cheerily. 'Wait until the child is born. If it speaks in Welsh, then Owen Elias is our man. If it has aristocratic poise, Sylvester Pryde is unmasked. And if it has a face like a full moon and sighs like a furnace, then it is Edmund Hoode who has been a-leaping.'

'I think you will find it is none of them.'

'Whoever he is, he cannot hide for ever. I rely on you, Nick.' He punched Nicholas playfully on the arm. 'You will root him out in the end.'

'Someone may do that office for me.'

'Who is that?'

'Our landlord's wife,' said Nicholas. 'She will hound her daughter until she gets the name out of her. Rose Marwood is in desperate straits. Prisoners at the Tower endure a milder interrogation than the one the girl must weather.'

'God's lid!' exclaimed Firethorn putting both hands to his face and shivering with horror. 'I have just had a gruesome thought.'

'What is it?'

'Suppose that the child bears a resemblance to either of the girl's parents? Suppose it has the same unsightly features as Marwood and his wife? It was better to drown the monster at birth in the Thames. No child should be forced to go through life with such a cruel handicap. Have you ever seen two such hideous human beings in one marriage?'

'They are not well-favoured,' said Nicholas tactfully.

'Yet they are very well-matched. Duplicate ghouls.' He gave a shudder. 'You are right, Nick. Rose's predicament is dire. How can she hold out against them? Her parents only have to leer at the girl and they will fright the name of her lover out of her.'

Sybil Marwood hovered over her daughter like a giant eagle, pecking away at her with painful questions and constant reproach.

'For the last time, Rose,' she said, 'who is he?'

'I cannot tell you, mother.'

'Stop protecting the knave!'

'I gave him my word,' bleated the girl piteously. 'I have to honour my promise.'

'Honour!' shouted Sybil. 'You dare to talk of honour! Have you so soon forgot your Ten Commandments? Honour thy father and mother. The Bible enjoins us so. Yet you have dishonoured us in the most dreadful way. And now you make our suffering all the worse by lying to us.'

'I have not lied, mother.'

'Then what else have you done?'

'Told you the truth.'

'Half of it,' said her mother angrily, 'and the worse half at that. The half we do not know concerns the father. Now cease this prevarication and surrender his name.'

'It is a secret that must remain locked away.'

'Rose!'

'I am sorry, mother.'

'Stop torturing me like this.'

'It is you who is torturing me.'

'I have been sainted,' blustered the other.

'You and father have done nothing but revile and condemn me,' whined the girl. 'This was not intended to happen. It was a terrible accident. I am frightened to death by it. I hoped for some comfort from my mother, at least, but you have been a greater scourge than father. I can take no more of it. Leave me be. *Please*. Leave me be!'

Rose Marwood flung herself on the bed in a flood of tears. She was utterly distraught. They were in her bedchamber, an attic room with only meagre light permitted through the small window. Rose was still in her night attire, forbidden even to stir outside the door, lest her shame be seen and voiced abroad and lest her example somehow corrupted the maidservants. A girl who had been a dutiful and obedient daughter until now had brought scandal and disgrace to the Queen's Head.

The initial shock had sent her mother into a frenzy of recrimination but that shock was slowly wearing off. As she saw the pathetic figure before her, sobbing convulsively, on the edge of despair, even Sybil's flinty heart began to crack a little. Maternal instinct, which had hitherto produced nothing more than a long list of rules to govern her daughter's conduct and safeguard her chastity, now prompted a softer and more caring approach. Sitting on the edge of the mattress, Sybil put a clumsy arm around Rose's shoulder.

'There, there!' she soothed. 'Do not cry so.'

'I am terrified, mother.'

'We are here to help you.'

'But you have treated me so harshly.'

'That was wrong of us,' admitted Sybil, stifling the urge to remind Rose of the gravity of her offence. 'These are grim tidings, to be sure, but you are still our daughter and you should be able to turn to us for some kindness.'

Rose lifted her head to look up with tentative gratitude, only half-believing what she had just heard. Her mother so rarely touched her that she felt like a stranger. Sybil took one more step towards true maternalism by enfolding her in a warm embrace and rocking her gently. Because it was such a novel situation for both of them, neither knew quite what to say but some of the damage in their relationship was gradually repaired during the long silence.

When she sensed it, Sybil tried to take advantage of it.

'You were such a beautiful baby,' she recalled fondly.

'Was I?'

'Yes, Rose. You were adorable. Your father and I did our best for you and brought you up to lead a Christian life. You were a credit to us.' She heaved a sigh. 'Until now.'

'I'm sorry, mother. I'm so sorry. I would not hurt you or father for the world.'

'I know, I know.'

'It has been an ordeal,' she continued. 'A horrid nightmare that has kept me awake night after night. I had no idea what was happening to me. I thought I was sick or even dying. I feared that it was a punishment for my sins. It was only when I went to see the physician that he told me the truth. Do you know what I did, mother?'

'What?'

'Fell to the ground in a faint. He had to recover me.'

'Poor child!'

'I felt so *alone*. So completely alone.'

'Not any more.' Sybil held her more tightly and felt some of her daughter's resistance fading. It was time to exploit the unusual moment of closeness. 'We are here for you, Rose. Your father and I will always be here. You were so right to tell us when you did.' She stroked Rose's hair. 'Does he know about the child yet?'

'He?'

'The father.'

'No.'

'Why not? He has responsibilities.'

'He is not able to discharge them, mother.'

'Nevertheless, he has a right to know.'

'That is true,' murmured Rose.

'Is he so heartless that he would cast you off?'

'No, no, he is the kindest man in the universe.'

'Then why is he not here to help you through your time of trial?' asked Sybil. 'I see no hint of kindness in him.'

'That is because you do not know him.'

'Tell me his name and I will.'

'No.'

'I am your mother, Rose. Would you deny me this?'

'I must.'

Sybil squeezed her even tighter. 'You have never hidden anything from me before. Do not betray me now, child.' She deposited a token kiss on Rose's head. 'I love you.'

The declaration fell so awkwardly and unconvincingly from her lips that it put Rose immediately on the defensive. She gritted her teeth and shrunk back slightly from the embrace. Abandoning the gentler strategy, Sybil reverted to a direct assault, taking her by the shoulders to shake her hard.

'I'll beat the name out of you!' she threatened.

'You're hurting me!'

'This is only the start, you ungrateful girl!'

'I will never tell you who he is.'

'Why?' challenged her mother, releasing her. 'Are you so afraid to admit his name. Are you so ashamed of him that you pretend to forget all about him?'

A curious serenity seemed to fall on Rose. She smiled.

'I will never forget him,' she vowed dreamily, 'and I am certainly not ashamed of him. This baby was unlooked for, mother, I swear it, but I will tell you this. It was conceived in love with a man I worship. I will be proud to bear his child.'

'Not if I have anything to do with it!'

Rose was checked. 'What do you mean?'

'This child has no business making its way into the world. I was not able to prevent it from being conceived,' she said with asperity, 'but there may be a way to stop it from being born!'

Chapter Four

The performance of *Mirth and Madness* that afternoon bordered on disaster. While not sinking to the depths they plumbed during the rehearsal, Westfield's Men waged a losing battle against fatigue, indifference and lack of concentration. A hilarious comedy produced scant hilarity. What mirth there was arose largely from the errors with which the performance was littered. Nobody entirely avoided them. Actors collided, cues were missed, lines were forgotten, weapons were mislaid, tankards were dropped and the wrong music was played at the wrong time on three glaringly obvious occasions. Even Barnaby Gill disappointed, stubbing his toe during one of his celebrated comic jigs and hopping off the stage on one foot to blame everyone in sight for his mishap.

Madness, too, was in short supply. The audience saw almost none that was called for in the play. It was reserved for the tiring-house where Lawrence Firethorn, guilty at his own merely adequate performance and frothing at his company's untypical incompetence, ran mad and scolded his colleagues in the most florid language. Nicholas Bracewell did his best to restore an element of calm but his was a lone voice. *Mirth and Madness* was a doomed ship which sailed on to certain calamity with its crew clinging to its bulwarks with an air of resignation.

It was left to George Dart to provoke the most mirth. The smallest and least talented member of the company, he was its natural scapegoat. He was a willing assistant stagekeeper who could work well behind the scenes under supervision but, as soon as he stepped out onto a stage, Dart was always prone to misadventure. His duties in Act Four were relatively simple. Dressed as a forester, he had to carry on the five miniature trees which Nathan Curtis, the carpenter, had made and painted to indicate a woodland setting. The trees were crude but vital properties since they allowed characters to hide behind them and eavesdrop in what was felt to be the funniest scene in the play. George Dart rewrote it in his own unique way.

When he placed the last tree in position, his coat became entwined in its branches and he sought to disentangle it, only managing to get himself more caught up than ever. In an effort to get free, he pulled so hard that he sent the tree hurtling into its neighbour which, in turn, buffeted its own neighbour and so on. All five trees went crashing to the ground like a set of skittles, exposing the young lovers who had been hiding behind them to instant ridicule. In a blind panic, Dart tried to flee but his coat was still snared and it was torn noisily in two by the urgent movement. In the space of a few seconds, he had felled the entire wood, deprived the lovers of their hiding place, ruined his coat and utterly destroyed the scene. When Dart came charging in terror into the tiring-house, Firethorn had to be held back from trying to strangle him.

Yet, oddly, it had a beneficial effect. The woodland scene was their nadir and sheer embarrassment made the company wish to atone for it. Though the last act was still strewn with mistakes, it was a vast improvement on what went before it and partially helped to redeem Westfield's Men. Firethorn led the revival and George Dart was banned from setting any further foot on the stage. Tepid applause greeted them when they came out to take their undeserved bow. Their poor performance severely disappointed their devotees and won them no new admirers. It was an afternoon of sustained blunders.

A grim silence fell on the tiring-house. Players were usually exhilarated by a performance, tumbling off the stage in a mood of excitement which carried them all the way to the taproom. Regret and remorse now prevailed. They were all to blame and they knew it. Lawrence Firethorn, the first to upbraid them for any falling off from their high standards, was too depressed to even address the company. When most of them had changed out of their costumes and drifted away, he confided in Nicholas Bracewell.

'That was atrocious, Nick!'

'I have seen better performances of the play.'

'A worse one is hardly conceivable. We left the piece

in absolute tatters. Everyone – and I include myself – was quite disgraceful. Why? What came over us?'

'We do not feel secure,' said Nicholas. 'Yesterday, on the verge of signing a new contract, the company was at its best. Today, with the threat of eviction hanging over us, our fellows lost heart and walked through a play that demanded a fast pace and concerted action.'

'Yes!' moaned Firethorn. 'The only concerted action the audience saw was when that pea-brained George Dart knocked down five trees simultaneously. Had a rope been to hand, I'd have hanged the idiot from the upper gallery.'

'Do not single George out. All were at fault.'

'Too true, Nick.'

'We must put this afternoon behind us.'

'If we can,' said Firethorn. 'I begin to wonder if the landlord has put a curse on us. Nothing went right.'

'Lack of spirit was to blame. It is a trusty old play but their hearts were not in it. Tomorrow, it will be different.'

'Will it?'

'Westfield's Men will be on their mettle.'

'I hope so, Nick,' said the other gloomily. 'Or we are done for. Marwood will not need to drive us out. We will lose our audience and be deprived of an occupation.'

'There is no chance of that,' said Nicholas confidently. 'We have suffered far more serious reverses than this and always come through them. Today was a minor blemish on our reputation. It will soon be erased and Westfield's Men will resume its position as the leading troupe of the day.'

Firethorn was reassured. 'Yes,' he said, gritting his teeth

and thrusting out his jaw. 'We will fight back hard and win through to glory once more. What is one bad performance in a long catalogue of triumph? We are invincible. That is what we must always remember. Nothing can halt the majestic progress of Westfield's Men.'

At that moment, a stranger came into the tiring-house. They recognised his distinctive livery at once. The servant came over to them and gave a slight bow.

'Master Lawrence Firethorn?' he enquired politely.

'I am he,' confirmed Firethorn.

'I was asked to deliver this to you, sir.'

Firethorn took the letter from him and quailed inwardly.

While one theatre company suffered, another was at the height of its powers. Banbury's Men were the resident company at The Curtain. It was one of the two playhouses built in Shoreditch outside City jurisdiction and therefore free from the petty legislation which hampered work at the inn yard theatres such as the Queen's Head. The Curtain also provided its actors with a far more imposing stage than the makeshift arrangement on barrels which was used by Westfield's Men and enabled them to use a whole range of technical effects denied their inn yard competitors. Giles Randolph was the acknowledged star of Banbury's Men, a tall, slim and slightly sinister individual who shone in roles which allowed him to hatch evil plots and to ooze villainy. *The Spanish Contract* was tailored perfectly to his skills and he led his company superbly that afternoon, earning such a thunderous ovation that it was five minutes before he was allowed to quit the stage at the end of the performance. Randolph bowed long and low, tossing out smiles of gratitude and drinking in the applause.

He was particularly pleased to notice his patron in attendance, giving only a token clap from his position in the upper gallery but evidently delighted with the reception accorded his company. The Earl of Banbury was not a regular playgoer, preferring to lend the company his noble name instead of gracing it with his presence, but *The Spanish Contract* had enticed him to The Curtain and he could not have chosen a more auspicious time to come. Giles Randolph made sure that the lowest and most obsequious bow was directed at their patron. The Earl's vanity had to be propitiated.

Having congratulated his actors and reminded them of the time of rehearsal on the morrow, Randolph dismissed them and shed the regal attire of a Spanish king for his own apparel. He was soon climbing the stairs to a private room at the rear of the upper gallery. The Earl of Banbury was alone with a couple of court beauties whom he had brought along as his guests, flirting outrageously with them and ignoring the huge gap which existed between his age and theirs. When Randolph joined them, their giggles turned to sighs of awe as they were introduced to the actor and whimpers of delight followed as he kissed their hands in greeting.

The niceties were soon concluded. A servant was summoned to conduct the ladies to the earl's waiting carriage while he himself stayed behind to speak with Randolph.

'You were superlative, Giles,' said the Earl.

'Thank you, my lord.'

'My guests were overwhelmed by your performance.'

'That is very gratifying.'

'You carried the whole play on your shoulders.'

'The role was expressly written for me.'

'That was clear,' said the Earl. 'Praise was unstinting. Some dolts choose to argue about who is the finest actor in London – Lawrence Firethorn or Rupert Kitely. Had they been at The Curtain, they would have seen that neither of those actors can hold a candle to you. Giles Randolph is incomparable.'

'You are too kind, my lord.'

'Where is the kindness in honesty? I speak but truth.'

'I endeavour to live up to your high expectations.'

'You do, Giles.' The Earl gave a cackle of pleasure and beckoned him closer with a crook of his finger. 'But I have brought some interesting tidings for you.'

'I long to hear them.'

'Mere rumours at this stage but ones with substance.'

'Tell me more, my lord.'

'First answer this. Who are our most dangerous rivals?'

'Westfield's Men, no question of that.'

'Not Havelock's Men?'

'No, my lord,' said Randolph firmly. 'They have a fine actor in Rupert Kitely and a tolerable stock of plays but they offer no serious threat to us. Lawrence Firethorn does. His company has strength in abundance and far too many playwrights first take their new work to Westfield's Men.' A supercilious note crept in. 'Firethorn has a meagre talent which is, alas, mistaken for something of grander proportion but he lacks true character, he is wanting in those qualities which make for greatness.'

'In short, he is no Giles Randolph.'

'By his own account, he is far superior.'

'Lord Westfield never stops boasting about him,' said the other with a sigh. 'He worships Lawrence Firethorn.'

'Then he worships a false god.'

The Earl of Banbury enjoyed the tart comment so much that he gave a brittle laugh and treasured the remark for use against Lord Westfield himself. He plucked at his goatee beard and peered at Randolph through narrowed lids.

'Do you hate them enough, Giles?' he wondered.

'Hate them?'

'Westfield's Men.'

'I utterly despise them, my lord.'

'What of Lawrence Firethorn?'

'A contemptible man, not fit to lead a company.'

'Then you would like to see him humbled, I think?'

'Humbled and humiliated.'

'Both may be possible,' said the other with a snigger. 'But much depends on you, Giles. It is time to harness your hatred and strike at Westfield's Men. You have many old scores to settle with them, I know, and many slights to avenge. Now then, sir,' he hissed. 'How far would you go?'

'All the way, my lord.'

'No holding back?'

'Not an inch.'

'And the company would support you?'

'To a man.'

'Then hear the news that I bear,' said the Earl, clapping his palms gleefully together. 'If my informers are to be believed – and they have never failed me before – fortune has smiled on us at last. It is time to take decisive action but it must be carefully considered beforehand. Once embarked upon, there is no turning back. You understand me?'

'Very well, my lord.'

'Good. I knew that I could rely on your loyalty, Giles.' He licked his lips. 'Serve me faithfully and Westfield's Men may not only be humbled and humiliated. They will be destroyed!'

Lord Westfield drank the first glass of wine in a single desperate gulp and filled his cup again from the jug. He was in a private room at the Queen's Head, so often a place for a discreet assignation before a performance or for joyous celebration after it, but now a cold and cheerless chamber which served to intensify his dejection. He sat at the little table and buried his head in both hands. Lord Westfield was not mourning the untimely demise of *Mirth and Madness* in front of its audience that afternoon. The performance had scarcely impinged upon his consciousness. Deeper matters agitated him.

He was on his third glass of wine when there was a tap on the door. The servant entered, bowed, then stood aside to admit Lawrence Firethorn and Nicholas Bracewell before bowing once more and withdrawing from the room. The newcomers inclined their heads politely and got a nod of acknowledgement in return. Their patron did not rise from his chair.

'Your letter summoned me, my lord,' said Firethorn.

'It did.'

'I took the liberty of inviting Nicholas Bracewell along. If this concerns the company, there is nobody more well-versed in its inner workings.'

'Then he is welcome,' said their patron. 'I know what a valuable member of Westfield's Men he has become.' He waved a hand. 'Pray take a seat, gentlemen. This news is too heavy to bear standing up.'

Nicholas and Firethorn lowered themselves onto the bench on the opposite side of the room. Fearing criticism, the actor-manager elected to defend himself before the attack came.

'A thousand apologies, my lord,' he said effusively. 'I know that the company fell far short of their best this afternoon but there are reasons for it. The problem will be addressed and solved, I give you my word. At our performance tomorrow, we will be worthy of your name once again.'

Lord Westfield was baffled. 'What are you talking about?'

'*Mirth and Madness.*'

'I have never heard of it.'

'Did you not watch it being played today?'

'I watched something but my mind was far away.'

'Then you have not come to censure us, my lord?' said Firethorn with relief. 'This is heartening.'

'You may not think so when you have listened to the intelligence I have gathered,' said the other. 'Westfield's Men are in grave danger. There could be a serious threat to the company's very existence.'

Firethorn blenched. 'You will surely not withdraw your patronage?' he pleaded.

'Never, Lawrence. I take pride in my company.'

'Then where does this threat come from, my lord?' asked Nicholas. 'You said that it *could* exist. Does that mean there is an element of doubt?'

'Only a small one, Nicholas.'

'Who is after us this time?' said Firethorn pugnaciously. 'We will beat them off, whoever they may be. We have done it before and we will do it again now.'

'That may be not be possible,' said Lord Westfield.

'Why?'

'We are up against the Privy Council.'

Nicholas and Firethorn exchanged an anxious glance.

'Are you certain of this, my lord?' asked Nicholas.

'The signs were infallible.'

'What signs?'

'Those little indications of how the wind blows which I have learnt to pick up,' said their patron. 'The Earl of Banbury was at Court yesterday and looked at me as if I were about to be led to the block for his amusement. Others did the same and so I turned to Sir Patrick Skelton for confirmation of my fears. He lied to me.' His cheeks coloured with anger. 'A man in whom I put complete trust actually lied to me. That was the most infallible sign of all.'

'Of what, my lord?' pressed Nicholas.

'The menace that confronts us. It so disturbed my slumbers in the night that I resolved to know the worst. This morning, I sought a meeting with Sir Edmund Tilney.'

'The Master of the Revels?' said Firethorn.

'The same. A man of power and influence in these matters. And one not given to deviousness or dishonesty. When I confided my worries, he was only too candid.'

'About what, my lord?' said Nicholas. 'Is the Privy Council displeased with our work? Do they wish to shackle us even more? Have the Puritans finally managed to persuade them that playhouses are dens of evil and places of corruption?'

Lord Westfield shook his head. 'I do not know how or why they have come to their brutal decision, Nicholas. Sir Edmund Tilney was not at liberty to divulge the full details to me.'

Firethorn gaped. 'Brutal decision, you say?'

'Brutal, savage and quite unnecessary.'

'What is the Privy Council's decree?'

'It has yet to be finalised,' said Lord Westfield, 'so there is a faint ray of hope that it may yet be softened but it seems unlikely. This is their edict. Believing that London has too many theatres, they are planning to close down all but two playhouses, one north and one south of the Thames. Other companies will be summarily disbanded.'

'This is barbarous!' howled Firethorn.

'What is the reasoning behind it?' asked Nicholas.

'They claim a superfluity of players when most of them, as you well know, lack proper employment. The Privy Council also sides with the City authorities in wanting to close down all the inn yard theatres because – a specious argument, this – they draw people away from their work and are likely to promote violent affray.'

'We have never had a violent affray at the Queen's Head!' roared Firethorn, reining in his ire at once. 'I am sorry to shout in your presence, my lord, but this has cut me to the quick. Close us down! It is unthinkable.'

Nicholas pondered. 'Something more is behind this,' he said. 'Why only two playhouses? That means one in Shoreditch and one in Bankside.'

'No,' said Lord Westfield, 'it means one in Shoreditch and The Rose. Havelock's Men are safe, of that we may be sure. The Viscount's uncle sits on the Privy Council. He would hardly condone a decision which would dispossess his nephew. That leaves only one other company to escape the rigour of this decree.'

'Westfield's Men!' affirmed Firethorn.

'Not if they close down the Queen's Head,' said Nicholas. 'A company with no place to perform would never win the approval of the Privy Council. They would choose one of the playhouses in Shoreditch and we know which one that would be.'

'The Curtain,' sighed their patron. 'Banbury's Men.'

'Over my dead body!' growled Firethorn.

'We will have to battle for our survival, Lawrence.'

'With every sinew in our bodies, my lord.'

'These are bleak tidings.'

'The bleakest possible.' He turned to Nicholas. 'They make our dispute with the landlord and a shabby performance of *Mirth and Madness* seem trivial by comparison.' Firethorn sagged visibly. 'The end of Westfield's Men? At one fell swoop?'

'It may come to that,' said their patron.

'What are we to do, Nick?' whispered Firethorn.

Nicholas took a moment to gather his thoughts.

'First of all,' he suggested, 'we learn the true facts of the situation. This edict is not yet declared and may assume a different shape when it has been framed. The second thing we must do is to shore up our defences.'

'Defences?' said Firethorn.

'Yes,' said Nicholas, 'and hastily. What Lord Westfield has learnt is news already in the possession of our rivals. That is apparent. Banbury's Men and Havelock's Men will each want to strengthen their own positions and the best way to do that is to take captives from Westfield's Men.'

'Nobody would desert us, Nick, surely?'

'I fear that they may. Think of the temptation. Given the choice between work with a new company or certain unemployment with an old one, there may well be those who might defect. We must speak to each of them in turn,' advised Nicholas, 'at the earliest possible opportunity and appeal to their loyalty. We must close ranks. If our actors start leaving us now, we will bleed to death long before the day of our execution.'

The Devil Tavern near Temple Bar served delicious food and fine wine to its patrons. Lucius Kindell rarely dined in such style. His brave decision to support himself as a poet and playwright had not endeared him to his father who, having paid for his education at Oxford, had expected him to join one of the learned professions and carve out an impressive career. Now virtually disinherited, Kindell eked out a living of sorts but it contained more excitement for the mind than sustenance for the body. To be invited to the Devil Tavern, and to be plied with as much food and drink as he could reasonably consume, was a treat to be savoured.

He was the guest of one John Ransome, a friend from his Oxford days who was now at the Inns of Court. A young man of independent wealth, Ransome had a passionate interest in the theatre and wanted to know all that Kindell could tell him about Westfield's Men. The company's apprentice dramatist was so inebriated with the wine and so intoxicated with the heady conversation that he did not notice the third person who joined them at their table. It was only when Ransome excused himself and departed that Kindell could take stock of the newcomer, a short, slight and rather anonymous figure.

'My name is Rupert,' said the stranger.

'Well-met, sir!'

'You are a friend of John Ransome, I hear. He speaks highly of you and that is commendation enough for me.'

'Thank you.'

'How do you like it here?'

'Very much.'

'You must come here again, Lucius.'

'I could not afford to do that too often, sir.'

'That situation may change,' said the other levelly.

Kindell leant forward to peer at his companion through the fug of tobacco smoke. He had seen the man before though in a dozen different guises. His heart began to pound. Was he really seated at the same table as the leading actor from Havelock's Men?

'Your name is Rupert?' he asked.

'It is.'

'Would that be Rupert Kitely, by any chance?'

'Chance is not involved, Lucius,' said the other, honestly. 'I am indeed the man you take me to be and I came here, with John Ransome's connivance, in order to meet and befriend you.'

'I am duly honoured, sir. I have seen you play at The Rose a dozen times or more. Each time you have astonished me.'

Kitely smiled. 'I seem to have done so again.'

'I cannot believe that you should wish to meet me.'

'Why not?'

'You are an established player and I am a mere beginner.'

'Even the best of us has to start somewhere,' said Kitely, 'and I will freely admit that my own introduction to the stage brought nothing like the success which has attended you. I stumbled where you have walked sure-footedly.'

'But all that I have done is to collaborate on two plays with Edmund Hoode. He is my mentor.'

'You could not have chosen better, Lucius. Master Hoode will teach you well until the time comes when you outgrow his tutelage. That time, I suspect, is not too far distant.'

'You think not?'

'I hear wondrous reports of *The Insatiate Duke*.'

'It was a collaboration.'

'But who set it in motion?' asked Kitely. 'Did you not tell John Ransome that you devised the plot and provided the title? Come, Lucius. No modesty here. Take due credit.'

'If you say so, Master Kitely.'

'Rupert,' said the other softly.

He poured more wine into Kindell's cup and more flattery into his ear, slowly winning his confidence and breaking down his defences. The inn was slowly filling and the prevailing mood of jollity spilt over into raucous noise. Kindell was too fascinated by his companion to hear any of it. That someone as distinguished as the actor should show such a keen interest in him was an overwhelming compliment. It never occurred to Kindell to wonder what lay behind it.

'What is your favourite tavern, Lucius?' said Kitely.

'The Queen's Head,' returned the playwright.

'What others do you frequent?'

'None, sir. I have been to the Red Bull and the Dolphin. And we gathered at the Cross Keys Inn yesterday. But I do not know the taverns of London well enough to have many favourites among them.'

'Have you not heard the famous poem?'

'Poem?'

'It will serve as a useful guide to you.'

Rupert Kitely sat upright and began to declaim the lines in a melodious voice, turning banal verse into something that was at once amusing and lyrical.

> *The ladies will dine at the Feathers,*
> *The Globe no captain will scorn:*
> *The huntsmen will go to the Greyhound below,*
> *And some townsmen to the Horn.*

The plummer will dine at the Fountain,
The cooks at the Holy Lamb:
The drunkards at noon to the Man in the Moon
and the cuckolds to the Ram.

The rovers will dine at the Lyon,
The watermen at the Old Swan:
The bawds will to the Negro go
And the whores to the Naked Man.

The keepers will to the White Hart
the mariners unto the Ship:
The beggars they must take their way
to the Eg-shell and the Whip.

The Taylors will dine at the Sheers,
The shoo-makers will to the Boot:
The Welshmen will take their way
And dine at the sign of the Goat.'

Kindell burst into laughter and the other broke off.

'You know a Welshman, I think.'

'Yes, Rupert. His name is Owen Elias.'

'By report, a fine actor.'

'But he also has a goatish disposition,' said Kindell. 'The rest of the company jest about it. Whenever a new wench serves at the tavern, Owen is the first to accost her. The man who penned that verse must have had Owen Elias in mind.'

'Tell me about him,' coaxed the other.

'A wonderful man and a good friend.'

'But what of his talent? Is this goatish Welshman really as gifted as some say? There are even those who call him a second Lawrence Firethorn.'

'Nobody could aspire to that title,' said Kindell. 'There is only one Lawrence Firethorn. He has no peer. But Owen does have rare gifts and would shine in any company.'

'I am pleased to hear it. Tell me why?'

Lucius Kindell talked at great length about his friends, quite unaware of the fact that he was being expertly pumped by the actor. Wine and wooing conspired to lower his defences. His naivety was subtly exploited. When it was all over and Rupert Kitely had been given a detailed insight into the membership and activities of Westfield's Men, he rose from his chair and helped Kindell up after him.

'Come, my friend,' he said. 'Let us walk to the river.'

'The river?'

'We can take a boat across the Thames.'

'To what end, sir?'

'I wish to show you our playhouse, Lucius.'

'But I have seen The Rose many times.'

'Only through the eyes of a spectator. Never as a prospective member of Havelock's Men. Here,' he said as Kindell tottered, 'lean on me, Lucius.'

When they came out into the street, the cold air hit Kindell with the force of a slap and he recoiled slightly. His companion supported him and they made their way unsteadily towards the river. The young playwright was still too flattered by Rupert Kitely's attentions to probe their true meaning. He glanced over his shoulder.

'There was no mention of the Devil in your poem.'

'Was there not?' said Kitely. 'We can soon amend that.'

'There is a verse about the tavern?'

'Yes but I choose to improve it a little.'

'Improve it?'

> *'The weavers will dine at the Shuttle,*
> *The bellmen go straight to the Bell;*
> *The hounds of hell to the Devil repair*
> *With Kitely and Lucius Kindell.'*

Their laughter mingled and echoed along the street.

They were all there. The eight sharers were crammed into the parlour of Lawrence Firethorn's house in Shoreditch to discuss the latest crisis which had befallen Westfield's Men. For once in his life, Barnaby Gill did not object to the presence of Nicholas Bracewell, sensing that the hired man might be the one person who could affect their survival. Refreshment had been provided by Firethorn's wife, Margery, who closed the door on the debate and scattered the apprentices who were trying to eavesdrop outside it. Many important meetings had been held at short notice in her home but Margery knew that none had greater significance than this one. Westfield's Men were engaged in a battle against extinction.

Lawrence Firethorn stood in the middle of the room as if he were at the centre of the stage at the Queen's Head. He ran his eye over the visitors.

'You all know why we are here,' he said solemnly. 'The Privy Council is poised to strike us down. We must decide how best to protect ourselves from its blow.'

'There is no protection,' moaned Edmund Hoode. 'How can we resist an edict of the Privy Council? It is the supreme power in the land. We are defeated.'

'No, Edmund,' said Owen Elias truculently. 'Never talk of defeat while there is breath in our bodies to fight.'

'Against whom?' said Barnaby Gill. 'The Privy Council? I side with Edmund here. We are minnows against a giant whale. We will be gobbled up at the first bite.'

'You might be, Barnaby,' said Firethorn, 'but I'll not. Nor will Westfield's Men. Should they try to gobble us up, we'll cause such havoc in their mouth that they will be forced to spit us out again.'

'How do we do that?' challenged Gill.

'That is what we are met to decide.'

'The decision has already been made for us, Lawrence.'

'That is not quite true,' Nicholas Bracewell reminded them. 'All that we have been given by Lord Westfield is a timely warning. No decree has yet been issued by the Privy Council and our patron has sworn to use what influence he has to prevent that decree from ever seeing the light of day. Whether or not he will succeed, we do not know, but he may at the very least put in an eloquent plea for Westfield's Men.'

'The most eloquent plea comes from our audience,' said Sylvester Pryde, looking around the room. 'I am new to this company, gentleman, and feel a natural diffidence in speaking out on its behalf but I do have one advantage. Until recently,

I was a complete outsider, able to observe and enjoy every theatre company in London before choosing to tie my future to this one. None of your rivals has such a large and faithful following as Westfield's Men. Popularity must surely be a touchstone here. The Privy Council would not dare to put to death the most loved and respected troupe in London.'

Hoode rolled his eyes. 'They would and they will.'

'Why?'

'That, Sylvester,' said Nicholas, 'is what Lord Westfield is endeavouring to find out for us. If we learn the motives behind this edict, we will have a clearer idea of where we stand and how we may best respond.'

'We stand in the shadow of the gallows,' sighed Hoode.

'There is nothing new in that,' said Firethorn. 'We have inhabited that shadow for a long time and always managed to cheat the headsman in the past.'

'How can we do so again?' asked Elias.

The lively debate was tempered with a general sadness. Hoode and Gill were already resigned to their fate and James Ingram, one of the younger sharers, shared their pessimism. Firethorn tried to inject some hope, Elias lent his usual jovial belligerence and Pryde supported their readiness to struggle by any means at their disposal to rescue Westfield's Men from the threat of the axe, but their arguments did not carry real conviction. Behind their bold assertions lay a recognition of cold reality. If the edict were passed, their chances of survival were perilously slim. An air of melancholy hung over the whole room. There was a long, painful silence during which they all reflected on their doom.

It was Nicholas Bracewell who finally spoke up.

'There *is* a solution,' he said thoughtfully. 'It is no guarantee of our survival but it would enhance our position greatly. We are fettered here. Havelock's Men and Banbury's Men hold the whip hand over us because they have playhouses where we have an inn yard.'

'Owned by a lunatic landlord!' snorted Firethorn.

'And soon to be closed to us,' noted Hoode.

'Let's hear Nick,' said Pryde, his interest aroused. 'I know that look on his face. I believe that he has a plan.'

'A burial service would be more appropriate,' said Gill.

'Speak up, Nick,' urged Firethorn. 'Tell us what to do.'

'It is only a suggestion,' said Nicholas, 'and I know that it is fraught with all kinds of difficulties but it would at least put us on an equal footing with our rivals. In my opinion, there is only one way to compete with Havelock's Men and Banbury's Men.'

'Aye,' said Elias. 'Murder the whole pack of them!'

'No, Owen. We meet them on their own terms.'

'And how do we do that, Nick?'

Nicholas gazed around his drooping companions.

'We build a playhouse of our own,' he said quietly.

'If only we could!' said Firethorn.

Gill was dismissive. 'A preposterous notion!'

'Is it?' rejoined Nicholas. 'Consider it well.'

'We have, Nick,' said Hoode wearily. 'Many times.'

'Always without success,' said Elias.

'Nothing would please me more than to have our own playhouse,' announced Firethorn dramatically. 'And it would gladden the heart of our patron as well. But we might as well wish for a palace of pure gold. We have no site, Nick. We have no builder. We have no money.'

Nicholas was undeterred. 'A site can be found,' he argued, 'and a builder engaged. And there must be ways to raise the money that would be needed.'

'Do you know how much the enterprise would cost?' asked Firethorn sadly. 'Far more than we could ever muster.'

'I still believe that we can do it,' said Nicholas. 'With a playhouse of our own, we could mount a challenge against any company in London and compel the Privy Council to grant us a reprieve. I know full well what cost would be entailed and how much the company would be able to put towards it from the profits. The rest can be sought from elsewhere. We simply need to secure a loan.'

'Out of the question, Nick,' said Firethorn with a shrug. 'Who on earth would lend an impecunious theatre company that amount of money?'

Sylvester Pryde rose to his feet and shared a warm smile among them. He spoke in a tone of ringing confidence.

'Tell me how much you need and I will find it for you.'

Chapter Five

Alexander Marwood was a soul in torment. Clad in his night attire but fearing that he would never again know the joys of slumber, he paced relentlessly up and down, his face so animated by nervous twitches that it changed its shape and expression with every second. His wife, Sybil, was propped up in bed in a state of ruminative anger, her features set in stone but her eyes gently smouldering. Marwood travelled aimlessly on. A bedchamber which had long been an instrument of torture to him now inflicted further refinements of pain. The agony reached the point where it burst out of him in a piercing yell.

'Arghhhhh!'

'What ails you, sir?' asked Sybil.

'Everything,' he moaned. 'My debts, my troubles, my misery. The whole of my life ails me! I am in Purgatory.'

'No,' she scolded. 'You are in a bedchamber with your wife. Do you think that is Purgatory?'

Marwood bit back an affirmative retort.

'Look at my situation,' he wailed. 'A daughter who has brought shame and ignominy down on me. An actor who was responsible for her condition yet whom I am powerless to evict. And now this latest threat to my sanity. A rumoured decision of the Privy Council to close all inn yard theatres.'

'I would have thought you would welcome that decision.'

'Welcome it, Sybil!'

'It achieves what you and that costly lawyer, Ezekiel Stonnard, have failed to do. It throws Westfield's Men out of the Queen's Head and rids us of the father of Rose's child.'

'Yes, my love, and I would give it my blessing if it did not also deprive us of such a large part of our income. I long to sever my contract with Westfield's Men but only in order to replace them with another company, much more trustworthy and amenable.'

'You have always hated players.'

'I hate beer but I have no qualms about selling it.'

'You are perverse, Alexander.'

'I have to look to the future,' he said. 'As you have so often pointed out to me, a theatre company brings custom here in abundance. To lose that source of money would be ruinous.'

'What do you intend to do about it?'

'Register my complaint in the strongest language.'

'To whom?'

'The Privy Council.'

'Ha! What notice would they take of a mere innkeeper?'

'I am wounded by this decision, Sybil.'

'We both are, sir,' she said sharply, 'but not so deep a wound as the one inflicted on us by our own daughter. That is what vexes me night and day.'

'And me. And me.'

'Then why have you not found the name of the father?'

'I might ask the same of you.'

'Rose is headstrong. She will not tell me.'

'Press her more closely.'

'Do you dare to instruct me?' she said warningly.

He backed off at once. 'No, no, Sybil. You know best how to handle the girl. You always have. But it is a wonder to me that you have not prised the name out of her.'

'It is protected by a lover's vow.'

'This lover's vow is more like a leper's handshake.'

'Rose is young and vulnerable,' said his wife with a grim nostalgia, 'as I once was. Vows exchanged in the heat of passion can bind for life. I found that out to my cost.'

Marwood did not dare to probe her meaning. When he thought of his daughter, he remembered that the last time his wife had given him the delights due to a husband was on the night when Rose was conceived. The girl was a living symbol of his years of deprivation. The fact that she herself, unmarried and not even betrothed, had savoured the pleasures of carnal love came as a huge shock to him. His lip curled vengefully.

'We must find the villain!'

'That was your office, Alexander.'

'I taxed Master Firethorn by the hour.'

'What has he done?'

'Asked his book holder to look into the matter.'

'Did Nicholas Bracewell not track down the villain?' she said in surprise. 'Then the man is more cunning than we thought. If he can elude someone as sharp-eyed as Master Bracewell, what hope do *we* have of finding him?'

'Rose.'

'Her lips will not speak his name.'

'Nor will those of the players,' said Marwood, 'though some of them must surely know who the rogue is. Such men always boast of their conquests. Half the company have probably heard the story of how he seduced Rose Marwood.' He came to a sudden halt and stamped both feet in turn. 'This is unbearable. I am in Hell itself!'

'Keep your voice down, Alexander.'

'I will expire from a broken heart.'

'You will do nothing of the kind, sir. You will stay on the trail of this man until you run him down. It is only a question of time. Rose admitted that he was an actor so we know that he is a member of Westfield's Men.'

'Or was, Sybil.'

'Was?'

'That was Nicholas Bracewell's thought. Haply, the man is no longer with them. The company changes all the time. In the course of a season, they take on and release a number of hired men. Rose's lover could have been one of them.' He plucked recklessly at his few remaining tufts of hair. 'He may not even be in London any more. He may be sowing his vile seed a hundred miles away.'

She became indignant. 'Spare me such foul language, sir.'

'I am sorry. Despair got the better of me, Sybil.'

'Then take your despair elsewhere if it makes your tongue run with such filth. I expect purity in my bedchamber.'

Marwood did not have the courage to mention his own blighted expectations with regard to the marital couch. They had withered on the vine many years ago. When he looked at Sybil now, a lump of human granite in billowing white linen, he marvelled at the fact that they had somehow, somewhere, in the distant recesses of time and by a grotesque error, actually had a semblance of affection for each other which had enabled them to produce a child. Marwood gurgled. Every second of illusory pleasure which he experienced that night had cost him hour upon hour of excruciating pain.

Sybil had closed her eyes and fallen so eerily silent that he supposed her to be asleep. After another frantic stroll up and down the room, he went to the bed and climbed carefully in beside her. His wife let out a deep murmur.

'Master Pryde!'

'Who?'

'Sylvester Pryde,' she said firmly. 'I have come to believe that he was Rose's downfall.'

'Which one is he, Sybil?'

'The handsome man with airs and graces. He wears fine apparel and has a quality most of his fellows lack. His beard is always well-trimmed. He is more liberal with his purse than the others, more courteous, too. Rose noticed him.'

Envy stirred. 'It seems that she was not the only one!'

'I was only displaying a mother's vigilance.'

'I know, I know,' said Marwood with a mollifying touch on her arm. 'What astounds me is how he managed to evade your vigilance. It has kept Rose safe from harm for so long. The man we seek is clearly Deception itself.'

'Sylvester Pryde may fit that description.'

'But he was questioned along with the others and found innocent of the charge. Nicholas Bracewell would have put serious questions to him.'

'I would like to do that myself,' said Sybil darkly. 'This Sylvester Pryde is altogether too plausible. I have a strong sense that he is involved here. When I mentioned his name to Rose, she blushed crimson.'

'Let me at him!' said her husband, flaring into life again. 'I'll take a pair of shears and geld the knave.' He made such a violent gesture with his hands that the bedside candle was blown out by the displaced air. 'I'll insist that Master Firethorn expels the miscreant at once.'

'We have first to be certain of his guilt, Alexander. And that can only be done by wresting a confession from Rose. I'll work more craftily on her.'

'Do so, Sybil. Practice on her. Wear her down. You are well-versed in that black art.'

'What black art?' she asked.

'I spoke in jest,' he said, regretting his momentary lapse into honesty about his wife. 'What I was praising was your gifts of persuasion.'

'I hope so, sir. I am in no mood for censure.'

118

'I have complete confidence in you,' he assured her –
then an image of his daughter came suddenly into his mind.
He gave an involuntary shiver. 'When is the unbidden child
due?'

'Forget the child.'

'How can I forget it when she carries it before her?'

'We may soon rid ourselves of that burden.'

'How? That devilish grandchild will be around our necks
for the rest of our days. With the whole parish pointing
their fingers and laughing at us. We will have to feed, clothe
and bring up a bastard child, Sybil.'

'I'll not endure that.'

'You will have to, my love. There is no cure.'

She turned to face him and opened a bulging eye.

'There is.'

Nicholas Bracewell returned to Bankside that night at a far
later hour than he had intended. Having nobly waited up
for him, Anne Hendrik, tired and slightly tetchy, was about
to scold him for breaking his promise to get back earlier
when she saw the deep concern etched in his face. Tiredness
fled, tetchiness disappeared and a surge of sympathy
ensued. After giving him a welcoming kiss, she led him to
the parlour and sat beside him.

'Something terrible has happened,' she guessed.

'It *may* happen, Anne.'

'What may?'

'Extinction.'

When he explained the situation to her, she cursed

119

herself inwardly for imagining for one moment that he had been delayed by some roistering with his fellows in the taproom. Anne knew that she should have had more faith in her lodger. Only a serious crisis would have made Nicholas default on his promise and nothing could be more serious than threat of dissolution.

'What does Lawrence Firethorn say?' she asked.

'I would not care to repeat his words in front of you.'

'And the others?'

'Most are resigned to their doom.'

'Without even fighting for survival?' she said with spirit. 'That does not sound like Westfield's Men. You have overcome plague, puritan attacks, disapproval by the City authorities, a fire at the Queen's Head, even the imprisonment of Edmund Hoode for seditious libel. Your inn yard playhouse has been closed down before but it has always opened again.'

'Not this time, Anne.'

'Only two theatres to remain? It is a scandal.'

Nicholas pursed his lips and nodded. 'There are those in the Privy Council who believe that theatre itself is a scandal,' he said philosophically, 'and they have strong support from the Church. We are up against the great and the good, Anne. They have the power to muzzle us completely.'

'Is there no way out of this predicament?'

'Only one and even that might not save us. But at least it would give us a fair chance against our rivals. They would think twice about ending the career of Westfield's Men so abruptly if we had our own playhouse.'

Anne was incredulous. 'Your own playhouse?'

'Yes,' he said with a wan smile, 'I know it may sound like a wild dream but it is not outside the bounds of possibility. First, we need a site. Next, we must hire a builder. And then there is the small problem of paying for them both and buying the materials for construction.'

'Can this be done, Nick?'

'If we want it enough, it can.'

'But where would your playhouse be?'

'Here in Bankside, Anne.'

'When we already have The Rose?'

'But that is all you have,' he said. 'Shoreditch has two theatres close by each other. If we build a third there, we have to compete with both of the others.'

'In Bankside you would be up against Havelock's Men.'

'True.'

'And you told me even now that they had some influence with the Privy Council.'

'Viscount Havelocks' uncle is a member of it.'

'Then your cause is lamed from the start.'

'No, Anne,' he reasoned. 'One man does not make the final decision about which two companies survive. The whole Privy Council will sit in judgement and they will take the advice of the Master of the Revels. Sir Edmund Tilney admires our work greatly but deplores our inn yard. In their own playhouse, Westfield's Men would shine like a jewel in a proper setting.'

'You would certainly outshine Havelock's Men.'

'That is why we must come here.'

'How was this idea received?' she asked.

Nicholas grinned. 'With utter disbelief at first,' he admitted. 'Edmund Hoode thought I had taken leave of my senses. Even Owen Elias was sceptical. Most of the others thought the project hopelessly beyond us until I listed some of the advantages with which we start.'

'Advantages?'

'We have a company of able-bodied men, Anne. With Nathan Curtis to teach us, we could all turn carpenter and help to build the structure ourselves. That would save us a great deal of money.'

'You would still need to find a considerable sum.'

'Sylvester Pryde came to our rescue there.'

'Sylvester? He has that kind of wealth?'

'No,' said Nicholas, 'but he is acquainted with many people who have. He swore to us that he could raise the bulk of the money for us. I believe him.'

'Sylvester is the best advantage of all.'

'Not quite.'

'What do you mean?'

'We have another good friend on whom we may call.'

'Who is that?'

'Anne Hendrik.'

She was startled. 'Me!'

'Yes,' he explained, 'the labour is vital and the money imperative but something comes before both.'

'Choosing the site.'

'That will be your contribution.'

'But I know nothing about the building of a playhouse.'

'You know Bankside better than any of us, Anne. Your trade brings you into contact with people all over Southwark. You have an instinct for business and an eye for a bargain. I'd willingly put my trust in you.'

'I would not know where to start, Nick.'

'Here and now,' he said, kissing her lightly on the lips. 'I will tell you what features a site must have and you will be well-prepared to begin your search tomorrow. Speed is of the essence here, Anne. A project like this must quickly gather its own momentum or it is lost.'

'It is certainly an exciting proposal,' she said.

'Exciting and inspiring.'

'With one huge drawback.'

'What is that?'

'You might go to all the trouble and expense of building a playhouse, only to find that the Privy Council closes it down again and sends Westfield's Men into the wilderness.'

Nicholas sat back in his chair and heaved a sigh.

'That is a risk we will have to take, Anne.'

A pall seemed to hang over the Queen's Head next morning. Word of their precarious position had seeped down to the lowest ranks of Westfield's Men and robbed them of all spirit. George Dart walked around as if in a dream. Nathan Curtis wielded his hammer without purpose as he converted the high-backed chair which had been used in *Mirth and Madness* into a regal throne. Hugh Wegges, the tireman, wondered if it was worth mending costumes which might never be used again. Peter Digby and his musicians were matching portraits of dejection and Thomas Skillen, the ancient stagekeeper, a man who had weathered so many threats to his livelihood in his long career in the theatre, felt that he could at last hear the funeral bell.

Alexander Marwood added to the general melancholy, circling the inn yard like a mangy old dog moping over a dead master. His wife glared down on them from a window, a hovering vulture who waited to pick their bones. When they erected their stage, there was a queasy feeling that they might be doing so for the last time. Superstitious by nature, actors saw bad omens on every side. Nicholas Bracewell did what he could to raise their morale but all that he could conjure into being were pale smiles on the faces of corpses.

Edmund Hoode arrived in a state of gibbering terror.

'It has started, Nick,' he confided.

'What has?'

'The fight to the death with our rivals.'

'In what way, Edmund?'

'They have got at Lucius Kindell.'

'They?'

'Havelock's Men,' said Hoode with disgust. 'Or, to speak more precisely, that scheming fiend they call Rupert Kitely. He has led poor Lucius astray.'

'How do you know?' said Nicholas in mild alarm.

'They were seen together at the Devil Tavern last night and I doubt that Lucius had the wit to sup with a long spoon. When I called at his lodging this morning, I was told that he had gone to The Rose.' Hoode looked betrayed.

'What more proof do we need? They have seduced him away.'

'Did he expect you to call this morning?'

'Yes, Nick. It was arranged that he would watch the rehearsal of *The Loyal Subject*. Lucius has written a couple of speeches he wanted me to include in the play. There is no hope of that now. He has sold his soul to Havelock's Men.'

'We are not certain of that, Edmund.'

'Why else consort with Rupert Kitely?'

'Do not rush to condemn him,' warned Nicholas. 'There may yet be another explanation. Lucius is himself a loyal subject. He acknowledges the debt he owes to Westfield's Men.'

'Then what is he doing at The Rose?'

'We will soon find out.'

'I nurtured him,' said Hoode sadly. 'I taught him all that I knew about my craft. It would have been impossible to find an apprentice playwright more eager to learn and willing to work. And no pupil could have been more grateful to his master than Lucius Kindell.' His voice hardened into a bark. 'Until this happened. I have been stabbed in the back.'

'It is worrying news, certainly.'

'A tragedy, Nick. And only the beginning.'

'Yes,' agreed the other. 'I said that we had to shore up our defences. Our rivals are predators. They will swoop down and seize whoever they can in their beaks.'

Hoode ran a despairing eye over the rest of the company.

'Lucius is our first loss,' he said. 'Who is next?'

At that moment, Lawrence Firethorn came clattering

into the yard on his horse to take control. Sensing at once the mood of despondency, he tried to dispel it by issuing crisp orders to all and sundry. Response was immediate. The assistant stagekeepers built the stage with more urgency, the carpenter hammered with more enthusiasm, the tireman picked up his needle and thread, the musicians began to practise and the hired men who had been standing around in disconsolate groups now made their way swiftly to the tiring-house. Leaping down from the saddle, Firethorn handed the reins of his horse to a waiting ostler and crossed to his friends.

'Good morrow!' he said cheerily.

'I see no goodness in it, Lawrence,' said Hoode.

'That is because you spent the night in a cold and lonely bed, Edmund. Had you shared the hours of darkness with a wife as warm as Marjory, you would have been up with the lark and throbbing with energy to greet the new day.' He gave a ripe chuckle. 'Marriage has many pains but its pleasures are truly beyond compare.'

Hoode grimaced. 'How can you talk of pleasure at such a time? Westfield's Men have no future ahead of them.'

'We have a far more glorious future ahead.'

'If we all work together for it,' said Nicholas.

'Yes,' said Firethorn. 'Unity is our strength. Let them all come at us. The company will triumph. Ah, what a sublime difference a night of bliss can make to a man! I retired to bed as the manager of a troupe which might soon become defunct and I awoke as the leader of a happy band of lads who may soon have their own playhouse.'

'You will not find much happiness here, Lawrence,' said Hoode gloomily. 'Most of our fellows do not share your optimism.'

'Then it will have to be beaten into them. Eh, Nick?'

'A good performance is the best remedy.'

'Then we will have it,' vowed Firethorn, punching the air with a clenched fist. 'By heaven! We'll set the stage alight with our skills. *Mirth and Madness* was a travesty. We owe our audience a superlative performance to atone for yesterday's disgrace. And what better play to offer them this afternoon than *The Loyal Subject* by a certain Edmund Hoode?'

'What better play?' echoed Hoode. '*The Insatiate Duke*.'

'They'll have that again, too, before the week is out.'

'They may have the play, Lawrence, but not the author.'

'You are the author, Edmund.'

'I am one of them. The other was Lucius Kindell.'

'Well?'

'He has turned traitor.'

'That is not so,' said Nicholas, jumping in to prevent Hoode from reciting his mournful news. 'Lucius is a rising talent who is bound to be courted by our rivals. But he will always choose Westfield's Men over them, especially when he hears that we are to have our own playhouse.'

'Will that miracle ever come to pass?' said Hoode.

'Yes!' affirmed Nicholas.

'No question but that it will,' added Firethorn. 'I will strain every fibre of my being to bring it about.'

'Everybody will do the same,' said Nicholas. 'When they

see that we have a choice between survival or disappearance, the whole company will rise to the challenge.'

'That may be so, Nick,' said Hoode, 'and you will not find me wanting. But I have grave doubts about our ability to raise the necessary money.'

'Sylvester Pryde will find most of what we need.'

'He will not let us down,' said Firethorn confidently.

'Then where is he?' asked Hoode.

'What?'

'Sylvester is not here, Lawrence. I was the first to arrive this morning and I can assure you that he has not come in through that gate.' Hoode shrugged. 'Nobody likes Sylvester more than I. He is a cheerful companion and a generous friend. But he does too often try to seize attention and ingratiate himself. What if his offer was no more than an idle boast to gain a momentary lustre?'

'It was made in good faith,' insisted Nicholas.

'Then where is he?'

'Sylvester will be here any moment.'

'Yes,' said Firethorn airily, 'and he will expect to rehearse *The Loyal Subject*. Let us begin, gentlemen. Nick, gather the whole company into the tiring-house. I'll put some heart into them and assure them that Westfield's Men are not destined for the grave.'

Firethorn stalked off but Hoode's scepticism remained.

'Where is Sylvester?' he said.

'He will be here,' replied Nicholas.

'I thought that about Lucius.'

He walked forlornly away. Nicholas went after him and

collected all the members of the company into the room at the rear of the stage which was used as the tiring-house. Everyone but Sylvester Pryde was there and his absence was worrying. In his short time with Westfield's Men, he had been unfailingly punctual. At such a critical time in the company's fortunes, it was vital for him to be there.

Firethorn spoke to them like a warrior king addressing his army on the eve of battle. There was pure steel in his voice. When he told them about the project to secure a playhouse of their own, heads lifted and frowns vanished. They were also reminded of their shameful performance on the previous day and they resolved to make amends. By the time Firethorn had finished, even the wilting Edmund Hoode and the cynical Barnaby Gill were enthused. They donned their costumes with alacrity.

Yet there was still no sign of Sylvester Pryde. Hiding his concern behind a broad smile, Firethorn took Nicholas aside.

'Where *is* the fellow?' he whispered.

'I do not know.'

'Can he be sick?'

'I think it unlikely.'

'Still lying in the arms of some woman?'

'Sylvester has never let anyone distract him before.'

'Then why is he doing so now?'

'I have sent George Dart to his lodging in search of him,' said Nicholas. 'Meanwhile, I would suggest that we reassign Sylvester's roles to other members of the company for the rehearsal. Owen Elias and James Ingram can most easily take over those roles and both are experienced at doubling.'

'Instruct them to that effect, Nick.'

'I will.'

'And pray that Sylvester turns up,' said Firethorn. 'He must not desert us in our hour of need.'

'There is no possibility of that.'

Nicholas's reassurance sounded hollow. Both men were now having serious doubts about Pryde and they knew how important it was to start the rehearsal before those doubts spread throughout the entire company. Busy actors would have no time to brood. When the musicians were in position, therefore, Nicholas gave the signal and the fanfare sounded. Owen Elias stepped out in a black cloak to deliver the Prologue to a couple of ostlers and four curious horses.

They were well into Act Two before a breathless George Dart came staggering into the tiring-house. Nicholas gave the cue for the Queen and her train to make an entry then he beckoned the diminutive figure across to him. The perspiration was running in rivulets down Dart's face.

'What news, George?'

'None that will please you, alas.'

'Was Sylvester not at his lodging?'

'No. He left at first light, it seems.'

'Where did he go?'

'His landlord did not know. Nor does he understand why Sylvester Pryde quit the house for good.'

Nicholas was shaken. 'For good, you say?'

'When he left, he took his belongings with him.'

'No word of explanation?'

'None, I fear.' Dart wiped an arm across his glistening brow. 'I am sorry I could not bear happier tidings.'

'You have done well, George. Change into your costume as a guard in the royal retinue and be ready for the first scene in Act Three. Oh, and one thing,' cautioned Nicholas. 'Do not mention to anyone that Sylvester has quit his lodging. It might cause unnecessary alarm.'

Dart nodded and went off to find his costume. Nicholas turned his full attention to the rehearsal and put the disappearance of Sylvester Pryde from his mind. There was no point in worrying over a problem he was powerless to solve while he as engaged in his duties as the book holder. It was only when the play came to an end that the subject took on a new urgency. Having thanked the company for the sterling effort which they had put into the rehearsal, Firethorn dismissed them and sought a quiet word with Nicholas.

'Well?' he said.

'Sylvester is still not here.'

'Where can the man be?'

'Not at his lodging, that much is certain. He left at dawn and took his belongings with him.'

Firethorn blenched. 'Has he fled London?'

'I hope not.'

'Why else quit his lodging?'

'I have no idea,' confessed Nicholas, 'What surprises me is that he sent no word to us. Sylvester has always been so considerate. This sudden flight is disturbing.'

'And may bring all our ambitions crashing down,'

said an anxious Firethorn. 'Without Sylvester, there will be no money. Without that money, there will be no new playhouse. Did he deliberately raise our hopes in order to dash them, Nick?'

'That would not be in his character.'

'What is he playing at?'

'We will discover that in time,' said Nicholas. 'Until then, we must not unsettle the others by telling them he has disappeared. I will devise an excuse which will cover his absence.'

'Your excuse would not fool me for a moment,' said a voice behind them. 'However prettily it was phrased.'

They turned to see Barnaby Gill entering the tiring-house.

'You were eavesdropping!' accused Firethorn.

'I have a right to know the truth, Lawrence.'

'By lurking outside a door?'

'Sylvester has fled the sinking ship,' said Gill wryly. 'I could have foretold this. He was all noise and pretence, a man of fashion who liked to disport himself upon a stage, a strutting peacock with no real belief in the actor's art.'

'That is not so,' countered Nicholas. 'Sylvester was keen to study and improve. He was committed to Westfield's Men.'

'Where is that commitment now?'

'We begin to wonder,' said Firethorn ruefully.

Gill was sardonic. 'Wonder no more, Lawrence. He has ridden out of London as fast as he can. That promise to secure a loan for us was no more than a vain boast. It gave him a moment of ascendancy over us. Having enjoyed that, he has left the rest of us floundering.'

'So it seems, Barnaby.'

'I have more trust in Sylvester,' said Nicholas.

Gill snorted. 'Then it is misplaced.'

'He loved this company.'

'Until he discovered that there is no longer a company to love. He has gone. Such men are rovers. They never stay long in one place.' Gill sniffed at his pomander. 'I wager that we never set eyes again on Sylvester Pryde.'

Nothing more could be said. They went off to the taproom to seek refreshment before the afternoon's performance. No mention was made of the missing actor but he was clearly on the mind of the whole company. Their sharer had deserted them and the projected playhouse lay in ruins. Everyone sensed it. There was no way that the company itself could raise such a substantial loan on their own. They had tried and failed many times. Their patron, Lord Westfield, was even less likely to come to their aid. Crippled by debts, he was more concerned with seeking loans for his own purse than for any building plans conceived by his troupe. Their plight was hopeless.

Yet they did not surrender to despair. The prospect of dissolution seemed instead to fill them with determination to give a good account of themselves in what might be one of a series of valedictory performances. Westfield's Men were determined to be remembered, to write their signature boldly and vividly on the memories of London playgoers.

When they returned to the tiring-house, there was

a mood of resolution. Firethorn strengthened it with another rousing speech but it was Nicholas who perceived another side to the new sense of purpose. While keen to serve Westfield's Men to the best of their ability, they also wanted to attract the attention of their rivals. Havelock's Men and Banbury's Men were the favoured survivors of the Privy Council's edict and they would divide the spoils of Westfield's Men. That being the case, it was highly likely that both companies would have someone in the audience to study the company and select the most likely recruits. Westfield's Men were auditioning for their individual survival.

The yard was full, the galleries bursting and the actors straining at the leash. *The Loyal Subject* was a fine play, first performed at Court during the Christmas festivities and a reminder that the company had been favoured with royal patronage. With a mere ten minutes to go before the drama started, the tension was broken in the most unexpected way.

'I am sorry to keep you all waiting, lads!'

Sylvester Pryde strode cheerfully into the tiring-house to be met by a tidal wave of questions. He raised both hands to silence the company then motioned them in close to him.

'I went in search of money,' he explained. 'That meant an hour's ride out of London. I left a message with my surly landlord but I see from your faces that he never delivered it. The rogue was too angry at my sudden departure to oblige me. No matter, friends. I am here now and so is our saviour.'

'Our saviour?' said Firethorn. 'Who is he?'

'That must remain a secret,' warned Pryde, 'but this I

134

can tell you. The loan is all but secured but nobody can be expected to advance so much money without some proof of your genuine quality. I brought him to the Queen's Head to watch you this afternoon. Your saviour sits up in the gallery. My part is done,' he said with a grin. 'The money is there but you must show yourselves worthy of it.'

'God's tits!' said Firethorn with a laugh. 'We'll dazzle like sunlight. You heard him, lads. It is up to us now. Seize this opportunity with both hands. Follow me!'

Owen Elias and James Ingram gladly relinquished the roles they had taken over from Pryde and the latter quickly changed into his costume for the first scene. Determination now shaded into euphoria. At the eleventh hour, they believed, they had been rescued by the man whom they had all foolishly suspected of deserting them. When the performance commenced, they hurled themselves into it as if their lives depended on the outcome.

It was a sensation. Inspired by Lawrence Firethorn, the whole company shone brilliantly, bringing out every facet of *The Loyal Subject* and attesting once again their supremacy on the London stage. The audience was alternately harrowed and amused as tragic events were interleaved with comic diversion. Somewhere in one of the galleries was the person whose money could reprieve them and they directed their performance at their invisible saviour. At the end of the play's final dramatic scene, they were given an ovation which set their blood coursing.

While the rest of the company went off to the taproom to celebrate, Sylvester Pryde slipped quietly away to seek out their benefactor. They were kept waiting for a long time before he appeared again. When he finally did so, his face was clouded, his shoulders hunched and his gait halting. His every motion signalled rejection. Profound disappointment fell on the company. Pryde dispelled it with a wicked grin.

'The loan is secured!' he announced.

'Did he enjoy our performance?' asked Firethorn.

'Our saviour exulted in it. The money is ours.'

'The man is our guardian angel!'

'We will have our playhouse after all,' said Hoode with a giggle of pleasure. 'But what shall it be called?'

Suggestions came thick and fast and Nicholas Bracewell waited until the separate imaginations had run dry. He then stepped into the middle of the group.

'Master Firethorn has already named it,' he said.

'Have I?' asked a bemused Firethorn.

'You described our benefactor as a guardian angel. That must surely be the name we choose. The Angel theatre.'

Firethorn beamed. 'The Angel.'

A roar of acclamation went up. The christening was over.

Chapter Six

Rose Marwood felt like a prisoner in her own home. It was a frustrating situation. She shared a hostelry with dozens of other people yet she was not allowed to see any of them apart from her mother. Even her father was denied access to her, though that was in the nature of a gain rather than a loss. Having been shouted at and cursed by him in the most robust language, she was glad to be spared his ire and his whining self-pity. Neither of her parents seemed to be able to think about anything but the effect of her pregnancy upon them. She detected no real sympathy for her and it was what she most needed at that delicate time.

The ordeal which lay ahead was made far worse by her ignorance of the full implications of childbirth. Terrible fears assailed her. She remembered all of the blood-curdling tales she had overheard passing between older women. She thought of all the gravestones she had seen in the church cemetery, pathetic monuments to young brides who had died while trying to bring a child into the world. Would that also be her fate? Would they allow her to lie in consecrated ground? And what of the child itself? Would it survive or go with its mother to the grave? Whenever she contemplated the moment of birth itself, she was terrified.

Yet it was his. That thought anchored her terror. The child was conceived in love with a man on whom she doted and it was a great consolation. There was still hope for her. If Rose could get word to him of her condition, she was sure that he would come to her rescue and carry her away from a home she had come to detest. A God-fearing girl, she knew that she should be more obedient to her parents but they had virtually disowned her since she confessed her secret. Forced into a choice between them and her lover, she wanted him.

Wonderful memories washed over her and soothed her anguished mind. Until she had met him, she did not know what happiness was. Only when she was lying in his arms did she realise how much pleasure had been denied to her by watchful parents who kept her on an invisible chain. Her lover had snapped that chain for her and she would be eternally grateful to him for that. Whatever horrors might be inflicted upon her, Rose knew that she could bear them for his sake and she was convinced that he would one day bring her travail to an end. All that she had to do was somehow to make contact with him but that was impossible when she was entombed in her bedchamber. If he came in search of her at the Queen's Head, he would not be allowed anywhere near her.

Grief claimed her again and she flung herself down on the bed, sobbing quietly and whispering his name to herself over and over again. A sharp tapping sound made her sit up and look around but the source of the noise was a mystery. After a brief pause, she heard the sound again and realised that it came from the window. Crossing quickly to it, she peered out and saw the massive figure of Leonard below in the street. Leonard was an affable giant of a man who worked at the inn. Kind, willing but slow-witted, he had a brute strength which was held in check by a gentle disposition. He sent a warm smile of greeting up to her.

After wiping a hand on his leather apron, he slipped it inside his shirt to bring out a hunk of bread and a slice of cheese. He gestured for her to open the window so that he could throw the food up to her. Rose was touched. Leonard was taking a risk in trying to comfort her. Servants had been forbidden to speak with her and faced instant dismissal if they disobeyed. In his own shambling way, Leonard had ignored the order and sought her out. Rose was no longer wholly alone. She had a friend.

She opened the window and popped her head out.

'Thank you, Leonard,' she said.

'This is all that I could find,' he said, holding up the food. 'But I'll bring more another time.'

'I am not hungry. I have victuals enough.'

'Oh!'

'But I thank you for your kindness.'

He shrugged his huge shoulders. 'I wanted to help.'

'I know. I am very grateful.'

An idea began to form in her mind but she had no time to discuss it with him. The sound of a key in the lock brought the conversation to an abrupt close.

'Someone is coming,' she called. 'Go at once!'

'I will,' he said, backing away.

'But Leonard . . .'

'Yes?'

'Will you come again?'

He nodded enthusiastically before vanishing around the corner. Rose shut the window but her mother had already come into the room and sensed a breach in her security. Rushing to the window, she flung it open and glared out but the street was now empty apart from a few stray dogs. Sybil rounded smartly on her daughter.

'Who were you talking to?' she demanded.

'Nobody, mother.'

'Do not lie, girl. I heard your voice.'

'You must be mistaken.'

'Was it *him*?'

'Alas, no,' said Rose, head bowed.

'Then there was someone. I knew it.' She pulled the window shut. 'I'll have a lock put on this. That will stop you.' She flicked a hand. 'Get dressed.'

'Why, mother?'

'Do as you are told. We are going out.'

'Where to?'

'You will soon find out. Now dress yourself.'

While her daughter shed her night attire, Sybil kept vigil at the window. Rose dressed as quickly as she could, fearful that Leonard would return and be discovered. He was the one faint hope she had of getting a message to her beloved and she did not want him thrown out of his employment at the inn. That would be a cruel reward for the kindness he had shown her.

'I am ready, mother,' she said at length.

'Then let us go.'

Sybil took her firmly by the wrist and almost dragged her out of the room. They were soon leaving by a rear exit and plunging into the labyrinth that was London.

'Their own playhouse?' Giles Randolph was aghast. 'Westfield's Men intend to build their own playhouse?'

'That is what I have heard, Giles.'

'Where will it be?'

'The site has not yet been found.'

'Surely not here in Shoreditch? We have to contend with The Theatre as it is. A new playhouse could put our own position in jeopardy.'

'That is why I brought the tidings to you at once.'

'You did well, Henry.'

'I know where my loyalties lie.'

Henry Quine gave a fawning smirk then raised the glass of canary wine to his lips. He was a slim, young man of medium height with dark hair which curled attractively around his ears and a vestigial beard. If his eyes had not been so close together and his nose so long, Quine might have been accounted a handsome man but he had a smile which redeemed his features and a deep, melodious voice which stroked the ear. The two colleagues were supping at a tavern in Shoreditch.

Giles Randolph was patently annoyed by the news.

'Their own playhouse?' he said. 'That is impossible.'

'They do not think so.'

'How could they raise the money for such a venture? Lord Westfield is more penurious than our own patron and Lawrence Firethorn's credit will not extend that far.'

'They have secured a loan, Giles.'

'From whom?'

'I cannot say but I know who has been their broker.'

'Who?'

'Sylvester Pryde.'

'Their new sharer?'

'He has wealthy friends.'

'So it seems, Henry,' said the other, 'and that wealth might make Banbury's Men poor indeed. As long as Westfield's Men play at the Queen's Head, we are in no danger. Inn yard theatres will be closed down in due course. Give them their own playhouse, however, and it is a different story.'

'Only if it is built here in Shoreditch.'

'North or south of the river, it is a threat.'

'Not to us,' said Quine. 'If they choose a site in Bankside, it is Havelock's Men who will suffer from their proximity. We will be safe here at The Curtain.'

'I am not so sure.'

'Two theatres only are to stand. One north and one south of the Thames. That is the promised edict.'

'Promised but not delivered, Henry,' said Randolph

with a sneer. 'The Privy Council is capricious. According to our patron, they have put off a final decision for some weeks. That gives Westfield's Men time to find a site and start to build. Security of tenure is almost certain to go to Havelock's Men. The Viscount's uncle sits on the Council. But what if the work of Westfield's Men is judged superior to our own? Such is the perversity of the Privy Council that they may even change their decree and permit both surviving playhouses to stand in Bankside.'

'That is highly unlikely, Giles.'

'It is a possibility we have to consider.'

'How do we counter it?'

'With cunning, Henry. We must disable them.'

'Tell me how and it will be done.'

Randolph smiled. 'You have been a loyal servant to us,' he said, pouring more wine into his friend's cup. 'The day when Henry Quine joined our company was indeed an auspicious one. You have tied yourself to Banbury's Men and will do anything to advance our cause.'

'Anything!' repeated Quine.

'Being made a sharer will be a just reward.'

'I long to have that honour.'

'It will come, Henry. It will come.'

'When?'

'When our own future is certain and when Westfield's Men are doomed. They are sides of the same coin.' He leant in closer. 'Sound out Barnaby Gill. He is a gem that must be stolen. Take him away and their company totters. Master Gill and Lawrence Firethorn are uneasy bedfellows. Let us drive a wedge between them.' He raised a finger. 'But do it carefully, Henry. Dangle promises before his eyes.'

'I will study how best to do that.'

'Be quick about it. Ours is not the only company which will try to take captives. Havelock's Men will do the same.'

'They have already struck.'

'Indeed?'

'Or so it is rumoured,' said Quine. 'One Lucius Kindell, a young playwright whom Edmund Hoode has taken under his wing – a sure sign of promise in itself – has been wooed and won over by Rupert Kitely.'

'Then we have no time to waste,' said Randolph irritably. 'Get to Barnaby Gill before Havelock's Men start to pour honey into his ear. Offer whatever you have to, Henry. Greedy men will lap up any lies.'

'Master Gill is greedier than most.'

They shared a laugh, then drained their cups of wine.

Randolph became serious. 'Will this damnable playhouse of theirs ever be built, do you think?'

'Yes, Giles. They are resolved and already have a name.'

'What is it?'

'The Angel theatre.'

'The Angel!' said the other contemptuously. 'This angel could displace Banbury's Men from our place in heaven. We must act swiftly. Who is the man who secured their loan?'

'Sylvester Pryde.'

'Can we corrupt him?'

'I doubt that, Giles.'

'But he is the key to their good fortune.' He stroked his beard with the back of his hand. 'Tell me about him, Henry. Tell me all about this Sylvester Pryde.'

Sybil Marwood did not loosen her grip on her daughter until they reached their destination in Clerkenwell. Hustled along through an endless succession of streets, lanes and alleyways, Rose was in great discomfort. When her mother finally released the girl from her grasp, Rose rubbed her sore wrist. Before she had time even to look up at the dilapidated little house, she was helped inside it by a firm maternal palm.

As soon as they opened the door, the smell invaded their nostrils. It was a strong, rich, but not unpleasant aroma and Rose thought at first that someone was cooking a meal in the kitchen. They were in a dark, featureless room with only a few stools and a table by way of furniture. A ragged piece of cloth hung over the doorframe opposite and it was pulled back to reveal the gaunt face of an old woman with straggly grey hair trailing down from her mop cap. Rose recoiled slightly but Sybil seemed to know the crone.

'We are here at the appointed time,' she said.

'I am ready for you,' said the old woman, pushing the cloth aside to step into the room and scrutinise Rose. 'So this is your daughter, is it? A pretty girl without question and not like most of those who come to me for help. They have the mark of wickedness upon them but Rose does not.'

'Yet wicked she has been,' grunted Sybil.

'I beg leave to doubt that,' decided the old woman, giving Rose a gap-toothed grin of reassurance. 'A man is to

145

blame here. She was led astray. Rose is only the victim of another's wickedness.' She indicated a stool. 'Sit there, girl.'

She bustled out of the room and Rose hesitated.

'Do as she bids you,' ordered her mother.

'Who is she?'

'Mary Hogg. A wise woman of Clerkenwell.'

'Why have you brought me here?'

'She will medicine you. Now sit down.'

Sybil used both hands to ease her onto the stool. Rose was in a mild panic, sensing that she was in danger without quite knowing what that danger might be. When Mary Hogg reappeared, she was carrying a cup that was filled with a steaming liquid. Setting it down on the table, she turned to Sybil and snapped her fingers. Money was passed between them and the old woman counted it before slipping it into the pocket of her filthy apron.

Mary Hogg turned her full attention upon Rose.

'Do not be alarmed, Rose,' she soothed. 'I will help you as I have helped so many others in the past. I am a wise woman and know the art of saving a girl's reputation.'

'Reputation?' murmured Rose.

'This child comes before its time. You are unwed.'

'And no husband in sight,' added Sybil.

'Do you know what would happen if this baby were born?' continued the old woman. 'It would be condemned to a life of misery and you with it. Bastard offspring are spurned by one and all, Rose. You would be the mother of an outcast. It would be a cruelty to bring such a child into the world. A cruelty and a sin. For you have been sinful.'

'I have prayed for forgiveness,' said Rose.

'Prayer is part of my remedy,' explained the other. 'And the old religion furnishes us with the best supplication. Do not be afraid to make use of what would be forbidden in a church. God will bless you for it. When I have given you my cure, you must say five Paternosters, five Aves and a Creed for nine consecutive nights, taking herbs in holy water at the same time. Only at the end of nine days will we know if the cure has been effective.'

'What cure?' asked the trembling girl.

'Release from this shame!' said Sybil.

Rose stood up. 'You would kill my child!'

'It is an act of Christian kindness,' said Mary Hogg. 'Besides, I cannot kill what is not really alive. I simply prevent it from taking on any shape and form. Do not fret,' she whispered, easing her back down onto the stool. 'It will not hurt you, Rose, and my cure has the approval of God or He would not hear the prayers.'

'I want to go home, mother!' exclaimed Rose.

'Not until this is done,' said Sybil, restraining the girl as she tried to rise again. 'Not until you take the remedy.'

'Keep her away from me! She frightens me!'

'Not as much as that child in your belly frightens me and your father. You have shamed us, Rose, and we are paying to rid ourselves of that shame. Now keep silent!'

Rose struggled to get up but she was held firm. Mary Hogg took something from the pocket of her apron and stepped in close to the girl. Her voice had a gentle persuasiveness.

'Do not hold her so,' she said to Sybil. 'Rose must not be compelled. She knows what must be done. It is in the interests of everyone but, most of all, it advantages Rose herself. When she is wed, she will bear as many children as she wishes. She is clearly fruitful. This first apple will soon be forgotten when it has been plucked down.' Motioning Sybil back, she bent over Rose and held up the object in her hand. 'Open your mouth a little so that I may place this on your tongue.'

'What is it?'

'The bill of a white duck. It has potent charms.'

'I do not want it in my mouth.'

'It will only be for a minute or two.'

'It offends me.'

'You will find its taste both sweet and comforting.'

Mary Hogg began to intone a strange prayer, waving the duck bill to and fro in front of Rose's face until the girl was slowly lulled into a state of relative calm. The old woman used delicate fingertips to part the patient's lips then carefully inserted the duck's bill. When it lay on Rose's tongue, the prayers were replaced by a series of charms which were chanted in a high, lilting voice.

The girl's mouth stayed open when the duck bill was removed and her eyes stared straight ahead. She seemed to have gone off into some sort of reverie. Mary Hogg dipped a finger in the cup to test the heat of its contents. Nodding her approval, she lifted the cup to Rose's lips and tipped it gently upwards. Before she was able to resist, the girl had swallowed a mouthful of the hot, black, curdled liquid.

Jumping to her feet, she spluttered a protest and held both hands over her mouth as she started to retch.

'Must she drink it all?' asked Sybil.

'No,' said Mary Hogg complacently. 'My work is done. Make her say the prayers each morning, as I instructed, on her knees. In nine days' time, her problems will be at an end.' She put the duck's bill back into her pocket. 'And so will yours.'

Westfield's Men underwent a complete transformation. In less than a week, their fortunes improved out of all recognition. The loan was secured and the relevant document signed, a site was located, a builder hired and detailed plans drawn up for the immediate construction of The Angel theatre. Jaded actors who feared extinction now became proud members of a company which would have what they believed would be its own permanent home in Bankside. It was the stuff of dreams.

Anne Hendrik was instrumental in finding the site for them. On Sunday morning, therefore, after they had attended church together, Nicholas Bracewell escorted her to the river to take a closer look at the property.

'I knew that you could do it, Anne,' he said proudly.

'Luck played the greater part.'

'You asked the right people and looked in the right places. Where is the luck in that? Take due credit.' He gazed around. 'This site is not ideal but it has virtues which make its defects seem small.'

'I hope so, Nick,' she said.

'Let me tell you how the playhouse will look.'

The Angel theatre was to be built on the site of a disused boatyard which had been badly damaged by fire. Its wharf had collapsed into the Thames. Tenements stood either side of it and a row of houses, inns and ordinaries ran alongside the back of the site. Nicholas ignored the scene of devastation and saw only the tall playhouse which would replace it. One arm around Anne, he drew large pictures in the air with the other hand. The Angel theatre was conjured into existence.

'It will be one of the delights of Bankside,' said Anne.

'That would only be fitting,' he observed with a grin. 'For the site was discovered by another delight of Bankside.'

'Is that what I am?'

'What else, Anne?'

She gave a little laugh. 'Would you soil your tongue with flattery on the Sabbath?'

'I merely express our gratitude,' he said, squeezing her affectionately. 'Thanks to you, this old boatyard will have a new lease of life. So, we trust, will Westfield's Men.'

'Is your patron in favour of your venture?'

'He is consumed with delight. When the project was first mentioned to him, he took fright because he thought that we would ask him for money which he simply does not have. As soon as he realised that we could raise our own capital, he gave us his full support.' Nicholas let his gaze rake the riverbank. 'Can you not see that wharf when it is rebuilt?'

'Yes, Nick.'

'Playgoers will be able to come by boat and alight at the very door of the theatre. The watermen will bless us for the increase we will bring to their trade.'

'The watermen and the innkeepers of Bankside.'

'Yes, Anne. All will profit from The Angel.' He gestured towards the timbers which were stacked on the site. 'Including this builder you commended. Thomas Bradd has his materials in readiness. Work begins in earnest tomorrow.'

'He will not fail you, Nick. He repaired my own house and has worked for some of my neighbours as well. We all found Thomas Bradd to be an honest and trustworthy man.'

'That was my impression of him,' said Nicholas, 'but I took the trouble to examine some of the other properties he built in Southwark before we engaged him. He is without question a sound craftsman and is willing to let some of us labour alongside him to keep the costs down.'

'Us?' she queried. 'Does that include you?'

Nicholas chuckled. 'I was the first to volunteer my services, Anne. Do you think I would miss out on the chance to build a piece of theatre history? Do not forget that I am no raw beginner. When I sailed with Drake, we learnt to turn our hands to anything. That experience will stand me in good stead.'

'Who else will work here?'

'Nathan Curtis, for certain. He is our skilled carpenter and lives here in Bankside. Owen Elias is also eager to do his share of sawing and hammering. Edmund Hoode and James Ingram will not be left out. And, of course,' he added, 'there is Sylvester Pryde. He is not above earning himself a few blisters from hard labour.'

'Surely he has done more than enough already?'

'He insists on being involved in the construction.'

After surveying the site for another few minutes, they turned away and headed back towards Anne's house. Gulls flew overhead and cried out their hunger. The streets were busy. Entertainments which were curtailed on Sundays within the bounds of the city were permitted outside its jurisdiction. Nicholas was reminded that The Angel theatre would be able to open seven days a week in Bankside, thus increasing their takings and helping to pay off the substantial debt they were taking on.

'How did Sylvester raise the loan?' asked Anne.

'From an anonymous friend.'

'Have you no idea who he might be?'

'We can only guess, Anne. Some people believe that Sylvester himself has given us this money and that this guardian angel of ours is really a member of the company.'

'Is that what you believe, Nick?'

'No,' he said reflectively. 'On the day that he secured the money, he rode out of London for an hour. Our benefactor dwells in the country.'

'He must be a close friend indeed if he will advance several hundred pounds to Sylvester at such short notice.'

'That is my feeling, Anne.'

'Will you hazard a guess at his identity?'

'If you wish. I believe, in all probability, that he is a member of Sylvester's own family.'

'His family?'

'Yes, Anne,' he said firmly. 'If you press me closer, my guess would be that our guardian angel is his father.'

Sylvester Pryde was in his element. He was honest enough to acknowledge that he would never be lauded for his ability as an actor but there was another way to win plaudits within the company. He had effected a rescue. By arranging a loan on their behalf, Pryde had endeared himself to Westfield's Men and changed from a being a latecomer to the troupe into its hero. Whenever he arrived at the Queen's Head, he was met with smiles and words of praise. In the taproom, he was greeted with a round of applause from his fellows.

The play which was performed that afternoon was *The History of King John*, a stirring chronicle which offered him only two meagre roles, but Pryde was content. Simply to be a member of the company was a joy to him. To be its acclaimed champion gave him a deep gratification. He swept onto the stage as if he were playing the title role and declaimed his few lines with surging confidence. Liberated from their worst fears, Westfield's Men gave of their best yet again and made an old play vibrate with new significance.

Applause still rang in their ears as they took a final bow and retreated into the tiring-house. Everyone had a kind word or a pat on the back for him. Sylvester Pryde glowed. When they adjourned to the taproom, he was given a privileged position at the same table as the leading sharers and toyed with his cup of wine while rubbing shoulders with Lawrence Firethorn and Edmund Hoode. Barnaby

Gill sat opposite him and, when all his chores had been done, Nicholas Bracewell joined them. All but Gill were in a happy mood.

'What of our unfriendly landlord?' asked Pryde. 'Has he been told that we mean to vacate his premises?'

'Yes,' said Firethorn, 'and he was forced to approve. If inn yard theatres are to be closed, his contract with us is null and void. And since he still believes that we all took it in turns to seduce his daughter, he will be glad to see the back of us.' He slapped Pryde on the thigh. 'That is another boon you have bestowed on us, Sylvester. You have freed us from the domination of Alexander Marwood.'

'Has his daughter's lover been named yet?'

'No,' said Firethorn, 'but I know who he is.'

'Who?'

'Why, Edmund here!'

Hoode's cheeks became tomatoes. 'I deny the charge!'

'Then it must have been Barnaby!' teased Firethorn.

'Heaven forfend!' said Gill with disgust.

'Admit it, man. The night was dark and you mistook Rose Marwood for a pretty boy. It is your thrusts which help to swell that little belly of hers.' He let out a guffaw. 'The girl was well and truly Barnabied!'

'You are gross, Lawrence!' retorted the other.

'Then it was not you?'

Gill rose from his seat with dignity and excused himself.

'You put him to flight, Lawrence,' said Hoode.

'He would not have stayed much longer, Edmund. He has been sitting on coals since we arrived. Barnaby has an assignation. That is why he was so eager to quit our company.'

'An assignation or an invitation?' wondered Nicholas.

'What do you mean?'

'We are still under threat here. Lucius Kindell has already been snared and others in the company approached and blandished.'

'Nobody has offered me blandishments,' said Firethorn.

'Nobody would dare,' remarked Pryde.

'Master Gill is an easier target,' argued Nicholas. 'I know for a fact that both Banbury's Men and Havelock's Men covet him. Since word of The Angel went abroad, they may redouble their efforts to entice him away.'

'He has a contract with us, Nick,' said Hoode.

'We had a contract with the landlord but we are about to be in breach of it if we leave the Queen's Head.'

'Barnaby will not leave,' said Firethorn. 'He will rant and rave at us but he would never betray us.'

'Has he confided to you any approaches from our rivals?'

'No, Nick.'

'Is not that a form of betrayal?'

'Only if those approaches took place. My guess is that they did not,' decided Firethorn. 'Barnaby is never at ease with red-blooded fellows like us. His pleasures lie elsewhere and I believe he has gone off in search of them.'

Nicholas did not pursue the subject but he had noticed warning signs about Gill's behaviour which suggested that his commitment to Westfield's Men was not as absolute as it might have been. It caused him concern. The Angel theatre would be a lesser auditorium without Barnaby Gill to grace its boards.

Pryde was more interested in Rose Marwood's fate.

'What has happened to the poor girl?' he asked.

'She is kept under lock and key,' said Nicholas. 'They have even put a bolt on her window or so Leonard tells me.'

'How would he know?' said a jocular Firethorn. 'Was he in the girl's bedchamber at the time? That would be a revelation! The lumbering Leonard as the father of her child. Procreation must surely have taken place with the girl astride him for she would else have been suffocated beneath that monstrous body.'

'Leonard is a good friend to her,' said Nicholas. 'No more. I will miss him when we leave here. That bullish strength of his was put at our disposal many times.'

'Yes,' said Hoode, 'I have seen him lift a barrel of beer on his own when its weight would defeat two other men.'

'It is a pity that he cannot be employed on the site of The Angel,' said Pryde. 'Leonard's muscles are an asset that none of us could provide.'

A cheer went up from a nearby table and Pryde turned to see Owen Elias beckoning him over to join them. Half-a-dozen grinning faces endorsed the invitation.

'Go on, Sylvester,' said Firethorn easily. 'It is their turn to enjoy your company. You are common property now, my friend, and must be shared equally among us all.'

'Then I take my leave,' said Pryde courteously.

A yell of delight went up as he crossed to the others and room was immediately made for him on the settle. Elias put a proprietary arm around him and ordered him a drink. Pryde was soon at the centre of the merriest table in the taproom. Firethorn watched with approval then turned to Nicholas.

'You were right, Nick,' he said seriously. 'I did not wish to discuss it in front of Sylvester. He has rendered us a sterling service but we do not have to draw him too close into our affairs. There is still a whiff of mystery about him which I find disturbing.'

'Mystery?' echoed Nicholas.

'We know so little about him.'

'He found us that money,' noted Hoode. 'What else do we need to know, Lawrence?'

'The name of our guardian angel, for a start.'

'Sylvester is sworn to secrecy.'

'That is what irks me,' admitted Firethorn, 'but I will bear my irritation. Let us go back to Nick's comment. I think it was accurate. Barnaby *is* being courted.'

'By whom?' said Hoode anxiously.

'By Banbury's Men, by Havelock's Men or by one of the other companies. Does it matter? All that need concern us is that he is their chosen target.'

'How do you know, Lawrence?'

'He has been strangely silent of late.'

'Yes,' said Nicholas, 'and, alone of our fellows, he has shown scant enthusiasm for The Angel. It is almost as if he believes that he will never play there.'

'But he must,' insisted Hoode. 'He is one of us.'

'And will remain so,' said Firethorn. 'Barnaby and I have

our differences but I am all too aware of his contribution to our work. We would be impoverished by his absence. Keep a close eye on him, Nick.'

'That is what I have been doing,' confessed Nicholas. 'I saw how uncomfortable he was at this table. He kept glancing up as if expecting to meet someone else here. I think that he has doubts about The Angel. Even if it is built, we may still find ourselves without an occupation.'

'In London, perhaps,' conceded Firethorn, 'but we need not vanish into thin air. Westfield's Men can still tour.'

'Not with Barnaby,' said Hoode gloomily. 'You know how much he loathes life on the road. If he had to choose between a tour with us and a London playhouse, our hopes of keeping him would be slim.'

Firethorn sighed. 'What is the remedy, Nick?'

'We have to convince him that his interests are best served by Westfield's Men,' said Nicholas. 'We have to build The Angel and turn it into the most exciting playhouse in London. Then he will never even think of leaving us.'

Sylvester Pryde remained at the Queen's Head for most of the evening, moving from table to table to receive congratulations from all his fellows, carousing until the wine began to make him feel slightly drowsy. Pleading the need of some fresh air, he waved a general farewell then came out into Gracechurch Street and swung right towards the river. Pryde sauntered along in the cool night air with a grin of satisfaction on his face. He was not only accepted by his colleagues now. He was positively feted.

When London Bridge loomed up ahead of him, he walked on until he reached Thames Street then turned right. His legs were taking him where his heart wanted them to go. Minutes later he was standing at the river's edge, staring out across the broad stretch of water at the site of The Angel theatre. Pryde could see it rising boldly on the opposite bank, soaring above the buildings around it and advertising itself by its very ascendancy. He was immensely proud to have been able to instigate the building of the new playhouse and took an almost paternal joy in it.

'Boat, sir?' called a hoarse voice.

'What's that?' said Pryde, coming out of his reverie.

'Do you want to cross the river?'

'Why, yes,' he decided impulsively. 'Take me over, good sir. I want to view a property on the other side.'

'Come aboard.'

There were two watermen in the little vessel and they rowed with an easy rhythm. Pryde sat in the stern, his eyes fixed on the abandoned boatyard that would soon disappear beneath the foundations of his theatre, his mind filled with imagined triumphs for the company. It never occurred to him that he was being followed by someone in a second boat.

When he reached the other bank, he tipped the watermen handsomely and went ashore. He was soon picking his way in the half-dark around the site of The Angel. It was still largely covered with debris and there was little progress to note but Pryde still felt exhilarated by the experience. As he stood in the centre of the property, he could almost see the many sides of the theatre rising up around him and hear the applause that reverberated around its walls.

Huge timbers stood upright against a wall, waiting to take their place in the new structure. Pryde ran his hand against one of them, feeling its rough-hewn surface and estimating its immense weight. When he heard a noise behind him, he tried to turn round but something hard and broad struck him viciously across the back of the head. He collapsed in a heap on the ground with blood gushing out of the wound. Still half-conscious, he opened his mouth to cry for help but no words emerged. The last thing he ever saw was the timber, which he had so lovingly caressed, descending murderously towards him.

Chapter Seven

Nicholas Bracewell set off early next morning on the long walk to the Queen's Head. Instead of following his customary route to London Bridge, however, he took the opportunity to visit the site of The Angel to speak with the builder. Thomas Bradd was already there when Nicholas arrived, supervising some men who were clearing the site of its accumulated debris. Bradd was a short, sturdy man in his forties with a sense of power in his compact frame and the kind of weather-beaten face which suggested some years at sea. He gave Nicholas a lop-sided grin of welcome.

'We should make more progress today,' he said gruffly.

'Good.'

'There is no wind to worry about so we can burn all this rubbish without danger. By this afternoon, we will be able to start digging the foundations.'

'Some of us will join you when our play is done.'

'It will be hard work,' warned Bradd. 'It is not like standing on a scaffold and spouting fine words into the air.'

'We know that. We expect to sweat.'

'Sweat, bleed and swear oaths aplenty.'

'Whatever it takes,' said Nicholas with a smile. 'This playhouse means everything to us. We will put strong arms and willing hearts at your disposal.'

'I will use them mercilessly.' Bradd gave a dark chuckle then pointed at the pile of timbers which lay on the site. 'It is a pity that your actors are not here now. We could do with some of those strong arms to shift that timber. It stood upright yesterday but somehow it has tumbled in the night.'

'That seems strange.'

'It does. We stacked it with great care. A howling gale could not have blown it over.'

'Then why does it now lie on the ground?'

Nicholas watched two of the men begin to move the fallen timbers, slipping a rope around the end of the first one before dragging it clear of the pile then using a shorter plank to lever the timber back into an upright position. He could see the effort that it was costing them. Nicholas was no stranger to physical labour but some of his fellows had led a softer life. They would have a rude shock when they worked for Thomas Bradd on the site of The Angel.

'I wish that we did not have to build so close to the bank,' observed Nicholas. 'The water runs high at this point.'

'We will take account of that,' said Bradd.

'This would not be the only property to be flooded.'

The builder tensed. 'Do not tell me how to build, sir. I have had twenty years in the trade and know what precautions to take against flood and other perils. Besides,' he said, waving an arm, 'we have no choice. The site is not big enough for us to set the playhouse back from the river.'

'You are right and we have faith in your judgement.'

'I would not continue otherwise.'

Nicholas soothed him before taking his leave. He did not get far. When he was less than a dozen yards away, a cry of fear made him turn back again. One of the men who had been shifting the timbers was now pointing at something which protruded from the base of the pile. It was a human hand. Nicholas broke into a run and overtook the builder as the latter waddled towards the gruesome discovery. Only a man's left hand was visible but it bore a distinctive ring which Nicholas had seen many times before. His temples pounded and his mouth went dry as he identified Sylvester Pryde.

'Get him out of there!' he ordered.

Then he grabbed one of the timbers and began to heave.

It was strenuous work and they were soon perspiring but Nicholas drove them on. Thomas Bradd did his share, handling the rough timbers with seasoned hands and helping to toss them aside. Any hope that the prone figure might still be alive soon vanished. The sheer weight of the timber would have crushed him to death. One leg was uncovered, then a second, then part of his chest. Nicholas was horrified to see that his friend's bright apparel was now soaked with blood and caked with filth.

The last and heaviest timber obscured the face of the victim. All four of them lifted it clear and dropped it on the ground. The sight which confronted them made one of the men turn away in disgust and another vomit. Bradd was transfixed. Nicholas was overcome with anguish. Sylvester Pryde was unrecognisable. The handsome face was smashed out of shape, the long hair and beard were glistening with gore. A huge gash in the forehead indicated that it had taken the full force of the timber as it fell. Nicholas fought to master his grief.

'Poor devil!' muttered Bradd. 'Who is he?'

'A member of the company.'

'This is a fearful accident.'

'It was no accident,' said Nicholas. 'He was murdered.'

Rose Marwood lay in bed and drifted in and out of sleep as the doctor examined her. The fever seemed to have taken a hold on her. For the first few days after her visit to Clerkenwell, nothing had happened. All that she felt was the lingering aftertaste of the strange brew prepared for her by Mary Hogg. Irritating minor symptoms then began to appear before developing overnight into a raging fever. Rose's strength ebbed away. The only prayers that were said in her bedchamber now were the frantic entreaties of her mother, begging for forgiveness and pleading for her daughter's recovery.

Sybil was overwhelmed by remorse. The wild urge to get rid of an unwanted child was now replaced with true maternal concern. As she looked at the flushed face of

164

her daughter, she was shocked by the thought that she might have been responsible for the girl's illness. In trying to dispose of a child, the wise woman of Clerkenwell, it seemed, might also have brought about the death of its mother.

'How is she?' murmured Sybil.

'Let me examine her properly and I will tell you.'

'I have never seen Rose so sick.'

'Stand back, please,' said the doctor crisply. 'You are in my light. It might be better if you waited outside.'

'Do let me stay!' she implored. 'Rose is my daughter.'

'Then let me attend to her.'

Mouthing apologies, Sybil retreated to the other side of the room and watched with trepidation. The doctor was a small, wiry man in his fifties with a white beard and a wizened face. His instruments stood beside him in a leather case. After feeling his patient's pulse, he opened her mouth gently so that he could peer into it. Then he placed a cool hand on the fevered brow. Rose's eyes opened again but they lacked any expression. She dozed off within a minute.

The doctor was thorough. When his examination was over, he turned to question Sybil, sensing that she might in some way be responsible for the girl's sickness.

'What have you done to her?' he challenged.

'Nothing,' she murmured.

'She is grievously sick.'

'That is why we sent for you, doctor.'

'When your daughter came to visit me, she was strong and healthy. Rose thought she was ailing but I told her that she was with child. That produces changes in the body. I explained that such changes were quite normal and tried to still her fears.' He glanced back at the bed. 'But look at her now. These symptoms have nothing to do with motherhood. What has happened to her?'

'I do not know, doctor.'

'Has she eaten rancid food? Drunk foul water?'

'She is well-cared for,' bleated Sybil defensively.

'Then why is she locked away like this?' he said sternly. 'You used a key to let us in here and I see that bolt upon the window. It should be wide open to admit fresh air not shut tight like that.'

'It will be opened,' she promised. 'It will, it will.'

The doctor put his head to one side and studied her for a moment. Guilt made her shift her feet and rub her hands nervously together. He clicked his tongue in disapproval.

'What has been going on here?' he asked.

'Nothing, nothing.'

'Why has the girl declined so?'

'I wish I knew.'

'Let me give you a warning,' he said, fixing her with a cold stare. 'Do not try to meddle with nature. Rose is unwed and she was shocked to learn that she was with child. You and your husband must also have been shaken by the tidings. That is nothing new. I see it happen all the time to the parents of young girls who give birth out of wedlock. They are hurt,' he continued, 'they feel ashamed and desperate. They blame their daughters and make them suffer bitterly. In some cases, they are even driven to extremities.'

'Extremities?' croaked Sybil.

'I think that you know what I mean.'

'No, doctor.'

'Unwanted children are conceived all the time,' he said with a glance at the bed. 'London is full of quacks and charlatans who will offer to get rid of those children at a price. They are not only tricksters. Such people can cause great damage.'

'Can they?'

'What they do is to slaughter innocent babes in the womb. That is not only a heinous crime, it is a sin against nature and an offence before God.'

'I know that now,' she gabbled.

'Never expose your daughter to such witchcraft,' he insisted. 'Or you may put her own life in jeopardy.'

'Will she die, doctor? Will Rose die?'

'I hope not.'

'What must we do? Tell us and it will be done.'

'The first thing you must do is to love and cherish your daughter. Nurse her tenderly. It is always the best medicine.'

'I will sit beside her day and night.'

He crossed to open his case. 'I will leave a potion for her,' he said, taking out a little flask and handing it to her. 'Give her two drops of it in a small amount of clean water twice a day and make sure that she swallows it. Use a damp cloth to wipe her brow and keep it cool. And open that window to clear away this smell of sickness.'

'I will, I will, doctor. What else must I do?'

His instructions were long and specific. Sybil made a

careful note of them but avoided his piercing gaze because it made her sense of guilt almost unbearable. She plied him with questions of her own and stored up each answer in her memory. Before he left, the doctor casually slipped a hand under the pillow and extracted a battered Roman Catholic Prayer book. Sybil backed away and shuddered violently.

'This has no place in a Protestant household,' he chided. 'You know the law. We have put aside the old religion. How did this forbidden book come to be in the girl's bed?'

'I do not know,' she lied, snatching it from him. 'But I will throw it away at once, doctor. I give you my word.'

'Honour it,' he said sharply. 'Or I will have to report this to your parish priest. You will not save your daughter with Romish incantations or with concoctions sold by quacks. Medicine is the only cure.'

'Yes, yes.'

He looked at Rose. 'Call me if her condition worsens.'

'We will, doctor.'

'And remember that you are a mother.'

The words were a stinging rebuke and Sybil felt the full force of them. When the doctor scurried out of the room, she sat down on a stool and wept contritely. Rose seemed peaceful now, eyes closed and breathing regular. But the fever was clearly still upon her and Sybil suspected that it had originated in a Clerkenwell backstreet.

She was still sobbing when her husband eventually arrived.

Alexander Marwood was even more appalled than usual.

'The doctor asked for his fee,' he moaned. 'Do you know how much the man charged me?'

'It does not matter,' she said.

'It matters to me, Sybil. The fee was exorbitant.'

'If he can save Rose, I would give him every penny we have,' she said, crossing to the bed. 'We have wronged her, Alexander. We treated her like a criminal instead of a daughter. I feel so ashamed of what you made me do.'

'Me?'

'Yes,' she said, trying to shift some of the blame. 'You badgered me, sir. You forced me to punish Rose.'

Marwood was dumbfounded. No husband was less capable of forcing a wife to do anything than him. Obsequious requests were his only means of influencing Sybil. He peered over her shoulder at the slumbering girl. He was sorry that Rose was so ill but his first thought was still of his own humiliation.

'Has she lost the child?' he said hopefully.

'No, Alexander.'

'But you told me that she would.'

Sybil's words burnt into him like a branding iron.

'I told you nothing of the kind. Do you understand?'

When Nicholas Bracewell finally reached the Queen's Head, he found the company in a buoyant mood. The stage had been erected, properties had been set out and the actors were chatting happily in groups. Nicholas was given a mocking cheer when he appeared. Usually the first to arrive, he was now the straggler in the party.

Lawrence Firethorn sought to rub the message home.

'Ah, Nick!' he said good-humouredly, 'so you have risen from your bed at last, have you? You are unconscionably late, dear heart. It is not like you to put the caresses of a lady before the needs of your company. Why the delay?'

'I will tell you in private.'

'Secrets, eh? I long to hear them.'

Nicholas drew him aside to break the sad tidings. He explained that the delay was forced upon him. When the body of Sylvester Pryde was uncovered, constables were summoned and the crime reported. Nicholas supervised the transfer of the corpse to the morgue before giving a sworn statement to the coroner. It was only then that he was able to hurry to the Queen's Head.

Firethorn was thunderstruck by the news.

'God in heaven!' he murmured. 'This is a tragedy!'

'We must decide what to do,' said Nicholas quietly. 'My advice would be to cancel this morning's rehearsal so that we may appraise the situation. *Black Antonio* needs little enough attention. We have performed the play so often that we could do so at a moment's notice without any rehearsal.'

'Yes,' agreed Firethorn. 'We need time to think.'

'Let me speak to the company. They will have to be told sooner or later and I would rather they heard it from my lips. In any case,' he added, 'they will be able to help me.'

'In what way?'

'Someone must have seen Sylvester leave here last night. They can give me some idea of what time that was. I had already returned to Bankside so I have no knowledge of his movements. Sylvester Pryde was a good friend to us. I will track down his killer,' he vowed, 'and the trail starts here.'

'We will all want to follow that trail, Nick,' said the other vehemently. 'The culprit must be made to pay for this hideous crime. He has not only murdered Sylvester. He has killed our new playhouse stone dead.'

'That may not be so.'

'But Sylvester was our intermediary.'

'The loan is secured and the terms agreed.'

'Might not our benefactor wish to withdraw the money?' said Firethorn anxiously. 'His only reason for helping us was his friendship with Sylvester. That can no longer exist.'

Nicholas was calm. 'Let us not race to meet a problem that may not exist,' he said. 'Two things must be done as soon as possible. We must find this guardian angel of ours and acquaint him with this terrible event. My hope is that he will want the playhouse to be as much a theatre as a memorial to Sylvester Pryde. Our loan may still be safe.'

'You spoke of two things, Nick.'

'I did.'

'What is the other?'

'We must keep up the spirits of the company,' said Nicholas. 'These heavy tidings will tear at their hearts but we must not let them despair. Westfield's Men are under surveillance. If our work suffers, our chances of survival grow small. The company must strive to its utmost.'

'We will, Nick. For Sylvester's sake as much as for our own. He would not want us to betray our art.'

'I will impress that upon them.'

When they were herded into the tiring-house, Westfield's Men knew that something was seriously amiss. The lateness of Nicholas Bracewell and the absence of Sylvester Pryde were worrying signs but none of them suspected how the two were conjoined. Nicholas broke the news to them as gently as he could but there was no way that he could lessen its impact. The whole company was rocked. Richard Honeydew fainted, two of the other apprentices burst into tears and George Dart had a fit of uncontrollable shivering. Edmund Hoode offered up a silent prayer for the soul of the departed. Owen Elias pulled out his dagger and swore to avenge the murder. Barnaby Gill retreated into a watchful silence.

'We will not rehearse this morning,' explained Nicholas. 'We need time to make certain decisions and some of you, I know, will prefer to be alone with your thoughts. But remember this,' he said over the murmur of agreement. '*Black Antonio* must not suffer. Though we have lost a fellow, we still have a duty to our audience, our patron and ourselves. Mourn for Sylvester in your hearts. Do not take that sorrow onto the stage this afternoon.'

'You will answer to me if you do,' cautioned Firethorn. '*Black Antonio* is a fine play which must be well-acted. Let us dedicate the performance to Sylvester Pryde and make it worthy of his name. Are we agreed?'

A rousing shout of affirmation went up. Firethorn tried to lift their morale before dismissing them. He and Nicholas stayed behind with Hoode and Gill. Seated on benches in the tiring-house, they attempted to evaluate the full effect of their colleague's untimely death. Gill was despondent.

'This has destroyed us,' he concluded morosely.

'Only if we let it do so,' said Nicholas.

'Sylvester was the moving spirit behind The Angel.'

'He has gone to join the angels himself now, Barnaby,' mused Hoode. 'He may be looking down on us at this minute.'

'Yes,' said Firethorn, 'looking down and urging us to go on with the building. One of our rivals is behind this murder. I feel it in my bones. If they cannot beat us by fair means, they will resort to foul deeds. Do we leave the field and let Banbury's Men and Havelock's Men strut in triumph? Never!'

Nicholas was circumspect. 'We do not know that Sylvester was killed by one of our rivals,' he said softly, 'and we should not allot blame until we have learnt the true facts of the situation. The first thing I would like to know is what Sylvester was doing on that site.'

'Dreaming,' said Hoode. 'What else?'

'But when did he go there? Last night? This morning?'

'Was he taken there by force?' wondered Firethorn. 'Or did he go of his own accord?'

'And why kill him in such a brutal manner?' asked Hoode. 'Is there some significance in the manner of his death?'

'Yes,' decided Gill. 'It put a curse on the site. But you are wasting your time asking all these questions about Sylvester when the most important one remains unanswered. He came out of nowhere to join us and bought his way into our affections. We do not know from whom he raised this loan or how to make contact with our benefactor. When Sylvester quit his lodging, he told nobody where he went. In short, he went out of his way to cover his tracks.' He looked searchingly around the faces of the others. 'What we should be asking ourselves is this. Who *was* Sylvester Pryde?'

Lucius Kindell was learning what a handicap his diffidence could be. When he worked alongside the mild-mannered Edmund Hoode, he had no problems. Hoode treated him like an equal and encouraged him to express himself freely. Rupert Kitely came from a very different mould. Though he could be quiet and persuasive when the need arose, he could also be stern and authoritative and the young playwright found it difficult to talk to him, still less to contradict him. Consumed with anxieties, he was too shy even to voice them in Kiteley's hearing. It was a situation which had to change.

As he sat in the lower gallery of The Rose and watched Havelock's Men in rehearsal, he was afflicted yet again with guilt. Westfield's Men had launched his writing career at a time when their rivals viewed his work with less enthusiasm. Under the aegis of Hoode, he could feel his talent developing but his confidence in that talent was now waning. Had he been engaged by Rupert Kitely because the latter really believed that he would write wonderful dramas or was he simply being used as a stick with which to beat Westfield's Men? Kindell decided that it was time to find out and he screwed up his courage to do so.

His opportunity came during a break in rehearsal. Rupert Kitely beckoned him down with a lordly wave. There was an air of condescension about the actor now. When Kindell joined him, he was deliberately kept waiting for few minutes. His resolve began to melt away. Kitely eventually turned to him.

'Well, Lucius?' he said. 'Do you like what you see?'

'Very much, sir.'

'A competent piece but we will make it look a much more accomplished drama. That is our art, Lucius. To take base metal and turn it into gold.' He saw the distress on the other's face and laughed. 'That was no reflection on your work, my young friend. Lucius Kindell will give us gold which we will merely have to burnish. How fares the new play?'

'Slowly.'

'Why so?'

'I find it difficult to work alone.'

'You will soon grow accustomed to that.'

'Will I?' said Kindell meekly. 'I am not so certain. I have been deprived of my master and I miss him.'

'You have outgrown Edmund Hoode,' said Kitely with a reassuring smile. 'He has taught you all he can, Lucius. From now on, you will not have to work in his shadow. You will forge a play of your own and take full praise for its excellence.'

'That excellence has eluded me so far.'

'I will help you. Have no fear.'

Kitely broke off to distribute some orders among other members of the company. His authority was unquestioned and they treated him with the utmost respect. That only served to put Kindell even more in awe of him. That same awe had also been engendered by Lawrence Firethorn but it had been less of a problem. Though a much more flamboyant character, Firethorn was somehow approachable in a way that Kitely was not. The playwright found it hard to believe that he was with the man who had shown him such warm friendship at the Devil tavern.

After a few more commands, Kitely came back to him.

'You catch me at a busy time, Lucius.'

'I did not mean to disturb you.'

'No, no,' exhorted the other. 'Come as often as you like. Actors are the tools with which you work. The more you come to know about us, the better you will deploy us. Besides, you are one of Havelock's Men now.'

'Am I?'

'We have commissioned a new play, have we not?'

'Why, yes,' said Kindell, 'and I am grateful.'

'Then no more regrets about the Queen's Head. In this profession, survival is everything. We will still be here at The Rose when Westfield's Men are no more than a dim memory.'

'*I* will always remember them.'

'And so you should, Lucius. But they head for extinction.'

'Do they?'

'I told you what the Privy Council intends.'

'Yet I heard a rumour that they are building their own playhouse here in Bankside.'

Kitely was dismissive. 'Pay no attention to that.'

'Is it not true?'

'It is true that they *hope* to build a playhouse. They have even had the gall to christen it. But their Angel Theatre will be torn down before it is ever used.'

'How do you know?'

'Because the Privy Council has decreed that there will only be one playhouse south of the river. And I am in a position to tell you, Lucius,' he said with conviction, 'that you are at present standing in it.'

Nicholas Bracewell spent the rest of the morning trying to establish some details about Sylvester Pryde's movements. Several members of the company remembered his leaving the Queen's Head on the previous night and there was rough agreement on the approximate time of his departure. Assuming that he had headed for the river, Nicholas retraced his steps and pushed his way through the crowded Gracechurch Street. He followed his instincts and swung right into Thames Street then sharp left. He was soon standing on the riverbank, listening to the gulls and watching the dark water lapping at the wharves.

Boats were coming and going all the time as watermen delivered or collected passengers. Those who gave a tip to their ferrymen were rewarded with courteous thanks while those who failed to reward them suffered a torrent of abuse from the vociferous watermen. Nicholas began a painstaking search for a boat which might have taken Sylvester Pryde across the river. Since he often used that mode of transport himself, he was well known to the boatmen and called many by name but none was able to help him. Most had gone off to a tavern or home to bed at the time when Nicholas's friend might have wished to be rowed across the river. The book holder gradually came round to the conclusion that Sylvester must have walked over London Bridge.

He was just about to leave the riverbank when another boat pulled into the wharf. Two passengers paid their fare and alighted. Nicholas strolled over to the boatmen and put to them the questions he had already put to dozens of their colleagues. The two men in the boat traded a glance. There was such a close resemblance between them that they had to be father and son. The older one acted as spokesman.

'How much is it worth?' he asked.

'The fare across the river,' offered Nicholas.

'Why do you want to know about this man?'

'He was a good friend of mine.'

'Any other reason?'

'Someone murdered him.'

'Then we will help you all we can, sir,' said the boatman apologetically, 'and we do so at no cost. We did pick up a gentleman last night. Around the time you say and looking much as you describe. We saw him clear by the light of the torch. Apparelled in red and black with a black hat that bore an ostrich feather. Is that him, sir?'

'Yes!' said Nicholas. 'What happened?'

'We rowed him across and dropped him by the old boathouse. He was very generous, as my son will confirm.

When we went ashore, we drank to his health at a tavern.'

'Did he speak to you as you rowed across?'

'Not a word, sir.'

'Did you see where he went?'

'To that old boatyard. It was burnt down.'

'Was there anyone else there?'

'We saw nobody, sir, but it was growing dark. There may have been someone in the shadows.'

'Did anyone follow you?' asked Nicholas.

'Follow us?'

'Across the river.'

'Two or three boats, sir. We paid no heed to them.'

'Did any of them land near the boatyard?'

'Who knows? We left as soon as we were paid.'

'Is there anything else you can tell me?'

'Nothing beyond the fact that he was a gentleman, sir,' said the other. 'But you know that. A fine, well-spoken man. When we picked him up here, he was staring across the river at something over by the boatyard. Is that any help?'

'Yes,' said Nicholas gratefully.

He thrust a coin into the man's hand then hurried away. Progress had been made, albeit small. He now had a clear idea of the time when Sylvester Pryde must have reached the site of The Angel theatre and, most probably, was killed there. He could also guess what had impelled his friend to go there in the first place. Pryde was a romantic, deeply in love with the whole notion of theatre and fired by the thought that he would be involved in the construction of a new playhouse. Nicholas could imagine how completely caught up in the emotion of the moment he would have been as he walked around the site of The Angel. It would have left him off guard.

When he got back to the Queen's Head, the first person he met was Leonard, rolling an empty barrel across the yard before hoisting it without effort onto a waiting cart. Leonard's big, round face split into a grin when he saw his friend approaching. It was Nicholas who found him the job at the Queen's Head and he was eternally grateful to him, happily enduring the strictures of Alexander Marwood in return for a regular wage and a place to live.

'Well-met, Leonard!'

'It is good to see you again, Nicholas.'

'I am here almost every day.'

'That is still never enough for me.' The grin widened. 'But I thought to watch you at rehearsal this morning.'

'Evidently, you have not heard the news.'

'News?'

'Sad tidings, Leonard. We have lost Sylvester Pryde.'

'Lost him?' He blinked in surprise. 'He has gone?'

'For ever, I fear. Sylvester is dead.'

When he heard the details, Leonard's face crumpled and his eyes grew moist. Pryde was a popular figure in the taproom and always had a kind word for those who worked there. Leonard was stunned by the notion that he would never see him again.

'Why,' he said, running a hand across his chin, 'I bade him farewell less than twelve hours ago. Had I known I was sending him off to his grave, Nicholas, I would have held him back with both hands. Dear Lord! What a case is this!'

Nicholas was curious. 'You bade him farewell, you say?'

'Yes. Last night.'

'As he left the Queen's Head?'

Leonard nodded. 'I was here in the yard and called out to him as he passed. But I do not think he heard me for he made no reply and that was strange. I remarked on it to Martin.'

'Who is Martin?'

'You remember him,' said the other. 'He worked here as a drawer some months ago. As friendly a soul as you could meet. But Martin could not take the sharp edge of our landlord's tongue and he left.'

'What was he doing back here?'

'He drops in from time to time if he is passing. I think he lodges nearby. I told him how odd it was that Sylvester did not return my farewell.'

'Which way did he go?'

'Right, into Gracechurch Street.'

'That confirms what I have already found out.'

Leonard frowned in dismay. 'Could I have been the last person to see him alive, Nicholas? I would hate to think that.'

'Sylvester took a boat across the river. I talked with the watermen who rowed him across. Besides,' sighed Nicholas, 'the last person who saw him alive was his killer.'

'Who would want to murder such a kind gentleman?'

'That is what I intend to find out.'

'There is so much villainy in this world!' said Leonard.

His eye travelled to the upper storey of the inn and his voice became a conspiratorial whisper. 'Some of it has been taking place under this roof, Nicholas.'

'Here?'

'Mistress Rose. They have treated her wickedly.'

'Her parents?'

'Yes, and now she lies sick of a fever.'

'What have they done to the poor girl?'

'Locked her away like the vilest criminal. They even bolted her window so that she could not talk to anyone out of it. That was my fault, I fear.'

'Yours, Leonard?'

'I took her food and meant to toss it up to her. But someone caught her with the window open when I was below. One of the servingmen was ordered to fix a bolt on it.'

'This is harsh behaviour for a parent.'

'It is cruelty, Nicholas,' he said, 'and the saddest thing is that I cannot help Rose. She has been so good to me.'

'And now she has a fever?'

'I was sent to fetch a doctor.'

'Then it must be serious.'

'That is my fear.' He became sombre. 'The Queen's Head is changing. I said so to Martin. It is not the place I have so enjoyed working in. Friends have drifted away. Rose is hidden from me. Master Marwood has grown bitter. And now,' he said with a nod towards the makeshift stage, 'I hear that we are to lose Westfield's Men as well.'

'Not through choice.'

'I will miss you, Nicholas.'

'We will be sorry to leave.'

'Is there no hope that you will stay?'

'None.'

Leonard's head dropped to his chest and he emitted a long sigh of resignation. Nicholas was about to move away when a stray thought nudged him.

'Where does he work now?'

'Who?' said Leonard.

'Your friend, Martin?'

'At the Brown Bear in Eastcheap. Why do you ask?'

'No reason,' said Nicholas pensively.

Given the circumstances in which it took place, the performance of *Black Antonio* that afternoon was a small miracle. It was taut and dramatic, full of fire and deep meaning, and it kept the audience completely ensnared for the two and half hours of its duration. Since it was expressly dedicated to Sylvester Pryde, everyone in the company wanted to make an important personal contribution and it was left to Lawrence Firethorn, in the title role, to bring them all together into a unified whole. Such was their commitment that nobody would have guessed that it was a demoralised company in mourning for a dear friend.

Barnaby Gill was outstanding. In a play as dark and relentless as *Black Antonio*, the comic scenes took on an extra significance and Gill made the most of each one of them. He was as spry as ever during his jigs and his clownish antics brought welcome relief to an audience in the grip of high tension. When the company left the stage at the end of the play, Firethorn paid him the rare compliment of embracing him and showering him with congratulations.

'You were magnificent, Barnaby!'

'I always am, Lawrence,' said Gill tartly. 'But you have only just noticed me.'

'Sylvester would have delighted in your performance.'

'He appreciated true art.'

'So did our audience.'

Elation soon gave way to dejection again as the company remembered how Sylvester Pryde had been killed. They tumbled off to the taproom to celebrate the performance and to drown their sorrows. Drink was taken too quickly and a maudlin note soon dominated. Westfield's Men began to exchange fond stories about their murdered colleague and to speculate on the identity of his killer.

Gill stayed with his colleagues until the majority of them were too drunk even to notice if he was there. When Owen Elias fell asleep beside him, he slipped surreptitiously away from the table and made for the door. Only Nicholas Bracewell saw him go. Once outside, Gill made sure that he was not followed, then set off. It was a long walk but his brisk stride ate up the distance and he reached his destination when there was still enough light for him to see the tavern clearly.

As he looked up at the building and heard the sounds of revelry from within, he wondered if it was wise to keep this particular tryst. He hesitated at the threshold until self-interest got the better of loyalty. When he entered the taproom, he saw Henry Quine sitting alone at a table. Quine beckoned Gill over.

'Hello, Barnaby,' he said. 'I hoped that you would come.' He gestured for Gill to sit beside him. 'There is someone who is very anxious to meet you.'

A tall figure came out of the shadows.

'Welcome to Shoreditch!' said Giles Randolph.

He gave a quiet smile of triumph.

Chapter Eight

When he reached the site with his little band of helpers, Nicholas Bracewell was pleased to see that work had continued throughout the day. Overcoming the shock of finding a murder victim underneath their timbers, Thomas Bradd and his men had cleared the site, burnt most of the debris and begun to dig the foundations. The builder was delighted to have fresh labour at his disposal and he set them to work at once. They included Nathan Curtis, the carpenter, George Dart, the puniest but most willing of them, and Owen Elias, who did not think his position as a sharer with the company absolved him from hard work and who handled his spade with muscular assurance.

Nicholas watched them with a mixture of pride and affection. He had intended to put his own considerable strength at Bradd's service but another priority now existed. Their benefactor had to be traced, informed of Sylvester Pryde's death and persuaded to leave the loan intact. It was an onerous assignment, made all the more difficult by the veil of secrecy which was drawn across the whole transaction. He was not quite sure where to begin. Waving a farewell to his friends, he walked swiftly back in the direction of London Bridge, considering all the possibilities and wondering why Pryde had gone to such lengths to shield his own privacy.

He was halfway across the bridge when he was met by an extraordinary sight. Mounted on a horse, and having the greatest trouble in controlling the animal, was Leonard, sweating profusely and trying to find a way through the milling crowd and trundling carts which blocked the narrow thoroughfare between the shops and stalls. A poor rider, he looked profoundly embarrassed to be in the saddle of such a fine horse, feeling unworthy of the status it conferred on him. When he saw Nicholas, his face lit up with relief and he tugged at the reins before dismounting clumsily.

It was only when Nicholas reached him that he realised that his friend was not alone. Leonard's bulk had masked a second rider, a dignified man in a livery which seemed vaguely familiar. Nicholas also saw that the spirited animal which Leonard had been unable to master was Lawrence Firethorn's stallion. His friend ran the back of his hand across his forehead then gabbled his message.

'This gentleman came in search of you,' he explained with a gesture towards the other rider. 'He says that it is a matter of the greatest urgency. Master Firethorn knew where you had gone and loaned me his horse so that we could get to you fast.' He thrust the reins at Nicholas. 'You are to take him now to speed your own travel.'

'Where must I go?' asked Nicholas.

'Follow me,' said the other rider.

'Who are you, sir?'

'The steward of a household where a mutual friend of ours was known. Your presence is requested there immediately. I am not empowered to say any more.'

Nicholas had heard enough. When a steward was sent to deliver a message which could easily have been entrusted to a mere servant, then a matter of some importance was involved. The reference to a mutual friend was conclusive. Leonard was too obtuse to understand it but Nicholas knew at once to whom it pertained. It was his first piece of good fortune. Instead of having to follow a tortuous trail to their benefactor, he sensed that he might get to meet their guardian angel by a more direct route.

'Shall we go?' said the steward curtly.

'Lead on.'

Nicholas mounted the horse, thanked Leonard, then followed his guide over the bridge. His companion rode in silence and shrugged off every question that was put to him. Nicholas soon abandoned his interrogation. He was grateful for the loan of the horse and controlled it without effort as they headed up Gracechurch Street before turning left into Eastcheap. His guide towed him at a brisk trot along Watling Street, past the daunting grandeur of St Paul's Cathedral and on out through Ludgate. Fleet Street allowed them to break into a gentle canter and they were soon passing Temple Bar.

Stretching along the Strand was a row of some of the finest houses in London, stately mansions belonging to peers, bishops and men of wealth, coveted properties which gave their owners great kudos and an uninterrupted view of the Thames. Glad to be free of the city's stench, Nicholas inhaled fresh air into his lungs. The steward raised an arm to warn him that they would soon be leaving the road. Nicholas rode beside him down a wide track towards their destination.

The house was situated just beyond the Savoy Palace, now converted into a hospital but still possessing a degree of splendour. It was a smaller property than most in the Strand but it lacked nothing in elegance. Studying the impressive facade, Nicholas surmised that only a rich man could afford to buy such a home. Servants were waiting to take charge of their horses and the front door was opened for them. The steward conducted his visitor across the hall and into a large, low room with oak-panelled walls and exquisitely carved oak furniture.

Nicholas was left alone for a few minutes and occupied the time in looking at the portraits which were ranged around the room. The largest of them captured his attention. Against a background of leather-bound books, the face of an old, proud, resolute, white-haired man stared out from the canvas. There was nobility in his features and a hint of defiance in his expression. Notwithstanding the library setting, Nicholas felt that he was looking at a military man. He also thought that he detected a faint resemblance to a certain Sylvester Pryde.

The door opened and the steward came into the room.

'The Countess of Dartford,' he announced solemnly.

The woman who swept in had such striking beauty and wore such costly attire that Nicholas blinked in astonishment. Removing his cap, he held it before him and gave a courteous bow. The steward withdrew and closed the door behind him. While Nicholas stood in the middle of the room, the lady of the house walked around him in a circle to take a full inventory of him, giving off a fragrance that was quite bewitching. A faint smile of admiration touched her lips but she took care not to let her visitor see it. Lowering herself onto a chair, she adjusted her dress then looked up at him.

'You are Nicholas Bracewell?' she asked.

'Yes, my lady.'

'Thank you for answering the summons.'

Now that he could study her properly, he could see a slight puffiness around her eyes as if she had been crying but it did not detract from the sculptured loveliness of her features. It was difficult to put a precise age on her. Her clear skin was that of a young woman but there was an air of maturity about her which hinted at more years than were apparent.

'Can you be trusted, Nicholas?' she asked.

'Trusted, my lady?'

'Sylvester told me that you could. He said that you were honest and reliable. A good friend who knew how to respect a confidence. Is that true?'

'I believe so, my lady.'

'He also told me how modest you are.'

'Did he?' said Nicholas.

'Modest men have no need to boast. They can hold their tongues.' She appraised him again. 'I begin to think that he may have been right about you. Sylvester was a sound judge of character. He will be sorely missed.'

'Yes, my lady.'

There was a long pause as she gathered her strength for what might be an ordeal. The Countess of Dartford folded her hands in her lap and took a deep breath.

'Tell me what happened,' she whispered.

'Happened?'

'To Sylvester. How was he killed?'

Nicholas was astounded. 'You *know*, my lady?'

'Alas, yes.'

'But how?'

'Just tell me what happened,' she said, hands tightening their grasp on each other. 'You were there when he was found, Nicholas. You saw the body. Tell me about it.'

'I will, my lady.'

'Tell me *everything*.'

Edmund Hoode was racked with self-disgust. Having honoured a friend with his fine performance in *Black Antonio*, he had dishonoured himself by following his colleagues eagerly into the taproom in search of the oblivion of drink. Hoode had wallowed freely in sentimentality with the rest of them, recalling fond memories of Sylvester Pryde for the general ear then sighing afresh as others produced their own stories about him. It was only when he was about to drift off into a haze that he realised how disgracefully he was behaving. Others were praying for their dear departed friend or making practical efforts to build the theatre which Pryde had helped to initiate whereas Hoode was simply taking refuge in a drunken stupor.

Before it was too late, he stopped himself abruptly. While the others continued with their meandering recollections, he hauled himself up from the table and staggered out of the Queen's Head, anxious to make amends, to mark the passing of a good friend in a more seemly way. He was in no fit state to help on the site alongside the others and work on The Angel would in any case soon be abandoned for the day, but there was something which he could to do commemorate a fallen colleague. He could compose some verses in praise of Sylvester Pryde or write an epitaph for him.

Having made the decision, Hoode walked slowly towards his lodging through the evening air. By sheer force of will, he began to clear his mind of its woolliness and to frame the opening lines of his poetry. He was still deep in the throes of creation when he came to the street where he lived and did not even see the figure who stood outside his lodging.

Lucius Kindell came tentatively forward to meet him.

'Good even to you, Edmund,' he said.

Hoode gaped at him. 'Lucius!'

'I was hoping to catch you.'

'Why?' snapped Hoode, trying to pass him. 'We have nothing to say to each other.'

Kindell blocked his path. 'But I have something to say to you,' he murmured. 'I have come to apologise.'

'It is too late for that.'

'I know that you must feel let down.'

'I feel betrayed, Lucius. Cruelly betrayed.'

'That was not my intention.'

'You have cut Westfield's Men to the quick.'

'It is the last thing in the world that I wanted to do,' said Kindell, close to tears. 'I have been troubled by guilt ever since. But I had no future with the company.'

'Yes, you did.'

'No new play was commissioned from me.'

'It would have been. In time.'

'Only if Westfield's Men survived.'

'Ah!' sighed Hoode. 'We come to that, do we?'

'It is something I have to consider,' said the other defensively. 'Master Kitely explained it to me. He told me that I had to find another company to stage my plays and convinced me that that company was Havelock's Men. They are safe from the Privy Council's threat.'

'Do not be so sure, Lucius.'

'Viscount Havelock has influence at Court.'

'So does Lord Westfield,' retorted Hoode. 'But the crucial factor will be the quality of performance and we take all the laurels there. Rupert Kitely should look to his own survival. When The Angel theatre is built, it will put The Rose in the shade and turn it into a sorry flower that sheds its petals.'

'That is not what Master Kitely thinks.'

'I am not interested in him.'

'He gave me a solemn assurance that your playhouse will never be completed. When I asked him why he was so certain, he would not say but he was adamant, Edmund. You will fail.'

'We, too, are adamant.'

'That is what I always admired about Westfield's Men.'

'Indeed,' said Hoode with uncharacteristic irony. 'It is a pity that your admiration did not induce a degree of loyalty in your ungrateful breast. Once thrown away so callously, friendship can never be regained.'

'That is why I came to your lodging,' admitted Kindell. 'I was too ashamed to seek you at the Queen's Head. Too ashamed and far too afraid.'

'With good cause. Lawrence Firethorn would have eaten you alive, Lucius. He has no time for traitors.'

'Do not call me that.'

'You are a renegade, Lucius.'

'No!'

'A deserter, a rogue, a craven coward!'

'It is not true!' pleaded the other. 'I hoped that you at least would understand my decision.'

'All that I understood was the feel of the knife between my shoulder blades. You pushed it in so deep.'

Kindell burst into tears of contrition and it was some time before he recovered his composure. Hoode's anger slowly mellowed. He could see the dilemma in which his apprentice was caught and he remembered the start of his own career in the theatre when he, too, was subjected to the pull of rival companies. But that did not excuse what Kindell had done.

'I miss you, Edmund,' he said with a hopeless shrug.

'We are well rid of you.'

'I miss you all. Master Firethorn, Master Gill, Nicholas Bracewell, Owen Elias, Sylvester Pryde and every last member of Westfield's Men down to little George Dart. They will have a very low opinion of me now.'

'And rightly so,' said Hoode, 'but you have clearly not heard the worst news. Sylvester is dead.'

'Dead?' Kindell was appalled. 'Sylvester Pryde?'

'He was murdered.'

'This is hideous intelligence!'

'I am surprised that you did not hear it from the mouth of Rupert Kitely.'

'Master Kitely?'

'Yes,' said Hoode. 'Perhaps that is why he told you that our playhouse would never be built. Because he knew that Sylvester had been crushed to death on the site of The Angel and thought that it would stop us. Well, you may give him a message from us. Every member of Westfield's Men will have to be killed to stop our playhouse rising up in Bankside.'

Kindell was horrified. 'Are you saying that Master Kitely was somehow implicated in the killing?'

'Ask yourself this. *Cui bono*?'

'But he would never stoop to murder.'

'He would stoop to anything, Lucius. Mark him well.'

Hoode brushed past him and went into his lodging. Lucius Kindell stood outside in the street for a long time with his brain spinning uncomfortably.

She was a brave woman. The Countess of Dartford insisted on hearing details which would have unsettled more squeamish listeners but she did not flinch for a second. She remained calm and poised. Nicholas sensed her grief but saw no outward evidence of it. Her self-control was extraordinary.

'Thank you,' she said when he finished.

'That is all I can tell you, my lady.'

'It is enough for now, Nicholas.' Her jaw tightened. 'The only other thing I would like to hear is that his killer has been apprehended.'

'He will be,' promised Nicholas.

'You are a good friend to him.'

'He was our fellow.'

'You spoke with such affection of him. Sylvester was a rare man. He knew how to win everyone's good opinion. He made people love him.' She suppressed a sigh. 'What will happen now, Nicholas?'

'Happen, my lady?'

'To your playhouse?'

'We will continue to build it,' he affirmed. 'That is what Sylvester would have wanted us to do. Members of the company worked on site this very day and I will take my turn there when time permits. No, my lady,' he said, 'as long as our loan is forthcoming, we will press on.'

'What if it were withdrawn?'

'We have written promise, my lady.'

'A promise may be revoked.'

'True.'

'Sylvester was your intermediary, was he not?'

'Yes, my lady.'

'Without his persuasion, your benefactor would not have parted with a single penny. What reason does that benefactor have to pay the loan now that Sylvester is no longer involved with Westfield's Men?'

'But he is, my lady,' said Nicholas with sudden passion. 'He is part of our history. We will always revere his memory The Angel theatre will keep that memory alive in the most visible way. He died in its service. It must be built.'

'You are almost as persuasive as he was.'

'We need that loan, my lady.'

'And if it vanishes?'

'We would have to find the money elsewhere.'

'That will not be easy,' she pointed out. 'People are superstitious. They would take a foul murder on the very site of the playhouse as a bad omen.'

'We prefer to see it as a sign to carry on.'

'I admire your courage.'

'It will be needed in the weeks ahead, my lady.'

She sat back pensively in her chair and subjected him to a careful scrutiny. Nicholas was discomfited. She seemed to know a great deal about him and the company while yielding up little about herself. Sensing his uneasiness, she waved him to an oak bench against the opposite wall.

'You have been standing too long, Nicholas.'

'Thank you, my lady,' he said, sitting down.

'But I was not quite sure if you would be staying,' she explained. 'I had to test you first. I think that you can be trusted. You were honest with me.'

'I tried to be, my lady.'

'Sylvester held you in high esteem.'

'I am flattered.'

'How well did you know him?'

'As well as anyone else in the company,' he said, 'but that is no large claim to make, my lady. The truth is that none us really knew Sylvester. We saw him as a friend and as a valuable member of the company but we had no notion where he came from or what career he had pursued until he joined Westfield's Men. He talked little about himself, nor did we press him on the subject. It is not unusual, my lady.'

'Unusual?'

'Actors are strange creatures. It is not only vanity which makes them strut upon a stage. Many other motives impel them. Sylvester Pryde was not alone in using the theatre as a kind of refuge, a place where he could hide his true self and be someone else for an afternoon.'

'And what was that true self, Nicholas?'

'I am not sure.'

'Hazard a guess,' she encouraged. 'You have been here long enough to make observations and to pass a judgement What have you decided?' She smiled at his obvious reluctance. 'Do not be afraid to speak your mind. I will not be offended.'

'Very well, my lady,' he said, plunging in. 'I believe that Sylvester secured that loan from a member of his family. We have long felt that he came of aristocratic stock and noted a prosperity about him which could not be bought with his share of our takings. In short, I think that the money for our playhouse came from someone in this room.' He turned to indicate the largest portrait. 'From his father.'

The Countess of Dartford fought hard to contain her mirth. She rose from her seat and walked away from him so that he could not see the smile on her face. When she recovered her poise, she came back to rest a hand on the back of her chair.

'That is not his father, Nicholas, I do assure you.'

'Then I am mistaken.'

'Gravely,' she said, turning to the portrait. 'That gentleman has no children nor is he likely to produce any. He is well over sixty years of age and in extremely poor health. You are looking at Charles Bartram, Earl of Dartford,' she said levelly. 'He is my husband.'

'I do apologise, my lady.'

'Charles would be flattered by the compliment.'

'I spoke in ignorance.'

'Only because I urged you on, Nicholas. Let it pass.' She resumed her seat and became earnest. 'I will tell you about Sylvester Pryde,' she volunteered, 'but I must first extract a promise from you. Whatever I tell you must remain a secret between us. Is that understood?'

'Yes, my lady.'

'I will have to trust to your discretion.'

'You will not find it wanting,' he asseverated.

'I know.' She collected her thoughts before continuing. 'Sylvester hailed from Lincolnshire. His father, Sir Reginald Pryde, had his estate there and hoped that his only son would take it over after him. It was not to be. Sylvester was too free a spirit to spend the rest of his life in Lincolnshire. He and his father fell out. Sir Reginald settled a sum of money on him but left the estate itself to a nephew.' She gave a wan smile. 'You can imagine what Sylvester did with his inheritance.'

'He enjoyed spending it, my lady.'

'On others as much as on himself,' she stressed. 'He was the most generous person I have ever met and not only with money. Sylvester was a beautiful man. It was a joy to know him. As to what he did before he joined your company, I am not entirely certain myself. He dallied with the law. He even toyed with the notion of becoming a Member of Parliament. And there were doubtless other professions that held his attention for a short time. Only the theatre satisfied him,' she said. 'He found his true home with Westfield's Men.'

'We felt that, my lady.'

'Though he was never destined for real glory there.'

'He was a competent actor,' said Nicholas loyally. 'Short of the genius which makes a Lawrence Firethorn but an asset to any company. He worked at his trade.'

'That was a revelation to him,' she said. 'It was the only thing he ever dedicated himself to and it gave him rewards of the heart he had never imagined. That was why he was so eager to transact a loan for Westfield's Men. It was partly a repayment for all the pleasure and excitement you gave him.'

'He gave us pleasure and excitement in return.'

'Then you will not forget him?'

'Never!' vowed Nicholas.

She was content. She rose from her chair in a manner which indicated that the interview was over. Nicholas stood up and moved towards the door with her. In close proximity, he found her perfume even more alluring. She paused at the door.

'The loan will be paid.'

'Thank you, my lady.'

'Tell Master Firethorn that The Angel can be built.'

'I will.'

'But that is all you tell him, Nicholas. There is no need for anyone else but you to know that I provided that money. I have many reasons for maintaining my secrecy.'

'They are no business of ours, my lady,' he said, glad that their benefactor had finally been identified. 'Your kindness is appreciated and your wishes will be respected. But there is one thing I would like to ask before I leave.'

'What is it?'

'How did you know that Sylvester had been killed?'

'One of my servants made enquiries of the coroner.'

'But what made you send him to the coroner?'

The Countess of Dartford looked him full in the face.

'Instinct,' she said simply. 'Sylvester did not come back here last night. Only death could have kept him away.'

This time she could not hold back the tears.

Rose Marwood's fever broke in the night. A combination of the doctor's potion, her mother's nursing and the anguished prayers of her father eventually worked. Sybil sat beside the bed all night to tend her, trying desperately to atone for the pain and disease she believed she had inflicted on Rose by taking her to Clerkenwell. The doctor's reproaches had shattered her faith in Mary Hogg and she berated herself for her folly in trusting such a dangerous woman. Alexander Marwood had been given the task of destroying the Roman Catholic Prayer Book and he burnt it on the fire, wishing, as he stared into the yellow flames, that he could consign his daughter's lover to the same fate.

When Rose awoke next morning, she had visibly improved.

'How do you feel now?' asked Sybil solicitously.

'The pain has gone, mother.'

'Thank heaven!'

'I feel hungry.'

'That is a good sign.'

'I have been dreaming of food.'

'You shall have whatever you want.'

Rose felt a cool breeze stroking her cheek. 'The window is open,' she said in surprise. 'I thought you had it bolted.'

'It will stay open now to let in fresh air.'

'Thank you, mother.'

Sybil felt her daughter's brow then took both of her hands between her own. Apology never came easily to her and it cost her a tremendous effort of will.

'We were unkind to you, Rose,' she admitted.

'You frightened me.'

'Only because we were frightened ourselves. But I was wrong to take you to Clerkenwell. That was sinful. I see that now. I cannot find it in my heart to welcome this child but I should not have tried to get rid of it in that cruel way.'

'It is his, mother,' murmured the girl.

'Whose?'

'His.'

Sybil pulled herself back from further questioning. During her long hours of recrimination, she had come to see that she could never bludgeon the name out of her daughter. Only by winning back the girl's love and confidence would she have any hope of being told who the child's father was. Nursing Rose through her illness had been an important first step but there were several others to take.

'What food will I fetch you?' she offered.

'Anything,' said Rose. 'I am so famished.'

'Leave it to me.'

'Thank you, mother.'

'What else will I bring?'

'Something to drink, please. And mother?'

'Yes?'

'Could you open the window a little wider?' said Rose softly. 'The sun will shine onto the bed.'

Sybil was only too happy to oblige, opening the window

as wide as she could then going back to the bed to place on kiss on Rose's forehead. When she went out, she left the door slightly ajar to signal that the prison regime was at an end. Rose struggled to sit up and look around her bedchamber. She was still weak but the fever and the continual ache had faded away. For the first time since she had taken to her bed, she felt a degree of hope. That was a medicine in itself.

A scraping noise took her eyes to the window. Expecting to find a bird perched there, she was astonished to see something quite different. Lying just inside the window, as if placed there from outside, was a tiny red flower. Rose was overjoyed. Struggling to get out of bed, she supported herself with a hand on the wall as she made her way to the window to collect the flower. It was more eloquent than any message and she was certain that it came from him. He knew. He wanted to help. He was offering his love and support.

There was nobody outside the window but her disappointment was allayed by the flower. She inhaled its fragrance before making her way back to the bed, clambering into it with relief and holding the flower against her cheek. It was only when she heard her mother returning that she put the red rose hastily under the pillow. Sybil entered with a tray of food.

'You look so much better, Rose,' she said with a sigh of gratitude. 'You've got some colour back in your cheeks.'

The second performance of *The Insatiate Duke* had nothing like the success of the first. The acting was good, the effects startling and the stage management as smooth as ever but a key element was missing. Edmund Hoode no longer believed in the piece. Where he had been a moving Cardinal Boccherini on the first outing, he was now a rather sinister figure and it upset the whole balance of the drama. The audience was very appreciative but Westfield's Men knew that they were being given short measure at the Queen's Head that afternoon.

Nobody was more disappointed than Lucius Kindell, the estranged co-author of the tragedy. Too embarrassed to make himself known to the company, he sneaked into the yard and found a seat in the upper gallery. Given his involvement with a rival company, he had anticipated that his play would be dropped by way of retaliation but Westfield's Men were honouring their pledge to stage it again and that served to deepen his guilt. They were showing much more faith in his work than he had in theirs. The performance made him squirm in his seat, partly because it lacked any genuine passion and suffering, but chiefly because he could see what an ordeal it was for Hoode. A play on which the two of them had worked so hard for so long had turned sour for his co-author.

Lawrence Firethorn left the stage in a mild fury.

'We were abysmal, sirs!' he roared.

'Speak for yourself, Lawrence,' said Barnaby Gill. 'I will not hear a word against my performance. You saw those laughing faces. You heard that applause.'

'*The Insatiate Duke* was a shadow of itself.'

'Blame that on the insatiate duke.'

'We are all to blame,' insisted Firethorn.

'It is true,' agreed Hoode. 'This play is not for us. Give it to Nicholas to lock away in his box. It may stay there in perpetuity for all that I am concerned.'

They understood his rancour. Since his partnership with Lucius Kindell had been ruptured, he had become disenchanted with both the plays they had written together. Owen Elias sought to extract a jest from the situation.

'You are a changed man, Edmund,' he teased. 'We are used to seeing you moping over a woman who will not requite your love. Now you are weeping over the loss of a young boy. Take care you do not turn into a second Barnaby.'

'I resent that,' said Gill over the laughter.

'Why?' mocked Elias. 'Did Lucius reject you as well?'

'Yes,' said Firethorn, joining in the fun at Gill's expense, 'he sold his buttocks to Rupert Kitely instead. Barnaby will have to run off to Havelock's Men if he wishes have an assignation with our deserter.'

Gill fell silent and looked away guiltily. Firethorn and Elias continued to bait him but for once he did not rise to the taunts. Nicholas Bracewell noted his lack of response and was concerned. It accorded with Gill's reaction to the news that the loan to Westfield's Men would be paid in spite of the death of their intermediary. While the rest of the company had been thrilled by the reassurance which Nicholas was able to give them, Gill had sulked in a corner. It was almost as if he did not want Westfield's Men to have their own playhouse.

The company broke up to go their separate ways. A fresh detachment of volunteers went off to work at the site of The Angel for a few hours, relieving those who had laboured there to good effect on the previous day. When his chores were complete, Nicholas had intended to join the work party himself but Firethorn summoned him to a meeting with their patron.

They found Lord Westfield in his accustomed room, sipping a glass of wine and talking with some of his entourage. He dismissed the others so that he could be alone with the two newcomers. Anxiety flooded his face.

'What is this I hear about a murder in our ranks?'

'All too true, my lord,' said Firethorn sadly. 'Sylvester Pryde was crushed to death beneath some timbers on the site of our new playhouse.'

'Poor soul!'

'Nicholas was there when they found the body.'

Picking up his cue, Nicholas gave a concise account of what had happened. Their patron was deeply sympathetic. He needed no evidence to name the culprit.

'One of Banbury's Men,' he decided.

'We do not know that,' cautioned Nicholas.

'We know they envy us and we know that they will stop at nothing to disable us. Especially now that the Master of the Revels has spoken.'

'Has he?' said Firethorn with interest.

'Yes, Lawrence. That is what I came to tell you. I was at Court this morning when Sir Edmund Tilney confided in me the latest decision. It seems a just way to proceed.'

'How so?'

'The Privy Council have postponed their verdict,' said Lord Westfield fussily. 'They are masters of postponement because they can never make up their minds. Tilney feels that they need some help to come to judgement.'

'What does he recommend?' asked Nicholas.

'That the three major theatre companies be viewed alongside each other. This is his plan. Westfield's Men, Havelock's Men and Banbury's Men play at Court in turn. Other companies are not even in the reckoning.'

'I like this news,' said Firethorn.

Nicholas sounded a warning note. 'It may not favour us,' he said. 'If everything is to be decided on one performance, the slightest error might tell against us.'

'There will be no errors, Nick!'

'That is easier to say than to enforce. The importance of the occasion will make the company nervous and that is when unfortunate mistakes creep in.'

'It is so with the other companies,' said Firethorn. 'I have no fears. We will always outshine Havelock's Men.'

'And Banbury's Men,' added Lord Westfield truculently. 'They are nothing but a pack of murderers.'

Nicholas let the two of them enthuse about the plan. He kept his reservations to himself. Though delighted that they would have the honour of another performance at Court, he was deeply worried that the Privy Council's decision would take no account of their sustained excellence. Judged on their whole season, Westfield's Men could rightly claim supremacy over their rivals. When they were given only one chance to impress, they entered the realms of doubt.

There was another problem. Westfield's Men were a diminished force. When *The Insatiate Duke* was first staged, it was the headiest triumph they had enjoyed for a long time. Since then one of its co-authors had left, the other was profoundly depressed as a result, a sharer had been brutally killed and the company's resident clown was restless. He wondered how many more depletions there would be before the stipulated appearance at Court.

Firethorn's optimism knew no bounds. Striking a pose, he began to pluck plays out of the repertoire, nominating those in which he took the leading part and ignoring the contribution that others might make.

'*Hector of Troy*,' he concluded. 'That is our choice.'

'We should discuss this at greater length,' said Nicholas tactfully. 'The other sharers will want their say.'

'They will follow my lead, Nick.'

The book holder stifled his reply. He knew how outraged Barnaby Gill would be at the choice of *Hector of Troy*. Not only did it allow Firethorn to dominate the stage for the whole five acts, it confined Gill to two short scenes and one dance. The surest way to drive their clown out of Westfield's Men was to select a play which blunted his rich talents.

'What of this new playhouse?' asked Lord Westfield.

'It grows by the hour, my lord,' said Firethorn airily. 'Our fellows are taking it in turns to put their strong arms at the disposal of the builder. The Angel theatre will soon be a towering landmark on the riverbank.'

'And the loan?' said their patron.

'It is safe.'

'But was not Sylvester Pryde your intermediary?'

'That office has been taken over by Nick here.'

'You *know* who our mysterious benefactor is?' said Lord Westfield excitedly. 'Do tell us, Nicholas.'

'I am not at liberty to do so, my lord.'

'You may trust me. I am as close as the grave.'

'I have sworn an oath, my lord, and may not break it.'

'There's an end to it,' said Firethorn. 'Nick would not even confide in me. He is too honourable. What does it matter where the money comes from as long as we have it? This loan breathes new life back into Westfield's Men.'

'Yes,' said their patron wearily, 'but it is not only the company which is in need of a loan. Is our benefactor so wealthy that he can loan six hundred pounds to us at such a favourable rate of interest? Such a man is to be wooed, Nicholas. Cultivate him. Ask him if he would consider making a personal loan to a very dear friend of yours.'

'I think it unlikely, my lord,' said Nicholas. 'But for Sylvester Pryde, we would not have secured this loan. He was the pathway to our benefactor and Sylvester is dead.'

'Try, Nicholas. Even a small amount would be acceptable.'

'I understand.'

'Good.' He clapped his hands together. 'Meanwhile, I will continue to work away on your behalf at Court. The factions are already forming. Viscount Havelock has the largest but the Earl of Banbury is busy gathering his forces.' He gave a grin of self-congratulation. 'I, too, have assembled friends around me. Sir Patrick Skelton has been won over to our side and several others besides.'

'These are cheerful tidings,' said Firethorn.

'They are, Lawrence. And it is not openly among the men that I have recruited support. Several ladies have indicated a preference for Westfield's Men. Cordelia Bartram among them.'

Nicholas was taken aback. 'Cordelia Bartram, my lord?'

'Yes,' said the other. 'The Countess of Dartford.'

'Is she not a fabled beauty?' asked Firethorn.

'And rightly so, Lawrence. She is wasted on that old fool of a husband she married. No,' said Lord Westfield with a knowing chuckle, 'I was not at all surprised when Cordelia threw her weight behind us. It is one sure way to strike back at Viscount Havelock.'

'Why should she wish to do that?' said Nicholas.

'Revenge,' said the other. 'Hell hath no fury like a woman spurned. Before she was married, it is rumoured, Cordelia was his mistress until he cast her aside. The Countess of Dartford would love to see Havelock's Men perish.'

Chapter Nine

Viscount Havelock lived in a style which was the envy of his friends and foes alike. His house in Bishopsgate was palatial, surpassing in extravagance, though not in size, the neighbouring Crosby Place. The Viscount was a man of considerable wealth and a passion for displaying it. His theatre company were not simply a reflection of his devotion to the arts. They were a public statement of his importance, an expression of his vanity and a glittering jewel which he could wear to impress the rest of London. Viscount Havelock never resisted any opportunity to polish that jewel.

'Well, Rupert?' he enquired.

'All things proceed to our advantage,' said Kitely.

'I am delighted to hear it.'

'This latest device of Sir Edmund Tilney's makes our position ever more secure. We are to play at Court in sequence with Banbury's Men and Westfield's Men so that we may be judged side by side. Choice of the fare we select will be critical, my lord, and fortune favours us.'

'How so?'

'We have a play, fresh and new-minted, the sprightliest comedy which has come our way in years.'

'What is it called?'

'*A Looking Glass for London*.'

'I like the sound of that.'

'You will like it even more when you see it, my lord,' said Kitely with pride. 'It was to have been staged at The Rose on Monday but we will save it for Court. *A Looking Glass for London* is the ideal piece to set before Her Grace. Our rivals, meanwhile, will have no new offering ready in time. They will have to ferret through their old playbooks to find something fit. Our work will be fresh and lively against their dull, stale, careworn dramas.'

'This serves us well, Rupert.'

They were at the house in Bishopsgate and Kitely was extremely flattered to be invited there. At the same time, he was reminded of his position as the servant of his patron by being kept waiting when he first arrived then by being made to stand while his host lounged in a chair. They were in a small but well-appointed antechamber and Kitely could hear the sound of busy preparations in the adjoining dining room. The noble Viscount Havelock would never deign to invite the actor to his table. Though the theatre troupe brought them close, and even permitted a degree of friendship, the social distance between them remained vast.

'What of Westfield's Men?' asked the patron.

'They are beset by problems,' said the other complacently.

'And we will create more to vex them.'

'Have you been able to raid the company?'

'We have taken one prisoner so far, my lord. Their young playwright, Lucius Kindell. You saw his work at the Queen's Head recently.'

'Saw it and admired it,' recalled the Viscount. 'This fellow has talent. But I would sooner you had poached Edmund Hoode from their pantry. They feed chiefly off him.'

'Hoode will come in time, my lord,' said the actor. 'And Lucius will help to bring him there. My calculation was that Hoode would be desolate at the loss of his young apprentice. And so it has proved. Westfield's Men are a lesser company when their playwright is dejected.'

'You are a wise politician, sir.'

'I need to be in my profession.'

'And Banbury's Men?'

'They are of no account, my lord.'

'Do not dismiss them lightly, Rupert.'

'You know the terms of the edict better than I, my lord. One playhouse to stand north of the river and one south. Banbury's Men cannot hurt us while they are in Shoreditch.'

'But they must also have designs on Westfield's Men.'

'Indeed,' said Kitely, 'they have set themselves the task of stealing Barnaby Gill away.'

'How do you know?'

'Such information can be bought, my lord.'

'A spy in their camp?'

'He warns me of all that happens at The Curtain,' said Kitely with a thin smile. 'One Henry Quine, an actor with

214

the company, was used to see if Gill could be tempted. It seems that he can be. Gill has met with Giles Randolph.'

'I would sooner he met with Rupert Kitely.'

'That, too, will come in time, my lord,' promised the other. 'For the moment, I choose to let Banbury's Men work on our behalf. If they take Barnaby Gill from the Queen's Head, they disable the company badly and that serves our purpose. It is The Angel which threatens The Rose. Our rivals will help to clip its wings.'

Viscount Havelock rose to his feet to deliver his command.

'I want this new playhouse strangled in its cradle.'

'It will be, my lord.'

'The Rose must have no rival in Bankside.'

'Nor will it,' pledged the other. 'Havelock's Men will be unchallenged. The Angel theatre is the doomed project of a company which will soon be disbanded. Your company will reign supreme, my lord.'

'That will please me mightily.'

Viscount Havelock rose from his chair with a smile of satisfaction then gave his visitor a nod of dismissal before going off to join his guests. He would have something to boast to them about now.

Nicholas Bracewell was deeply troubled. His walk home from the Queen's Head was a series of recriminations. A casual remark from their patron had made him see their situation in an entirely different light. When he left the house in the Strand, he firmly believed that their benefactor was advancing

215

a loan to the company out of fondness for Sylvester Pryde but it now transpired that she might have another motive. Cordelia Bartram, Countess of Dartford, had struck him as a beautiful woman who was grieving over the death of a close friend and Nicholas had sensed that the friendship might well have been of the most intimate nature. He passed no moral judgement on that. It was not his place to do so.

If, however, the lady really was the discarded mistress of Viscount Havelock, and if she was using Westfield's Men as a weapon against him, then the company's position was precarious. They were mere pawns in a private quarrel between estranged lovers. When they had served their purpose and brought about the demise of the rival company, the scheming Countess might have no further use for them and the loan which she had so readily supplied might be recalled or laden with crippling additional interest payments. Instead of ensuring their salvation, Sylvester Pryde might unwittingly have loaded them with an intolerable burden.

What made his predicament worse was that Nicholas was unable to discuss it with anyone. Having given his solemn word, he was duty bound to stand by it and that meant holding back from his fellows any knowledge of the threat which their benefactor posed. He could now see all too well why the Countess of Dartford insisted on her anonymity. She did not wish Viscount Havelock to know that she was funding a campaign against his theatre company, nor, Nicholas suspected, did she want her husband to become aware of how she disposed of her money or how she spent her time away from him. Judging by his portrait, the Earl of Dartford was a proud, haughty man with a possessive nature. Had he realised that his wife had been entertaining a young lover at their London home, he would have been justifiably roused.

The more Nicholas reflected on the situation, the more complicated it became. Lord Westfield had his faults but he was a supportive patron. He could be weak, erratic and prone to interfere at times yet he never failed them in a real crisis. Nicholas could imagine how outraged he would be if he knew that one of the people he had recruited to his Court faction was secretly providing the money to build the new playhouse. If her identity were ever revealed, then Nicholas himself would come in for severe criticism from a patron who would not be above demanding his removal from the company. He was shaken by the thought that a vow given to the Countess of Dartford might turn out to be an act of professional suicide.

His meditations carried him all the way down to the river and he engaged a waterman to row him across. As they rode on the choppy water in the falling light, Nicholas recalled that Sylvester Pryde had made a similar journey to Bankside on the night of his murder. He could well understand the emotions which had surged through his friend. To be able to effect the survival of his company would have been deeply gratifying but it was the notion of the new playhouse which had fired him. The Angel theatre would not just be a marvel which Pryde had helped to bring into being. For a rootless actor, an outcast from his family, a wandering soul, a man who had finally discovered his true path in life, it was a spiritual home.

The boat landed him a hundred yards downstream of The

Angel but Nicholas felt a sudden urge to view the site himself. Little would be visible in the gloom but he knew that it would impart the same thrill of anticipation which Pryde had sought on his fatal visit. Instead of returning to his lodging, therefore, he walked briskly past the tenements which fringed the riverbank. When a gap in the buildings appeared, Nicholas thought for a moment that he saw figures moving about on the site and he came to a cautionary halt. No work could be done without torches and Thomas Bradd had dismissed his men some hours before. Who then could be trespassing?

Though he strained his eyes against the half-dark, Nicholas could no longer see anyone among the timbers and the piles of bricks. He decided that he had either been mistaken or that his arrival had frightened away any intruders. When he moved forward, he still took the precaution of keeping a hand on his dagger but he did not expect to have to use it. The site of the playhouse seemed deserted. Foundations had been dug and one wall had already been started. When he stood in the centre of the plot, Nicholas could envisage the great, many-sided structure rising up all around him until it matched The Rose in the middle distance. It was an inspiring moment but he was not allowed to enjoy it for long.

The sound of footsteps made him turn and he saw a burly figure hurtling towards him. Nicholas lowered his shoulder and struck his assailant so hard in the chest that the man was knocked off his feet. Nicholas pulled out his dagger but a second man struck his arm with a staff and forced him to drop it on the ground. He swung round to face the new adversary. Before Nicholas could even grapple with him, however, he was attacked from behind by a third man. All three now set on him, Nicholas resisted manfully, punching hard and drawing blood, using all his power to shake one of his attackers off and to wind a second with a blow to the stomach. But it was only a temporary respite and they came back at him with renewed ferocity.

Nicholas was outnumbered. As the brawl continued, the staff was used to club him to the ground. He tried to put his hands up to protect his head but his arms were drained of strength. A final blow knocked him unconscious. The men did not delay. Leaving him there, they set about their work with increased speed, kicking down the preliminary wall of the theatre then using ropes to drag and manoeuvre the heavy timbers into a pile in the middle of the site. Hessian soaked in oil was stuffed under the pile along with kindling. The bonfire was lit and the men retreated into the night.

By the time that Nicholas began to recover consciousness, the blaze was well-established. He opened a bleary eye to find that The Angel theatre was now a small inferno.

Giles Randolph was in a mood of unassailable smugness. His performance in the title role of *Richard Crookback* that afternoon had been hailed, the takings had been excellent, his patron had been indulgent and his favourite mistress had sent word that she was awaiting him. Only one source of pleasure was missing. He raised the topic with Henry Quine when the two of them met at The Elephant Inn in Shoreditch.

'You have done well, Henry,' he congratulated.

'Thank you,' said Quine.

'How did you charm Barnaby Gill so cunningly? I do not think that you did it at the Queen's Head under the very noses of his colleagues.'

'That would have been too dangerous.'

'Then how did you reach him? At his lodging?'

'No, Giles,' said Quine with a grin. 'Master Gill is not like us. He takes no pleasure from the society of women. His interests lie elsewhere and he frequents those haunts where he can pursue those interests. I met him at one of those secret gatherings.'

Randolph smiled. 'Did you turn apprentice and put on woman's apparel? Were you a practised coquette?'

'I simply approached him when he was in his cups and off guard. Flattery was my most potent ally. I showered praise on his work and told him what a tragedy it would be if his genius was swept off the London stage.'

'What was his reply?'

'The very notion mortified him.'

'So you whispered the name of Banbury's Men in his ear.'

'Yes, Giles,' said Quine, 'but that is all I whispered. I gave him plenty of time to think it over before I went to him again. Too much eagerness at first would have aroused his suspicion and frighted him away. Persuasion could not be rushed. Barnaby Gill has been with Westfield's Men a long time and deep loyalties still exist.'

'You found a way to defeat them, Henry, and I am most grateful to you for that. Well,' he said happily, 'he came. Master Gill's curiosity was such that he came here and met me. I told him all that he was hoping to hear.'

'You were masterly, Giles.'

'It seems that I could take lessons from you.'

'We won him over together.'

'Not quite, sir,' the other reminded him. 'We brought the horse to water but we have yet to make him drink.'

'He is ours.'

'That would be a twin joy, Henry. We would gain the finest clown in London and wound Lawrence Firethorn deeply. All hope would vanish for him. Westfield's Men would surely perish.'

'Even with their clown, they would not survive.'

'Can we be certain?'

'Oh, yes,' said Quine with a smirk. 'Absolutely certain.'

'Our patron asked me recently how far we would go to preserve the company and subdue our rivals.'

'What was your answer?'

'All the way.'

'That is mine, too. When war is declared, we must not be afraid to inflict casualties.'

Laughter at a nearby table made Quine look up. Some of the sharers from Banbury's Men were celebrating the triumph of *Richard Crookback* and savouring their forthcoming appearance at Court. Henry Quine felt a surge of ambition. It was only a matter of time before he became a sharer himself and joined the exclusive ranks of his profession. He turned to frame a question to which Randolph already had the answer.

'When will we have Barnaby Gill in our grasp?' he asked.

'That will be soon, Giles.'

'The day that it happens, I will have a contract drawn up for you, Henry. You will have the same privileges as all the other sharers. You will have your due proportion of the profits.'

'I yearn for that precious moment.'

'Nobody has earned it more than you,' said Randolph. 'You are accomplished in your art. When you have the opportunity to give full vent to your skills on stage, I will have to look to my own laurels.'

'No compliment could be higher than that, Giles.'

Henry Quine basked in the approval of his master.

'This was a fearful assault, Nick. You might have been killed.'

'No, Anne.'

'This wound is deep.'

'They could easily have murdered me if they had wished.'

'You should not have gone there alone.'

'I wanted to visit the site.'

'Hold still,' she said as he tried to turn his head. 'I have all but finished.'

Anne Hendrik was tending his wounds in the kitchen of her house. Having bathed his head with water, she was putting a bandage around it to stem the last of the bleeding. When that was done, she turned her attention to the bruises on his face and the grazes on his knuckles. Nicholas Bracewell endured the throbbing pain in his head without complaint.

'How do you feel now?' she asked.

'Much better after your ministrations, Anne.'

'You were in such a state when you staggered in here. I thought you had been set on by a dozen men and left for dead.'

'They wanted me alive.'

'And is the fire quite put out?'

'By the grace of God, it is,' he said sadly. 'But not before it had done its worst. Most of our timber went up in smoke. The site is derelict.'

Fire was an ever-present danger in Bankside where it could spread quickly through the rows of tenements with their timber frames and thatched roofs. When the blaze roared into life, dozens of people in the vicinity had streamed out of their dwellings in fear. To save their own property, and under the guidance of Nicholas Bracewell, they fought the fire with buckets and pans. The proximity of the river was the deciding factor, giving them a ready supply of water and helping them in time to douse the flames. It was only then that Nicholas felt able to lurch home to his lodging.

'I am almost done,' she said, bathing his hand.

He managed a smile. 'That is a pity. Your gentle touch blocks out the memory of the beating I took.'

'Promise me that you will not go to the site alone again.'

'Not alone, perhaps,' he said, 'but I will certainly return. I may well have to spend a night or two there.'

She was aghast. 'A night! Whatever for, Nick?'

'The site will need protection.'

'But there is nothing left to protect.'

'We still own the land. Once it has been cleared, we will have to buy fresh timber and start the work again.' He tried to rise. 'I must get word to Thomas Bradd.'

'You are not leaving this house tonight.'

'He must be told about this setback, Anne.'

'Then tell him from the comfort of that chair,' she said, easing him back into his seat. 'I will send a servant to fetch him. When he hears of your injuries, he will come post-haste.'

'That might be the best way,' he conceded. 'I still feel giddy when I stand. Master Bradd will be as angry as I am by this latest attack on us and I am sure that he will want us to mount patrols at night.'

'Must you be part of them?'

'I will insist.'

'Then I will join you.'

'Anne!'

'If you are to stand there in the darkness, I will bring food and drink to succour you. I may not be strong enough to fight off intruders but I can at least keep you all well-fed.'

'Thank you,' he said, kissing her hand affectionately. 'Your offer is appreciated but I would feel happier if I knew that you were warm and safe in bed here. Bankside at night is no place for a lady. Besides, Anne, I will not have to be there all the time. We will take it in turns.'

'You have done your share already, Nick.'

'I have a responsibility. I will not shirk it.'

'You are too dutiful.'

She gave him a hug then sat down opposite him, worried at the state he was in but relieved that she had been able to tend his wounds. The blows to the head had opened up deep gashes and he was badly bruised but no bones were broken. Anne knew from experience that he would not let his injuries slow him down. Nicholas Bracewell had shown his resilience on many occasions. A beating which would have cowed other men only put more steel into his resolve.

'I will find him,' he said quietly.

'Him?'

'The man who instigated this raid. I think he will be the same person who murdered Sylvester. That gives me an even larger score to settle.'

'Who could commit such hideous crimes?'

'Someone who is determined to ruin us.'

'Someone from The Rose?'

'Or from Shoreditch,' he said thoughtfully. 'Banbury's Men have equal reason to want us silenced for ever.'

'What of your loan?'

'Our loan?'

'Your benefactor gave you that money in good faith to build a new theatre,' she said, 'but all that it has produced so far is murder and arson. The whole project is smeared in blood. How will your guardian angel react to that?'

Nicholas made no reply but he was profoundly worried.

Lord Westfield arrived at the Palace of Whitehall with a new spring in his step. Word of the impending performances at Court by the three rival companies had been voiced abroad and it brought in support for his faction from some unexpected quarters. He firmly believed that his was no longer a theatre troupe with the mark of death upon it. It enabled him to meet the smirking Earl of Banbury and the smiling Viscount Havelock with equanimity. He could look both of them in the eye.

When he saw one of his allies, he detached himself from his entourage to steal a moment alone with her. Cordelia Bartram, Countess of Dartford, looked as gorgeous as usual but there was a faint air of sadness about her which even her vivacity could not entirely dispel.

'What is amiss, dear lady?' he asked courteously.

'Nothing, my lord. I am well.'

'You seem a trifle distracted.'

'My mind was elsewhere,' she said, shrugging off her melancholy at once. 'But I am delighted to see you. How fares your campaign?'

'Exceeding well.'

'Have you been gathering your forces?'

'Yes, Cordelia,' he said, 'and with encouraging results.'

'Tell me more.'

'I have had pledges of support from all quarters and Sir Patrick Skelton has hinted that he may be able to exert some influence over the Privy Council.'

'That is heartening,' she said. 'I am a mere woman but I am committed to your cause. What I can achieve on your behalf with my wiles, I certainly shall.'

He chuckled merrily. 'Then is the battle already won. No man alive can resist your wiles, Cordelia. I dare swear that you could win over the testy Earl and the handsome Viscount, if you put your mind to it.'

The Countess of Dartford hid her irritation behind a smile. Any mention of Viscount Havelock in her presence was tactless even if it was only in jest. Sensing that he might have offended her, Lord Westfield went off into a flurry of apologies but she waved them away.

'All that I want is the survival of your troupe.'

'That is assured, Cordelia, ' he said airily. 'Now that the three rivals will play here side by side at Court, our future is certain. Westfield's Men will tower above the others.'

'I expect no less,' she said quietly. 'Winning is paramount with me, my lord. I will not lend my support to a losing faction.'

'You have not done so.'

After issuing a dozen further assurances, he excused himself to move off to the Presence Chamber. His place was quickly taken by the immaculate Sir Patrick Skelton who eased himself alongside her to exchange niceties.

'Good morrow, my lady!'

'I am pleased to see you, Sir Patrick.'

'How do I find you?'

'In good spirits.'

'And your dear husband?'

'He is in poor health still,' she sighed, 'and likely to remain so. His physicians have no remedy for old age, alas. My husband will have to stay in the country.'

'At least we have the pleasure of your company here.'

'I crave excitement, Sir Patrick. I like to be involved. That is why I came back to our London house myself. And it seems that I arrived in time for some amusement.'

'Amusement, my lady?'

'This trial of strength between the theatre companies.'

'It is in earnest.'

'That is what makes it so interesting.' She lowered her voice. 'You and I are of the same party, I believe. That is reassuring. When as politic a man as you takes sides, I know that you will choose the right one.'

He gave her an urbane smile by way of a reply then fell in beside her as they strolled towards the Presence Chamber. She saw Viscount Havelock trying to catch her eye but studiously ignored him. It was another theatre patron who intrigued her.

'Westfield's Men are building a playhouse, I hear.'

'Yes, my lady.'

'Is that an expensive undertaking?'

'Very expensive, I should imagine.'

'And has Lord Westfield advanced the money?' she said artlessly. 'It is an act of wondrous generosity on his part.'

'It would be,' said Skelton, 'if it ever happened. But it did not. Lord Westfield is hounded by his creditors. He is in no position to lend his company one penny. If Westfield's Men depended on capital from him, they would long ago have vanished into oblivion.'

She absorbed the news with great interest. Her face was impassive but she was smiling inwardly as an idea formed.

The sight of Nicholas Bracewell's injuries caused fear and consternation among Westfield's Men. Their book holder had always seemed so solid and indestructible. If he could be reduced to the sorry figure they saw before them, there was little hope for the company. Nicholas's strength and courage were taken for granted as much as the control he exerted over their performances. To see their warrior so battered was a huge blow to their morale and their self-belief.

Nicholas countered the general misery with some stirring words of defiance then took up his book for the rehearsal and exerted even more authority over the proceedings than usual. He knew how important it was to take their minds off the assault he had suffered and to get them working hard at their craft. When the rehearsal was over, he lingered in the yard with Lawrence Firethorn, Edmund Hoode, Barnaby Gill and Owen Elias. George Dart, torn between sympathy and horror, lurked on the fringe of the discussion in the hope of offering a word of comfort to his one true friend in the company but Nicholas moved him gently away before Dart collected a more abusive dismissal from the rumbling Firethorn.

The actor-manager worked himself up into a fierce rage. 'This outrage will not be borne!' he vowed.

'You are not the one who has to bear it, Lawrence,' said Elias. 'That is poor Nick's lot.'

'He suffered those wounds while trying to defend our new playhouse. Our timber was destroyed, Owen. We all suffer that agony. Someone is determined to stop The Angel theatre ever coming into being.'

'I spy the work of Havelock's Men,' said Hoode.

'We have no proof of that,' said Nicholas.

'You carry it upon your head, Nick. Who most stands to lose if The Angel is built and prospers? The company at The Rose.'

229

'Edmund is right,' agreed Firethorn.

'Yes,' said Elias, adding his endorsement. 'Who else could it be? And men who commit arson will also lower themselves to murder. One of them probably killed Sylvester.'

'I wonder,' said Nicholas. 'His assassin followed him across the river before doing his work. That could mean that he lives here in the city and is familiar with the Queen's Head, where he must have lurked in wait for Sylvester. Most of Havelock's Men live in Southwark. One of them might have been dispatched here,' he continued, 'or some hired killer might have been engaged. But there are two further possibilities we must examine.'

'What are they, Nick?' asked Hoode.

'First, that the assassin hailed from Shoreditch.'

'Banbury's Men?'

'Several of them live cheek by jowl with us in the city. They know our territory and our habits. Their company even contains a few deserters from our own.'

Barnaby Gill looked distinctly uneasy. Silent so far, he felt impelled to enter the discussion. He waved a fussy hand.

'This is wild speculation,' he said. 'We should not accuse anybody without proper evidence. The Angel theatre is clearly a stricken enterprise. We should accept that it will never be built and look elsewhere for our salvation.'

'It *will* be built,' asserted Firethorn. 'If I have to put every brick and piece of timber in place myself, I will have that new playhouse.'

Gill was waspish. 'What use will a playhouse be if the

Privy Council's decision favours The Rose? You will be left with an empty shell on your hands.'

'Stop this talk of defeat, Barnaby!'

'I am merely facing the inevitable.'

'This is a time to be steadfast.'

'Is it?' said Gill sardonically. 'Look at Nicholas. He was steadfast and we can all see the result. Murder and arson have already taken place on that site. What will come next?'

'The burial of Barnaby Gill under its foundations!' roared Firethorn. 'Ye gods! This is treasonable talk. I want men around me who will fight to defend their livelihood.'

'Let us come back to Nick,' suggested Hoode, interceding in the quarrel before it distracted them completely. 'He said that we should examine two further possibilities.' He turned to the book holder. 'What is the second?'

'That the person or persons we seek have no connection whatsoever with any of our rivals,' said Nicholas. 'Indeed, they may not be involved in the theatre in any way.'

'What, then, is their motive?' wondered Elias.

Nicholas shrugged. 'Spite, malice, revenge. Who knows? We all assumed that Sylvester was killed in order to deter us from building The Angel theatre. But the scene of the crime might have been chosen at random by an assailant who took the opportunity when it arose.'

'What are you telling us, Nick?' asked Firethorn.

'That Sylvester may have been hunted down by an enemy. It was no deliberate attack on Westfield's Men at all. The sole aim was to kill one man.'

'But Sylvester *had* no enemies,' argued Elias. 'His real

talent lay in making friends. Who could possibly wish to raise a hand against him?' He gave a knowing leer. 'Unless it was some enraged husband whom he cuckolded.'

Nicholas thought for a moment about the Earl of Dartford.

'He had enemies,' he said, 'I am sure of that. And it might pay us to look more closely into his past.'

'This does not make sense,' said Hoode thoughtfully. 'If Sylvester was murdered by a personal enemy then the crime was an end in itself. Why, then, go on to set fire to our property?'

'The two attacks may be unrelated,' said Nicholas. 'I confess that I thought they were the work of the same villain at first but I am not so convinced now. And even if they are linked, it may not be through one of our rivals.'

'Who else could join the two together?' asked Hoode.

'Our benefactor.'

As soon as the word popped out, Nicholas wondered if he had stumbled onto something. Could murder and arson have been used as a means of attacking the Countess of Dartford? Was there someone in her past who was wreaking the havoc in order to blight her plans? How would they know of her involvement with Westfield's Men? Or of her relationship with Sylvester Pryde? The only way that he could probe the mystery was to visit her again. Cordelia Bartram had a right to know about the latest setback to the theatre she was lending money to build and she might conceivably be able to offer some insight into the outrage.

When they pressed him for more detail, Nicholas backed

off and deflected them from any further mention of their guardian angel. It was forbidden territory. Their immediate concern was to stage a play that afternoon and he urged Firethorn to rally his company beforehand. They must not be allowed to dwell on adversity.

'I'll speak with them now,' said Firethorn.

'And I will take refreshment,' said Gill, fastidiously.

'Do not take your pessimism into the taproom, Barnaby. We have enough of that from our landlord. Give your fellows a smile. Raise their spirits. When the play is done,' he announced, 'every man of us will repair to the site to work.'

Gill was scandalised. 'You will not get me near all that filth, Lawrence. It would ruin my apparel. And my hands are far too delicate for manual labour.'

Nicholas stepped in. 'There is no need for any of us to go to the site today,' he said. 'It would only depress our fellows the more to see it in such a parlous state. Thomas Bradd has men enough to clear the mess. Let us leave it to him.'

'I wish to view the damage for myself,' decided Firethorn.

'Then go alone,' urged Gill. 'You will not get me near a place which has brought so much horror down on our heads. I begin to think that it may be haunted.'

He went off to the taproom with Firethorn at his heels.

When Hoode and Elias tried to follow, Nicholas detained them.

'I need some help from you,' he said.

'Anne is the only person who can help you,' observed

Elias. 'You should be in your bed while she nurses you back to health, Nick. With injuries like yours, I would play the invalid for a week at least.'

'That is not an option which I can afford to take.'

'Tell us what to do, Nick,' said Hoode, 'and it will be done without complaint.'

'Thank you, Edmund. I want you to seek out Lucius Kindell.'

'If I do, it would only be to box his ungrateful ears!'

'School your anger,' advised Nicholas. 'He can be of considerable use to us.'

'But he is no longer involved with the company,' said Hoode. 'He took thirty pieces of silver from Havelock's Men.'

'That is why you must befriend him, Edmund.'

'Befriend the rogue! Never!'

'Listen to Nick,' ordered Elias. 'I understand his reasoning and it is sound. He wants a spy in Bankside.'

'Not a spy,' corrected Nicholas. 'Lucius will be an unwitting informer. Go to him, Edmund. Apologise for your coldness. Make much of him. Give out that you fear the demise of this company and must perforce look for another to stage your plays. Ask him to tell you all that he can of Havelock's Men. We may well learn much to our advantage.'

'I'll do it, Nick!' said Hoode. 'Though I'd prefer to strike him yet will I fall upon him with fond smiles and soft words. Lucius will be too innocent to know what I am about. He will be our intelligencer.'

'And what of me, Nick?' asked Elias.

'You have a more difficult assignment.'

'I am more than ready.'

'Then follow Master Gill.'

'Follow him?'

'When the play ends,' said Nicholas, 'wait until he leaves then act as his shadow. I fear that he is in league with Banbury's Men and would rather know the truth of it than trust to instinct. You were briefly a member of the company and know its haunts. Trail him. See if Master Gill takes you to one of them.'

Elias grinned. 'I'll stick to him like a limpet.'

'What will you do, Nick?' asked Hoode.

'Seek a meeting with our benefactor.'

'Are we never to be told who he is?'

'Not until I have permission to release the name, Edmund.'

'I will kiss him on both cheeks in gratitude.'

Nicholas smiled. 'I doubt that,' he said, imagining the incongruity of Edmund Hoode trying to kiss the Countess of Dartford. 'But let us meet again this evening when you have spoken with Lucius.'

'And I will join you when I have anything to report,' said Elias. 'Shall we meet here at the Queen's Head?'

'No,' said Nicholas. 'In Eastcheap. At the Brown Bear.'

Chapter Ten

Alexander Marwood truly believed that marriage was an excellent mystery but its excellence proved so elusive that he had ceased to expect it. Every day, however, he was given resounding proof of the mystery of holy matrimony. Sybil's behaviour was eternally puzzling to her husband. When the dreadful news about their daughter's child had first been received, they had acted in unison, fearing shame, expressing outrage and punishing the girl with joint severity. Marwood and his wife had together initiated a search, albeit fruitless, for the father of the child.

Without even consulting him, Sybil had then taken the errant daughter off to Clerkenwell after depriving him of a considerable sum of money but all that the journey had produced was a tearful girl who soon fell sick of a fever. Marwood found himself blamed both for her pregnancy and for her illness and had the galling experience of having to part with more money when the doctor was summoned to tend her. More blame was incurred by the bewildered landlord who was accused by his spouse of cruelly locking up their daughter and treating her like a condemned felon.

When the fever broke, Rose improved markedly but Sybil's behaviour became even more mysterious. Having closeted the girl and badgered her in vain to make a confession, her mother now rediscovered a sweetness and maternal concern which was utterly baffling to her husband. Rose's door was left open, her window unbolted and food sent to her whenever she called for it. Alternately castigated and coaxed, Marwood was further bemused when he retired to bed on the previous night to be given an absent-minded kiss on the cheek from the dry and normally inviolable lips of his wife.

He was even more befuddled when he went upstairs in search of his capricious partner and found Rose creeping uncertainly along the passageway.

'Where are you going, girl?' he said harshly.

'Mother told me to take exercise,' she said.

'Did she?'

'I have to build my strength up again.'

'But you are dressed to go out, Rose.'

'Fresh air is good for me, father. The doctor advised it.'

'He said nothing about fresh air when he pursued me for his fee.' A belated paternal concern brushed him. 'How are you feeling now, Rose?'

'Much recovered.'

'That would be good news were it not for the shame that you bear. Are you not penitent?'

'Yes, Father.'

'And do you not regret the pain you have caused us?'

'It grieves me more than I can say.'

'Then tell us who is the author of our misery.'

'The author?' It was her turn to be puzzled.

'The father of your child!'

His raised voice brought Sybil bounding along the passageway with the ferocity of a lioness defending a cub against attack. She gave Marwood such an earful of rebuke that his head was spinning and all memory of his wife's nocturnal kiss was obliterated. Pondering once more the mystery of the marital state, he beat a hasty retreat.

'You told me to stretch my legs, Mother,' said Rose.

'I did, Rose,' said Sybil watchfully. 'But stay on the premises and do not talk to any of the servants. Confine yourself to a greeting. We have kept them ignorant of your condition and gave out that you were sick.'

Rose nodded obediently but knew that everybody at the Queen's Head would be aware of what was going on. It made her highly self-conscious. While anxious to meet one member of the staff at the inn, she wanted to keep clear of the others lest she be assaulted with embarrassing questions. Sybil sent her on her way and watched with mixed feelings as her daughter slowly descended the backstairs. Then she went off to confront her husband with another slight change of attitude.

Rose soon found him. Leonard was in the cellar, rolling a barrel of ale noisily into position against the dank wall, his bulk magnified by the low ceiling and the narrowness of the storeroom. Rose shivered in the chill atmosphere.

'Good day, Leonard,' she said.

He spun round. 'Mistress Rose!' he exclaimed. 'What are you doing down here?'

'I came to thank you.'

'Are you allowed to leave your bedchamber?' he said, fearing reprisals from her parents. 'Do not take risks on my account.'

'But you took them on mine, Leonard.'

'Did I?'

'You offered me food.'

'I was afraid that you were starving. They told me in the kitchen that you had not eaten for a whole day. I thought you might be denied food.'

'You came to me because you cared,' she said.

Leonard blushed. 'I wanted to help.'

'You did.'

'But you took no bread and cheese from me.'

'I saw you there outside my window. That was enough. I knew that I had one friend at the Queen's Head.'

'You have many, Mistress Rose,' he told her. 'Everyone is talking about you. We think you have been harshly treated. It is not my place to say so,' he added quickly. 'I have no right to speak against your parents. Your father gave me a place here when nobody else would look at me and I am grateful to him for that.' He struggled to find the right words. 'But I was . . . worried about you. That was why I came.'

'It made a big difference.'

'Did it?'

'Yes, Leonard.'

A slow smile spread over his face until it shone in the

gloom of the cellar. Rose's gratitude was a bounty in itself. The risks he had taken on her behalf were more than worth it. Her friendship was one of the things which mitigated the grinding hardship and constant unpleasantness of working for Alexander Marwood.

Rose lowered her head slightly and bit her lip.

'What do they say about me?' she murmured.

'Who?'

'The others.'

'Kind things, Mistress Rose. Kind things.'

'They do not laugh at me, then?'

'No,' he said earnestly. 'They would have to answer to me if they did. They are very sorry to hear . . .' He cleared his throat and groped for the right words again. 'To hear . . . what befell you. The players, too, show sympathy.'

Rose was dismayed. 'Do Westfield's Men know of my shame as well?' she said. 'It will soon be the talk of the parish.'

'No,' he told her. 'And do not think the players make any jests about you. Nicholas Bracewell makes sure that your name is respected. He will have no foul talk about any young woman. Besides, Mistress Rose, the players have troubles of their own which put you quite out of their mind.'

'Troubles?'

'Have you not heard?'

Leonard put his hands on his hips and gave her a halting account of the woes of Westfield's Men. She was saddened to hear that they might be driven out of the Queen's Head by an edict of the Privy Council and horrified to learn of the fire at the site of their new playhouse but it was the death of Sylvester Pryde which upset her the most.

'He was such a courteous gentleman,' she recalled.

'An upright fellow, to be sure.'

'It was always a pleasure to serve him in the taproom. Master Pryde had a smile and a kind word for me every time. And is he really dead?'

'The funeral is tomorrow, as I hear.'

'Would that I could be there to pay my respects!'

'We will miss Sylvester Pryde,' he said mournfully, 'but, then, we will miss the whole company when they leave here for good. Westfield's Men bring so much life and merriment to the Queen's Head.'

'They do, Leonard,' she enthused. 'When I lay sick in bed, the only thing which stayed me was the sound of a play being staged in our yard. That laughter and applause helped me through my ordeal.' Her eyes sparkled. 'I think there is no profession in the world more exciting than that of an actor. The inn will seem dead without the company.'

'I said as much to Martin.'

Her ears pricked up. 'Martin?'

'You remember him. He worked here briefly in the taproom. Martin chanced to call in and asked me how we were all faring at the Queen's Head. He enjoyed his time with us, I think.'

'Did he mention me?' she whispered.

'Oh, yes. And spoke with fondness.'

'What did you tell him?'

'That you were locked unjustly away.'

'And what did Martin say to that?'

'He was sad to hear it, Mistress Rose. And even sadder when he knew the reason.' He gabbled his apology. 'I hope I did not speak out of turn in telling him about your plight. But Martin was concerned for you. He pressed me. He will not breathe a word of this to anyone, I am sure. Martin is discreet.'

'Yes, Leonard. I am sure.' She made an effort to sound casual. 'What news did he have on his own account?'

'Very little.'

'Has his ambition been fulfilled?'

'He mentioned no ambition to me,' said Leonard, scratching his head. 'To tell the truth, I cannot think that any man would have an ambition to work at the Brown Bear.'

'The Brown Bear?'

'It is a scurvy inn in Eastcheap, full of wild company and wickedness. I would have thought that Martin could find better employment than that.'

Rose was hurt. 'Martin works at another inn?'

'Yes,' said Leonard. 'He would have been far happier to stay here. He was a fool to leave the Queen's Head. Do you not think so, Mistress Rose?'

'I do, Leonard,' she murmured 'I do.'

Lawrence Firethorn was glad to loan his horse to Nicholas Bracewell for the second time. The book holder was going to visit their benefactor's house and Firethorn was eager to do anything he could to make the journey there quicker and more comfortable. It gave him an excuse to pry and to probe.

'Do you have far to go, Nick?' he wondered.

'Far enough.'

'Outside the city, then?'

'Perhaps,' said Nicholas with a non-committal smile.

'Should you travel in your condition?'

'I have no choice.'

'You were badly beaten last night,' said Firethorn with regret. 'You must still be in pain. Let me come with you in case you falter on the way. We can borrow a second horse from the stables.'

'I prefer to go alone.'

'But is that wise?'

'Wise and necessary,' said Nicholas firmly. 'I was hurt in the attack but Anne was a kind nurse and I managed to walk all the way here from Bankside this morning. A ride will not tax me in the slightest.'

'Shall I bear you company at least part of the way?'

'No.'

'Will our benefactor agree to see you?'

'I hope so.'

'What manner of man is he?' fished the other.

'I must be on my way.'

'Is there *nothing* you will tell me, Nick?'

'Only that I have to keep my word.'

Firethorn contained his frustration. It irked him that a vital part of the company's financial situation was wreathed in secrecy. He could not understand why he, of all people, was kept in the dark about the source of their loan. At the same time, he did not wish to imperil it at such a delicate period by forcing Nicholas to break a confidence. He had complete faith in his book holder's ability to represent Westfield's Men fairly and firmly.

'We are undeterred,' said Firethorn.

'I know.'

'Impress that upon our benefactor. The fire last night was a minor setback that will only spur us on. Make him appreciate that, Nick. He must not take fright and withdraw his loan or we are laid low.' He looked worried. 'One thing more.'

'What is that?'

'May good fortune attend you!'

Firethorn slapped his horse on the rump and it trotted off across the inn yard. He waited until it was out of sight before he went off ruminatively to the taproom. Nicholas, meanwhile, rode off towards the Strand on his mission. It was not one which gave him any pleasure. Some of the bandaging around his head was concealed by his cap but his face still bore vivid souvenirs of the attack and he collected a number of ghoulish stares from passers-by. He wondered how the Countess of Dartford would react when he presented himself in such a bruised condition.

Yet she had to be kept abreast of developments at The Angel theatre and the visit might have an incidental bonus. Nicholas hoped that he might learn more of her relationship with Sylvester Pryde and some indication of whether it might be responsible for some of the ills which had befallen Westfield's Men. He also intended to find out more about her precise motives for lavishing so much money on a struggling theatre company. One thought buoyed him up. The performance that afternoon had vindicated the company's high reputation. Led by Firethorn and supported by Nicholas, their response to the arson attack had been refreshingly positive. They refused to be cowed into submission.

When he reached the house, Nicholas had some difficulty persuading the servants to let him in. It was only when the steward was sent for that the visitor was allowed over the threshold and that was done with blatant reservations. The Countess was at home but the steward had the severest doubts that she would consent to admit Nicholas. He went off with measured strides. When he returned from her, however, he was slightly abashed and he told the visitor, with dignified reluctance, that the mistress of the house insisted on seeing him at once. Nicholas was conducted to the chamber where he had met the Countess during his earlier visit.

He doffed his cap in deference and she was shocked.

'What has happened to you, Nicholas?' she cried.

'That is what I have come to tell you, my lady.'

'Then do so in comfort,' she said, motioning him to a seat and dismissing the steward in one gesture. 'Should you not be abed with such injuries?'

'They appear worse than they are,' he said bravely.

The Countess of Dartford was impatient to hear all. Nicholas was concise but accurate. He did not play down the extent of the setback but he stressed how well the company had come together in the crisis. Volunteers to work on the site and to guard it through the night were ready and numerous. He was able to assure her that their new playhouse would be fully protected from any further assault. Her main concern was for his safety.

'You put your own life at risk, Nicholas.'

'I survived.'

'Only because of your obvious strength,' she noted. 'A weaker man might well have perished from such an assault. They murdered Sylvester. Why did they spare you?'

'I do not know, my lady,' he said. 'Nor can I be sure that Sylvester's assassin was party to the attack on me. The two crimes may yet be unconnected. On the other hand,' he added, 'one reason for my reprieve did occur to me.'

'Well?'

'If the fire was started by one of our rivals, I may have been recognised and spared on that account. Havelock's Men and Banbury's Men are both confident of their future. If it falls, they expect to pick over the bones of Westfield's Men. I have been approached by both companies in the past,' he confided modestly. 'Haply, I was kept alive by someone who purposed to employ me at a later date.'

'Battering you like that is a strange way to endear you to a new company,' she observed drily. 'And if they coveted Nicholas Bracewell, why did they not also let Sylvester live to join their ranks? He was a sharer and you, with respect, are merely a hired man.'

'That is so.'

'What then, is the explanation?'

'Sylvester could transact the loan which could save us and I could not. He was murdered in order to scare off our benefactor. Fortunately, that did not happen. Also . . .'

'Be candid,' she urged. 'I know what you are about to say. Sylvester would not have been so eagerly sought after by another company.'

'He was a good actor but he had limitations.'

'No,' she said fondly, 'he was an able actor who was made to look inadequate in the presence of Lawrence Firethorn and Barnaby Gill and the others. I am not blind. I have seen Westfield's Men perform a number of times, Nicholas, at the Queen's Head and elsewhere. I know your quality. I did not need to watch you play *The Loyal Servant* in order to judge if you were a sound investment. I was at Court when the same piece was acted there. What drew me to your inn yard that day was the opportunity to watch Sylvester Pryde upon a stage.'

'You saw him at his best,' said Nicholas.

'But his best was several leagues below greatness.'

Nicholas hesitated. 'Yes, my lady,' he said at length.

'The consolation is that Sylvester did not know it. In his mind, he was the next Lawrence Firethorn, another titan of the theatre. Oh, heavens! What a magnificent sight he is at full tilt upon the boards! Firethorn is supreme and a proper man in every respect. I could watch him all day!' Her fulsome praise was commuted to a sigh. 'But dear, dear Sylvester! His ambition so far outran his talent but he never lived to face that ugly truth. It may have been a blessing.'

'I would sooner have him with us, my lady.'

'So would I, Nicholas. I *loved* the man!'

Her sudden passion took them both unawares and there was a long pause. The Countess went to a chair and lowered herself gently into it while she recovered her poise. Nicholas bided his time and adjusted his view of her. Cordelia Bartram was not the impulsive woman he had imagined, obliging an intimate friend with a substantial loan on the basis of a single visit to the Queen's Head. She was a seasoned admirer of Westfield's Men and – if there had been an entanglement with Viscount Havelock – she would be familiar with the work presented at The Rose as well.

'What do you want from me?' she asked calmly.

'Reassurance, my lady.'

'You came to give it and to take it away. Well, have no worries about the loan. It will take more than a few charred timbers in Bankside to frighten my money away.'

'I am deeply grateful to hear that, my lady.'

'There will be ample recompense for me.'

'Will there?' he said with interest.

'I will have the satisfaction of helping the company which took Sylvester to its bosom and I will satisfy a yearning of my own.' She gave an enigmatic smile. 'But that will come in time. What will you do now, Nicholas?'

'Endeavour to track down Sylvester's killer.'

'Who may or may not have been one of your assailants.'

'Yes, my lady.'

'Do you have any clues at all to guide you?'

'I believe so.'

'And do they point in the direction of Bankside?'

'Some of them.'

'Then take care, sir,' she warned. 'You contend with a viper. His bite is poisonous. Those fangs of his will sink into anyone who dares to obstruct him and Westfield's Men are doing just that.'

'With your help, my lady.'

'I do not like snakes. They are treacherous creatures.'

There was a black anger in her face which distorted its beauty for a while and left Nicholas feeling alarmed. The Countess of Dartford was involved in a bitter private feud and she had deliberately dragged Westfield's Men into it. At that precise moment, it was difficult to see how they could be extricated. Nicholas was sorely perplexed. His wounds began to smart afresh. The visit to their benefactor had left him at once reassured and disturbed. While his fellows could rejoice in the good news he took them, they would be blithely unaware of the silent menace which lay behind it. Nicholas was placed in an impossible position. It was mortifying.

'You may leave now,' she said rather brusquely.

'Yes, my lady.' He rose to his feet.

'But keep me well-informed.'

'I will.'

'All three companies appear at Court soon,' she remarked. 'Have Westfield's Men chosen the play they will present?'

'Not yet, I fear.'

'What of the other companies?'

'We do not know their intentions.'

'Might it not help you if you did?'

'Indeed, it might, my lady,' he agreed. 'To that end, I have taken action to ensure that both Havelock's Men and Banbury's Men are kept under surveillance.'

Owen Elias could hold his ale as well as any man in the company. When most of them were inebriated, he was only merry and the Welshman was always still on his feet when his fellows reached the stage of ignominious collapse. For the sake of appearances, however, he pretended to have drunk too much too fast in the taproom that evening. It enabled him to assume a drowsiness he did not feel and to keep a half-open eye on Barnaby Gill. The latter had joined his colleagues after the performance was over but he was patently restless. As soon as he believed that nobody would notice his departure, he stole quietly away and made for the stables.

Alert and still sober, Elias was lurking in the shadows by the gate to watch him leave. He could never trail Gill closely on foot but he saw that he did not need to do so. When the horse trotted in the direction of Bishopsgate, Elias knew that the rider was going to Shoreditch and the conclusion was unavoidable. Nicholas Bracewell's instincts were sound. Gill was on the run. Shocked by the attack on the site of The Angel, he had decided that Westfield's Men were on the road to destruction and wished to practise his art elsewhere.

It was a tiring walk to Shoreditch but Elias drove his legs on, knowing the importance of his assignment. There had been a period in his life when Giles Randolph dangled the prospect of being a sharer in front of him to wrest him away from Westfield's Men. Elias knew how cunning and unscrupulous Randolph could be and he was grateful that Nicholas Bracewell brought him back to the Queen's Head and contrived his translation to the status of sharer. It allowed the Welshman to have some fellow feeling for Gill. Both had responded to strong temptation from Shoreditch. Elias had been rescued but Gill might not be so easy to win back.

He was almost halfway there when he managed to beg a lift from a farmer who was returning home late from the market. It was a bumpy ride on the back of the cart and he had to endure the smell of unsold onions but Elias reached his destination much sooner than he would have done on foot. Gill's horse was tethered outside The Elephant. It was the confirmation he anticipated but it still upset him. Elias had been vaguely hoping that there was a mistake, that Gill was not fleeing to a meeting with another company at all but was simply visiting friends in Shoreditch, perhaps calling on Margery Firethorn at the family house in Old Street.

The sight of Gill's horse destroyed all hope. He would have only one reason to enter an inn which was the established haunt of Banbury's Men. Elias could never bring himself wholly to like the irascible Gill but he had great respect for his talent and a mocking fondness for the man himself. To lose him would be a severe blow to Westfield's Men but to have him stolen by their fiercest rivals would be a catastrophe. He crept towards The Elephant with his heart pounding.

The taproom was full and half-hidden beneath a fug of tobacco smoke. When Elias peered in through the window, he had difficulty making out anyone at first and reasoned that Giles Randolph would choose somewhere more private for such a sensitive transaction. Elias made his way around the outside of the building, peeping through each window while taking care not to be seen. Too many people in the company knew him. He never believed that he would actually manage to eavesdrop on a conversation between Gill and the actor-manager of Banbury's Men but the sight of them together would be positive proof of Gill's treachery.

It came much sooner than he expected. Three men suddenly stepped out of the rear exit of the inn, forcing Elias to dive behind a bush for concealment. He could hear Gill's voice without being able to make out exactly what he was saying. Had the betrayal taken so little time? Gill would hardly have ridden all the way to Shoreditch to turn down a seductive offer. Was he shaking hands on the deal? Elias inched forward to peer around the edge of the bush. Gill was mounting his horse and seemed to be in good humour. Giles Randolph was laughing softly. Raised in farewell, his colleague's voice did reach Elias this time.

'Adieu, sir! I thank you for your forbearance.'

'I am a patient man, Barnaby,' said Randolph, 'but I do need a final decision from you.'

'You shall have it very soon, I swear.'

'Do not disappoint us.'

'I have gone too far in this business to do that.'

'Play with Banbury's Men at Court in *Richard Crookback*.'

'The notion entices me.'

'Farewell! How will we hear from you?'

'I will send word!' said Gill as he rode away.

'Farewell, sir!' called a third voice.

Elias was about to pull back behind the bush again when he noticed the man who was with Randolph. His face was oddly familiar yet his name completely evaded the Welshman. There was something about the close-set eyes and the prominent nose which jogged his memory. Had he really met the man before or was he mistaken? Before he was able to make up his mind, the two friends went happily back into the inn, leaving him to ponder. Who *was* Randolph's companion?

The question teased him all the way back to the city.

The Brown Bear was a large, low, sprawling inn with overhead beams which obliged the patrons to duck and flagstones which had been liberally stained with hot blood and strong ale in equal proportions. It was the favoured resort of sailors, discharged soldiers and masterless men and the pert tavern wenches who swung their hips between the tables were willing to provide much more than drink. Edmund Hoode was deafened by its noise and unsettled by its sense of danger. The taproom at the Queen's Head could be rowdy but the Brown Bear seemed to be trembling continuously on the edge of violence.

He was glad when Nicholas Bracewell finally arrived.

'This place unnerves me, Nick,' he confessed.

'Strange,' said Nicholas with a grin. 'With my broken head and bruised face, I feel quite at home here.'

They bought drinks and found a corner where they could converse without having to shout over the din. Nicholas told him of his visit to their benefactor but said nothing beyond the fact that their loan was still intact. For the first time since he had sworn to maintain secrecy, he felt that it might have advantages. The Countess of Dartford was the sort of titled lady who should never be allowed near the playwright. His capacity for falling in love with unattainable beauties was alarming. Nicholas would at least be spared the discomfort of watching his friend endure yet another ordeal of unrequited passion.

'What of Lucius Kindell?' he asked. 'Did you see him?'

'I did, Nick.'

'And?'

'I gave a performance which Lawrence could not better.'

'Tell me all.'

'Lucius was at his lodging,' said Hoode, 'striving to put a scene together in a play they have commissioned. Think of that, Nick. Havelock's Men believe he has outgrown me. He is to pen a tragedy entirely on his own.'

'Is he capable of such a feat?'

'They think so but Lucius does not.'

'Lack of confidence was always his weakness, Edmund. That is where you helped him most. By instilling some self-belief in him.' Nicholas sipped his ale. 'Does he struggle?'

'Woefully.'

'He misses your guiding hand.'

'Lucius almost had it at his throat,' admitted Hoode, 'but I stayed it. I told him that I was no longer angry with him and that he was right to go to Havelock's Men. He was all tears. The only way I could stop them was to ask about his play and why it was becalmed.'

'Were you able to help him?'

'Listening was the greatest help I gave, Nick.'

'And was he grateful?'

'Thoroughly. He showered me with thanks and sought to justify his move to Bankside. Lucius is young but very observant. He has learnt much about Havelock's Men.'

'Does he know what play they will stage at Court?'

'*A Looking Glass for London*,' said Hoode. 'A new comedy from the pen of Timothy Argus. They let Lucius read an act or two and he was very excited by it.'

'I do not like the sound of that. Argus is gifted. He has written all of their best plays in recent years. If they have a new play to offer at Court, that gives them a hold over us for we have none.' He gave a smile. 'Even Edmund Hoode cannot conjure up five acts of wonder in so short a time. Tell me about *A Looking Glass for London*.'

Hoode repeated what he had heard from Kindell and added all the other information he had gleaned from his quondam apprentice. Even though his friend professed to loathe the young playwright, there was an affection in his tone which belied his hatred. The reunion had not merely shown Lucius Kindell how much he needed Hoode to advise him. It had reminded the latter of the happiness they had experienced when collaborating on two plays.

Someone jostled Hoode's arm and made him spill his drink. When he turned to complain, he found himself staring into the hirsute face of a sailor who was much taller and vastly broader than him. The man glowered at him. Hoode gave him a sheepish grin and leant across to Nicholas.

'Why did you ask me to meet you here, Nick?'

'It was close to Lucius's lodging and saves you the walk back to the Queen's Head.'

'I would rather have walked ten miles than come here. The Brown Bear is nothing but a den of vice. When I first came in, one of the serving wenches groped me familiarly.'

Nicholas laughed. 'She remembered you.'

'I am no pox-hunter! That lady would have fitted me out with a suit of French velvet as soon as I unbuttoned. I have learnt the value of a celibate life, Nick,' he said. 'No pox, no peril and no pain. The Brown Bear offers all three.'

'I came here for a purpose, Edmund,' explained the other. 'Bear with me a moment while I satisfy my curiosity.'

Nicholas hailed the landlord, a big, bearded, slovenly man with a bald head that was running with sweat and a face with more warts than space for them to occupy. He hobbled across and glared at Nicholas.

'What is your pleasure, sir?' he grunted.

'I wish to speak to Martin,' said Nicholas.

'Who?'

'Martin. One of your drawers.'

'We have no Martin here.'

'Are you sure?'

'I know who I pay, sir, believe me,' said the man firmly. 'And I have never parted with a penny to any Martin.'

'Has he left your employment, then?'

'He never came to the Brown Bear in the first place.'

The landlord was so certain and his manner so uncouth that Nicholas allowed him to be called away by another customer. Hoode had overheard the exchange.

'Who is this Martin you seek?' he said.

'He worked at the Queen's Head for a while.'

'I do not recall him.'

'No more do I,' said Nicholas, 'but Leonard spoke so warmly of him that I feel that I should have. Our landlord is the problem. He treats his servants so badly that they rarely stay for long. Martin came and went with the others.'

Hoode was annoyed. 'And *he* is the reason you brought me to this filthy hole? Some skulking menial whose face you cannot even remember?'

'Leonard told me that he sometimes called in at the Queen's Head to pick up news. Why?' asked Nicholas. 'And why choose Leonard as the man to tell it him?'

'I do not follow you.'

'Leonard is the most stout-hearted fellow alive. I love him as a friend and brought him to the inn because I knew he would give sterling service. But his brain is not the quickest thing about him, Edmund. He is easily gulled. I think that this Martin picked him out because Leonard would not suspect that he was being used.' Nicholas looked around. 'When I heard that Martin worked at the Brown Bear, I was surprised. You see it. A place of last resort. Beside this inn, the Queen's Head is a paradise even with Alexander Marwood in charge. No sane man would move from Gracechurch Street to splash about in this vile puddle.'

'We did!' protested Hoode. 'And for what reason?'

'To satisfy a whim of mine.'

'That blow to the head has unfixed your brain.'

'No, Edmund,' said Nicholas. 'I found exactly what I

257

expected to find. Martin does not work here. He is a liar who befriended the one man at the Queen's Head who would believe his lies without question.'

Hoode was still confused. 'So? Martin is dishonest. Was that wondrous discovery enough to make us endure the Brown Bear? London is full of liars.'

'But they do not all work at an inn which houses a troupe of players,' argued Nicholas. 'And they do not slink back to hear the latest news of the company from one who adores them so much that he watches them whenever he can steal a free moment. All I can plead here is instinct, Edmund, but that instinct tells me that we have been spied upon.'

'By Martin?'

'Who else?'

'But neither of us can even remember the fellow.'

'Exactly! When he was at the Queen's Head, he made sure that none of us got to know him properly. He kept in the background and held his peace.'

Hoode was unconvinced. 'This is folly on your part, Nick. I, too, can plead instinct and it urges me to get out of this evil place before I become infected. Let us go.'

'We must wait until Owen arrives.'

'Can we not do so in the street?'

Nicholas smiled. The boisterousness was too intimidating for his friend. Arm around his shoulder, he led Hoode back out into Eastcheap and away from the Brown Bear. A stentorian voice rang down the thoroughfare.

'I am coming!' bellowed Elias. 'Do not leave!'

They paused until he came puffing up to them.

258

'Hell's teeth!' he growled. 'I have been all the way to Shoreditch and back. Though a friendly farmer bounced my bum a part of the way, my feet still took a pounding.'

'To good effect?' asked Nicholas.

'Alas, yes. Barnaby is entwined with Giles Randolph.'

'Never!' denied Hoode.

'I saw it with my own eyes, Edmund. Heard them exchange words of friendship. What more do you need? A sighting of the contract which makes Barnaby Gill a sharer with Banbury's Men,' he said with sarcasm. 'Rest here while I go back to Shoreditch to fetch it for you.'

'What else did you learn, Owen?' said Nicholas.

'That my old legs do not like so much walking. I had forgotten how far it was, Nick. I tell you, I do not relish the idea of a daily walk to Bankside either. The city has its faults but I prefer to lodge here.'

'So do I,' said Hoode.

'To lodge and to work here,' continued Elias. 'I would not dare to say this to Lawrence now that we are so far gone with The Angel theatre, but the truth is that the prospect no longer thrills me as it once did.'

'Why not?' asked Nicholas.

'I like the Queen's Head,' said the other. 'We have played at The Curtain and at The Rose. Both have their virtues but I have to admit that I would choose the Queen's Head over them. Even if it were peopled with a hundred Alexander Marwoods.'

'I think I agree with you, Owen,' decided Hoode. 'My best work has been staged there. It inspires me.'

'It inspires us all,' said Nicholas sadly, 'but the Privy Council is like to turn us out. To stay here in London, we must have a playhouse of our own. The Angel answers that need.'

Owen was cynical. 'Barnaby does not think so. He would sooner throw in his lot with Banbury's Men than stay with us and risk all. They even talked of having him play at Court with them. In *Richard Crookback*.'

'Is that their choice?' Nicholas heaved a sigh. 'Report has it that *Richard Crookback* is their best achievement of this year. A new play from Havelock's Men and a fine one from Banbury's Men. We will have strong competition at Court. Tell us more about your findings, Owen?'

'May I do so with some ale in my hand, Nick? I need to sit down and search for solace in a tankard. Let us step back into the Brown Bear.'

'No!' shouted Hoode. 'It is a stinking pit! The only reason that Nick enticed me in there was to look for someone whom he knew we could not find. An arrant liar called Martin who once worked at the Queen's Head.'

The light of discovery came into Elias's eyes.

'What was that name again?' he asked. 'Martin?'

Chapter Eleven

The funeral was held at the Parish Church of St Leonard's, a place where more than one member of Westfield's Men had already been laid to rest. As a mark of respect to Sylvester Pryde, the day's performance was cancelled and the whole company filed into the nave of the church for the service. It was short but moving. An ancient priest who could never be expected wholeheartedly to approve of the wayward life of an actor nevertheless praised a man he had barely known in words that brought great comfort and many nods of agreement. Nicholas Bracewell was pleased that he had spoken to the priest about the deceased beforehand and he was interested to hear some of his own phrases coming back to him from the pulpit in such a sonorous tone.

Nicholas was too absorbed in his own grief to notice everyone around him and even when he acted as one of the pall bearers and helped to bear the coffin back down the aisle, he did not see the hooded figure who sat with a companion at the rear of the nave. It was only when they moved out to the cemetery and lowered the body of Sylvester Pryde into his grave that Nicholas was able to take stock of those around him. His fellows were overcome with emotion. Several were weeping, some were praying, others remained in a contemplative silence. George Dart was so distraught that he needed the physical support of Thomas Skillen.

Anne Hendrik was there and Marjory Firethorn accompanied her husband. What touched Nicholas was the fact that several people from the Queen's Head also came to pay their respects. Leonard was among them, his big face awash with tears, his mind trying in vain to grasp the meaning of such a violent and untimely death. Even Alexander Marwood turned up, prompted by the thought that the burial of one actor symbolised the imminent death of the entire company. It was a form of leave-taking and he was surprised how painful he found it. Having wished to expel the company so often in the past, he now felt strangely bereft.

Nicholas was gratified to see such a large congregation coming to the funeral of a man who had no family members to mourn him. It was a tribute to Pryde's capacity for making friends. Nicholas finally saw her when the burial service was over and people were beginning to disperse. Wearing a dark cloak with a hood pulled up to cover her face, she stood on the fringe with a young gallant in attendance on her. Before she left, she walked to the grave and tossed a valedictory flower into it. Nicholas guessed at once who she must be and he caught a whiff of her fragrance as she swept past on her way out. Alone of Westfield's Men, he knew that their benefactor had come to bid a sad farewell to a lover.

Lawrence Firethorn came across to him with his wife.

'Will you dine with us, Nick?' he invited.

'He must,' insisted Marjory. 'We can raise a glass to the memory of dear Sylvester. I invited Anne to join us but she has to get back to Bankside.'

'That is so, alas,' said Nicholas. 'Anne has a business to run but she wanted to pay her last respects to Sylvester. She was very fond of him.'

'Every woman was fond of him, Nick,' said Marjory with a wan smile. 'And the pity of it is that many of those whose favours he enjoyed will not even know that he is dead. When they find out the awful truth, there will be a lot of damp pillows in London. I wept a torrent myself.'

'Do not remind me!' sighed Firethorn. 'But will you join us, Nick? There is much to discuss. We have yet to choose the play we offer at Court and I would value your opinion in private before I argue with the others. Come to Shoreditch.'

'He will not dare to refuse,' said Marjory with a mock warning in her voice. 'Will you, Nick?'

'No,' he said with a smile. 'It is a kind invitation and I accept it with pleasure.'

She kissed him on the cheek and led the way out of the cemetery. Marjory was mother to the whole company and it grieved her to lose one of her children, however recent an addition to the shifting family that was Westfield's Men. They were the last to leave and threw a final, sad glance over their shoulders. Firethorn was indignant.

'I would have thought he might be here,' he complained.

'Who?' said Nicholas.

'Our benefactor. Sylvester died on the site of The Angel theatre. I am grateful that his friend advanced us the loan to build it but I think it a poor reflection on the name of friendship that he could not even turn up to see Sylvester laid to rest. Is our benefactor so heartless?'

'No,' said Nicholas, 'that is not the case at all.'

Doubt was a restless bedfellow. It kept Rose Marwood awake for most of the night as she thought of vows which were made and ambitions which were discussed with her beloved. Morning found her still twisting and turning on her bed. As the hours went painfully by, she could find scant relief for her anxieties. Had he forsaken her? When he was unaware of her condition, she could not blame him for keeping his distance as they agreed. But being apart was only a prelude to the closeness of marriage. Their union was blessed with a child and lacked only the sanction of the church. She would not be the first bride who went to the altar with child. He promised to come back and he promised to make her his. Where *was* he?

He knew. Rose could no longer make any excuses for him. He knew yet he neither came nor sent a message. She was desolate until she remembered once again the solitary flower. That was his message. That was a seal of his love. When he heard that he had fathered a child, he did not run in panic or turn away in disgust. He reached out to her. He found a way to leave the rose on her window sill at a time when she was so weak that she could hardly walk across the bedchamber to retrieve it. He knew, he loved, he sent a token. He was hers. Rose chided herself for losing faith in him and reached under the pillow once more to take out the rose and fondle it gently.

She was still entranced by it when there was a tap on the door. Rose sat up and hastily hid the flower away again. She tried to brush away the tears. There was a second tap on the door before it opened slightly.

'Are you there, Rose?' said a woman's voice.

'Yes, Nan.'

'May I come in?'

She did so without invitation and closed the door behind her. Nan was a scrawny old woman who worked in the kitchen at the inn and whose arched eyebrows gave her gaunt face a permanent look of surprise. Carrying a bowl of cherries, she bared her few remaining teeth and nodded excitedly.

'I brought these for you, Rose,' she said.

'Thank you, Nan.'

'I picked them myself. I was afraid to bring them before but your mother has gone to market and your father went to the funeral.' She gave an almost girlish giggle. 'So I came.'

'That was very kind of you.'

'Take them,' said the visitor, thrusting the bowl at Rose. 'You must keep your strength up. You're eating for two now.'

Rose blushed but consented to take the cherries from her. Peering more closely, Nan clicked her tongue in sympathy.

'Have you been crying?'

'No, no,' lied Rose.

'I know you must be worried. I was myself. I had my

first child when I was about your age. A little girl. Nobody told me what to expect. It was a shock.' A nostalgic smile touched the haggard features. 'But my daughter soon made me forget the pain. She was my little jewel, Rose. The most precious thing in my life. Until she died.'

'How old was she?'

'Barely two. None of my children lived beyond five. But they were all a great joy to me while they were alive.'

Rose felt more unsettled than ever. Nan was a friend and she had gone to some trouble to get the cherries for her but the last thing that Rose wanted to hear about were the pangs of childbirth and the woes of motherhood.

'You had better go, Nan. Mother may come back.'

'Yes, I don't want her to catch me here. But Leonard told me that you were allowed out now.'

'From time to time.'

'He was so pleased when you thanked him.'

'I had to, Nan. Leonard helped me.'

'Well, I hope that bowl of cherries is a help as well. You deserve them.' She giggled again and hunched her shoulders to pass on her gossip. 'Have you heard about Leonard?'

'Heard what?'

'We think that he is in love.'

Rose was astonished. 'Leonard?'

'It is absurd, I know. A man that size. A man as witless as poor Leonard. But I saw it in his face when he asked me.'

'Saw what?'

'That look,' said Nan.

'What was it that he asked you?'

'To pick one for him from the garden.'

'Pick one?'

'A flower,' said Nan, letting her eyebrows soar even higher. 'Those hands of his are far too big to snap a stem without damaging the flower itself and he was afraid he would be seen in the garden and mocked. But that's what he asked me to do for him.'

'To pick him a flower?'

'A red rose.'

'A rose,' gulped the other.

'Yes! Would you believe it? Leonard!'

Still giggling, she scurried out of the room and left Rose to absorb the shock. She was in great distress. Her cheeks were on fire and her breath was coming in short gasps. She felt as if she were about to choke with despair. The flower beneath her pillow was not a token from her beloved at all. He had failed her. She had drawn false succour from the rose. Leaping up, she backed frantically against the wall and stared in horror at her bed as if it had been defiled.

Marjory Firethorn knew when to leave them alone. She had always been exceptionally fond of Nicholas Bracewell, admiring his personal qualities as much as his invaluable service to her husband's company. It was a delight to her whenever he visited her home because he was invariably courteous to her and wholly free from the melancholy which plagued Hoode and the tantrums which Barnaby Gill often displayed. She cooked them a delicious meal and all three of them washed it down with a cup of wine. Having cooed over Nicholas's injuries once more, she then called the servant to clear the table and withdrew with her into the kitchen. Theatre was men's work.

Lawrence Firethorn had his first question ready.

'What shall we play at Court, Nick?'

'First, know what our rivals are offering,' said Nicholas. 'For that may determine our own choice. Banbury's Men will play *Richard Crookback*.'

Firethorn coloured. 'What! Will Giles Randolph try to ape me in the role of the hunchback? Such arrogance! I have made the part my own in our play about the same king. Those who saw Lawrence Firethorn as Richard III will laugh in derision at this pretender.'

'Nevertheless, that is their choice.'

'And Havelock's Men?'

'*A Looking Glass for London*.'

'I do not know the play.'

'How could you?' said Nicholas. 'It has not yet been performed. They are saving its novelty for the Court. It is written by Timothy Argus, always their most reliable author.'

'Alas, yes,' said Firethorn, wincing slightly. 'A new play gives them freshness that we others lack. But no matter,' he continued, flicking their rivals aside. 'How can those pigmies hope to tower over a giant like me? Whatever they play, they will barely reach my kneecaps.'

Nicholas was more cautious. 'We must give them some respect,' he advised. 'They may have nobody to compare with you but their companies are replete with talent. Expect them to give a good account of themselves or we are lost.'

'I will sweep them from the boards like dust!'

'The play we choose must suit our whole company.'

'Then it must be *Hector of Troy*!'

'Too long and wordy for an occasion like this.'

'*Vincentio's Revenge?* I shine equally in that.'

'It grows stale with overuse, I think.'

'Then it has to be *The Knights of Malta*. I will make the palace walls quake when I thunder as Jean de Valette.'

'It would not be my first suggestion,' said Nicholas tactfully. 'You soar to the heights in all three but none allows the whole company to show its true mettle. Banbury's Men present a history while Havelock's Men lean on comedy as their crutch. We should choose a tragedy to show our serious intent. The pity of it is that the best play for our purposes is no longer available to us.'

'Why not?'

'Because it is called *The Insatiate Duke*.'

'I spurn it, Nick!' yelled Firethorn with a gesture of disgust. 'We will not play it again until we have taken a knife to it and cut away everything that appertains to Lucius Kindell.'

'Then you cut away the very soul of it.'

'So be it. That vile traitor will not live to see me declaiming his verse again. Forget his work. It is past.'

Nicholas was not so ready to condemn Kindell, nor consign him to the company's history, but he did not defend him. There was no point in infuriating his host when he was manoeuvring him carefully towards a critical decision. After waving a few other titles in front of him, Nicholas came to the play which was his selection but he let Firethorn enthuse about it until the latter believed that he had chosen it himself.

'*The Italian Tragedy!* I have hit the mark, Nick!'

'I think you have.'

'What better piece to set before a Court than a tragedy of Court intrigue? By Jove, we'll do it! The play has been off the stage too long. We'll put it back where it belongs.'

'With help from Edmund.'

'But it is not his play.'

'He is contracted to repair as well as to create,' said Nicholas. 'Let him mend a few holes in its apparel and fashion a prologue by way of a new ruff. Edmund's wit is quicksilver. He will use the prologue to score off our rivals.'

'Done, sir! *The Italian Tragedy* it shall be!'

'A happy inspiration of yours.'

'When Marjory serves beef, my brain always whirrs.'

There were several other things to discuss, including the financial state of the company, but the main problem had been solved. When Nicholas had guided his host into some more important decisions, he took his leave.

'Will you walk back to the Queen's Head?'

'No,' said Nicholas. 'Having come to Shoreditch, I'll make a virtue of necessity and visit The Curtain.'

Firethorn goggled. 'Watch our rivals?' he howled.

'It is needful. I want to see the present strength of their company. The more we know about our rivals, the easier it will be to match them.'

'Match them and mar them!'

'I go to observe and not to enjoy.'

Firethorn's anger vanished and he embraced his friend warmly. Marjory came bustling out of the kitchen to collect compliments on her cooking and a farewell kiss. The couple waved him off down Old Street. Shoreditch's two theatres brought playgoers streaming out of the city and crowds were already gathering for the afternoon's entertainment. Nicholas made for The Curtain and paid to sit in the gallery. Instead of finding a place on a bench, however, he lurked near the door, confident that he would not be the only member of Westfield's Men who would appear. The gallery was filling up before his expected guest arrived. Concealing himself behind a post, Nicholas let the man choose his place before he moved across to sit beside him.

'Well-met, Master Gill!' he said.

'Nicholas!' Barnaby Gill paled. 'What on earth are you doing here at The Curtain?'

'I came to see a play.'

'Why, so did I.'

'No,' said Nicholas, whispering in his ear. 'You came to see a company you plan to join. Do not deny it, Master Gill,' he warned as his companion flared up. 'You were seen last night in the company of Giles Randolph. Seen and heard. If Master Firethorn knew of that meeting, he would not have been so civil to you at the funeral.'

Gill squirmed. He knew exactly how Firethorn would have reacted which was why his dealings with Banbury's Men had been conducted in secret. The time to announce that he was leaving the Queen's Head was when he had already quit the premises and not when he was still within

271

reach of an actor-manager with a vengeful temperament and the strength of a bull. Gill's exit was suddenly blocked by Nicholas Bracewell.

'Do not breathe a word of this to Lawrence,' he said. 'I have not yet committed myself to Banbury's Men. I merely heard their overtures as any sensible man was bound to do.'

'Is it sensible to betray your colleagues?'

'They are already betrayed by the Privy Council.'

'Their decree has yet to be enacted.'

'Westfield's Men will wither away,' prophesied Gill. 'This Angel Theatre is a cruel illusion. It will not save you. We will all have to find a new company. I merely lead where others will surely follow.'

'I will tell that to Master Firethorn.'

'No! I beg you!'

'His good wife, Marjory, will also have an opinion to give to you. She will censure you as much as he.'

'Keep the pair of them off me, Nicholas.'

'Then do not give me cause.'

'What else am I to do?' wailed Gill. 'Would you have me stay at the Queen's Head to watch the company sink into oblivion? Audiences love me. It is my duty to stay before them. And I can only do that by moving to The Curtain.'

'No,' asserted Nicholas. 'That is not the only remedy. There is another, if you are bold enough to take it. And it gives you a chance to make amends for this contemplated flight.'

'Another remedy?'

'It may answer all.'

'Pray, what is it, Nicholas?'

The flag was being hauled up its pole and the musicians were poised to begin. Nicholas chose deliberately to make his companion wait.

'The play commences. I'll tell you later.'

Lord Westfield was scurrying along a corridor at the Palace of Whitehall when someone glided out from an alcove to intercept him. Cordelia Bartram, Countess of Dartford, had shed her cloak and her expression of mourning, containing her grief inwardly while showing her old outward gaiety. Lord Westfield stopped at once to give her a vestigial bow of courtesy.

'Good morrow, Cordelia,' he said.

'My lord.'

'How does the day find you?'

'Tolerably well.'

'I hope to see your dear husband back at Court before too long. We have missed his wisdom and experience.'

'You will have to miss them even longer, I fear,' she said, 'and so will I. Charles weakens by the day. His physician begins to have serious doubts of his recovery. If there is no sign of improvement soon, I may have to return to the country to minister to him.'

'I pray that that will not be necessary,' he said with concern. 'The earl is a soldier and will fight this sickness with a soldier's courage. Besides, we should hate to lose you as well, Cordelia. I had counted on your being here when the three plays are presented at Court.'

'Nothing short of my husband's death would induce me to miss those, my lord. That is the time when I can be most useful to Westfield's Men. Mingling with the others to trumpet their virtues, making sure my opinions reach the Privy Council.'

'I will do the same.'

'Has your company chosen the play it will stage?'

'If they have,' he said, 'I do not know what it is. But I have tidings from the Master of the Revels.'

'What are they?'

'Westfield's Men will be last in order.'

'That gives them a clear advantage,' she said, thinking it through. 'Coming after the others, they will be fresh in the minds of the Privy Council when they withdraw to consider which companies will survive. This is a tasty morsel of news, my lord. It must have pleased you.'

'No, Cordelia,' he admitted, 'it causes me concern.'

'How so?'

'I believe that the decision has already been made. Look at the order in which the plays will be staged. Havelock's Men are first, then Banbury's Men, with my company last.' He sucked in air through his teeth and grimaced. 'That is clearly how we are viewed. Third and lowest in their estimation.'

'That is not so,' she argued. 'If a final decision has already been made, why invite the companies to Court in the first place? What happens here must affect the Privy Council's thinking. Do not be so downcast, my lord.'

'It preys upon my mind.'

'Westfield's Men have no peer. I have seen all three companies at work and admire them all, but your troupe will always seize the laurels. The others have brilliance,' she conceded, 'but you have Lawrence Firethorn and he exceeds all superlatives. How can you lose faith with such a man to lead your company?'

'He is my chiefest weapon, it is true.'

'A cannon matched against pistols.'

'Upon the stage, perhaps, Cordelia,' he said gloomily. 'But this war has not only been fought there. We have been sorely oppressed. One of my players was murdered.'

'I know it well,' she said, wincing at the reminder.

'Our book holder, Nicholas Bracewell, was attacked. And then the timbers for our new playhouse, The Angel, were set alight.' He shook his head worriedly. 'Our rivals have some terrible weapons of their own.'

'Do you have evidence that they were involved?'

'No evidence, Cordelia, but a deep certainty.'

'Well,' she said evenly, 'if that certainty can become firm proof, you are saved. The Privy Council will surely debar a company which uses such methods against a rival.'

'It is not the first time we have been abused.'

'Indeed?'

'Our rivals bite constantly at our heels,' he confided. 'I love my troupe but Westfield's Men have aggravated me beyond measure. Each day seems to bring a new source of anxiety. I will do all that I may to beat off our rivals and ensure our survival but I tell you this, Cordelia.' He glanced around to make sure that nobody overheard him. 'There are moments when the affairs of Westfield's Men trouble me so much that I would almost wish to be rid of the burden.'

The Countess of Dartford sounded calm and detached but her mind was already grappling with a bold new possibility.

'Would you yield the company to another patron?'

They were good. Nicholas Bracewell had always been willing to admit that. *The Fatal Dowry* was not the best play in their repertoire but Banbury's Men turned it into a stirring piece of theatre. Giles Randolph was in commanding form, marshalling his company around him with skill but rising above them without discernible effort. Lawrence Firethorn might scorn his rival but Nicholas took a more dispassionate view. Randolph was an actor to be admired and feared.

Barnaby Gill took less interest in him. What he saw was an actor of consummate skill who lacked the sheer animal power and charisma of Firethorn. Gill's attention was fixed on the comic characters in the play and they were disappointing. While Nicholas was murmuring with pleasure at taut dramatic moments, Gill was clicking his tongue irritably at the shortcomings of the clowns. He could see why Randolph was so keen to lure him to the company. Gill's comic expertise would enrich every play and make him the perfect foil for the actor-manager. As he watched, however, Gill was less convinced of the wisdom of a move to Shoreditch. The company was sound but it lacked the all-round excellence of Westfield's Men.

The play was well-advanced when Nicholas saw him. Taking the role of a spy, he wore a wide-brimmed hat which concealed much of his face to those in the gallery and there was nothing distinctive in his voice to disclose his identity at first. When the hat was removed, however, and when Nicholas was able to take a proper look at the close-set eyes and protuberant nose, he was in no doubt. The actor who now strutted so boldly at The Curtain had once been employed in a more menial capacity at the Queen's Head. Nicholas turned to Gill.

'Do you know the name of that fellow?'

'Which one?'

'Bellisandro, the spy.'

'Yes,' said Gill. 'That is Henry Quine.'

Leonard gazed around the inn yard at the Queen's Head with misgivings. Horses were coming and going, ostlers were flitting to and fro and a cart was rumbling in through the gate to deliver casks of wine. Yet the place looked strangely bare. Without the stage and the players who went through their intricate paces upon it every day, the yard seemed deserted. Leonard felt an emptiness in himself. Westfield's Men not only fascinated him with their work, they became good friends of his. When they were driven away, Alexander Marwood would be losing a source of income but Leonard would be deprived of the only family he knew. It was heart-rending.

As he helped to unload the wine from the cart, he tried to put his own anxieties aside. Rose Marwood was in a far worse predicament than he. Although her parents now allowed her a degree of freedom, they were still roaming the inn in search of the anonymous father and fulminating against him. They were poor support for a girl as frightened as Rose must be. There was little that Leonard could do beyond showing sympathy for the girl but she appreciated his gesture. He wondered if there was some more practical way in which he could help.

When his work was done, he made his way to the lane at the side of the inn and reached a spot below the window of her bedchamber. It was still open and he sensed that she was inside. The last time he visited the spot, he brought a ladder with him and clambered up it to leave a token on her sill. Only a stone could reach the window now and attract her attention. He bent down to gather a few missiles from the ground then froze in horror. Lying forlornly in the mud, its petals crushed and its stem broken, was the rose he had gone to such trouble to procure for her. His gesture of friendship had been summarily rejected.

Leonard walked sadly away to return to his chores.

Nicholas Bracewell was glad that he visited The Curtain that afternoon. His bandaged head and facial wounds earned him many inquisitive looks but he shrugged those off. *The Fatal Dowry* was a revelation. The performance also enabled him to accost Barnaby Gill and remind him of the virtue of loyalty. He was particularly interested to learn that it was Henry Quine who first approached Gill on behalf of Banbury's Men and who was a party to the negotiations with him. Nicholas realised why Gill did not recognise the actor from his role as Martin at the Queen's Head. Quine lacked the boyish charm which might have aroused curiosity in Gill who, in any case, frequented the taproom far less than any of his fellows and who treated the drawers and servingmen with lofty condescension.

Banbury's Men picked the right target. Any other member of the company might have remembered Martin. Owen Elias had done so when the name was spoken. Gill was safe to court and the most liable to respond. Nicholas was certain that in his time at the Queen's Head, Martin had watched them closely and searched for signs of weakness. Barnaby Gill's fluctuating loyalty was that weakness. Giles Randolph had cast his man well. Whether as Martin or as Bellisandro in the play, Henry Quine had been a most effective spy.

After the performance, Nicholas parted with Gill and made his way back to the city. Still suffering the aches and pains of his beating, he found the walk uncomfortable and called to mind what Elias had said about his preference for the Queen's Head. Most of the players, he suspected, would agree with the Welshman. The Angel theatre might help to secure their future but it would subject most of the players to a long daily walk. Nicholas made that journey every day and knew how tedious it could sometimes be.

He came through Bishopsgate and made his way along Gracechurch Street. Nicholas was in sight of the Queen's Head when a horseman came trotting towards him. It was the young gallant who had accompanied the Countess to the funeral.

'I have a message for you,' said the stranger.

'From whom, sir?'

'A noble lady whom we both know. She is most anxious to speak with Nicholas Bracewell. I have been waiting at the inn for you above an hour.'

'Must I visit her in the Strand?'

'No,' said the other. 'She stays nearby at the house of a friend. I will conduct you there.'

He nudged the horse and it loped off through the crowd with Nicholas behind it. The young man's manner was curt and patronising and Nicholas resented having to follow the rolling rump of his horse but an urgent summons from the Countess of Dartford could not be ignored and he was at least spared the ride to her property in the Strand. They reached the house in a matter of minutes. It was a sizeable dwelling set on a corner of two quiet streets but it had nothing of the grandeur which Cordelia Bartram favoured.

The young man gave his horse to a waiting servant then took Nicholas into the house and into the parlour. The Countess was waiting, seated in a window to keep watch for them. She did not rise when Nicholas doffed his cap and greeted her. The gallant lingered until she dismissed him with a light laugh. Nicholas noted the strained look which passed between them.

'Your friend was reluctant to leave,' he commented.

'It is his house. He feels dispossessed.'

'I see.'

'The property is convenient,' she said smoothly. 'I make use of it on occasion.'

'Your friend came to Sylvester's funeral with you.'

'I needed an arm to rest upon.'

'It was good of you to attend, my lady.'

'Sylvester was a special friend.'

But he was not, Nicholas surmised, her only lover.

The young gallant was peeved to be ejected from the room in which he felt entitled to stay for reasons beyond his ownership of the house. With no sense of shame, the Countess went to the funeral of one lover on the arm of another. Mourning one man clearly did not prevent her from offering her favours to a second.

'You were difficult to find, Nicholas,' she said.

'I have been to Shoreditch.'

'I am glad that you are here at last. Lord Westfield was at Court today. We talked at length about the company. What emerged from that conversation made me seek out you.'

'Is there any news from the Master of the Revels?'

'Just this. The order of performance at Court has been set. Westfield's Men will be the last in line.'

'That helps us,' said Nicholas keenly.

'I thought the same but your patron disagreed. He felt that it reflected the Privy Council's judgement on the troupe. Third, last and therefore destined for extinction.'

'Lord Westfield inclines to gloom at times.'

'I am glad to hear you sound a more cheering note.'

'Master Firethorn will be delighted by this.'

'Good,' she said with a smile. 'I will come to Lawrence Firethorn in a moment. My question is this. And bear in mind how much money I have loaned you because I believe that it entitles me to an answer. Has Lord Westfield ever talked before about ceding his interest in the company?'

'He has *talked* about it, my lady, but we are used to such moans. They amount to nothing in the end.'

'Supposing that they did?' she asked. 'Supposing that

281

Westfield's Men were forced to part with Lord Westfield?'

'Forced?'

'Circumstances change.'

'Our patron would never leave us.'

'He might, Nicholas. Inducements could be made. Lord Westfield is laden with debt and further burdened with the cares of his theatre company. Such things take their toll.'

'The burdens will ease when our future is certain.'

'Your patron did not think so. He was despondent.'

'Well, we are not,' said Nicholas firmly. 'Master Firethorn ensures that. Under his leadership, we are brimming with confidence and what I saw of Banbury's Men at The Curtain this afternoon has only strengthened that confidence.'

'I share it, Nicholas, believe me.'

He was cautious. 'Do I hear you aright?'

'I think you catch my meaning.'

'*You* would wish to become our patron?'

'Is that so strange a wish?' she said airily. 'Dartford's Men rolls off the tongue as sweetly as Westfield's and I would give you more support than ever the noble lord has managed. He will take much persuasion yet,' she admitted, 'but I saw him waver when I asked if he would yield up his troupe.'

Nicholas was too shocked to say anything. The thought of losing their patron was unnerving and he could find no enthusiasm for the notional replacement. What little he knew of the Countess led him to suspect that she would want to control and interfere in the company far more than Lord Westfield had done. His silence plainly irritated her.

'What is your problem, Nicholas?' she challenged. 'Can you not stomach the idea of a woman as patron? It is my husband's name that would be used for Dartford's Men but a woman's hand which would guide your fortunes. Your precious patron is not as enamoured with his troupe as you imagine. If his debts were settled as part of the bargain, I'll wager that he would snatch gratefully at the hand of someone who would rid him of his company.'

'That may be so, my lady,' said Nicholas. 'But it would be a very sad day for us if we lost the noble lord who brought us into being in the first place.'

'Would you oppose me, then?'

'It is not my place to support or oppose.'

'It is,' she insisted. 'I know what weight you carry inside the company. Sylvester instructed me well. Win you over and I have a powerful advocate. Win Lawrence Firethorn over and the game is settled.'

Nicholas was hurt. 'I am sorry that you see this as a game, my lady. We do not. It is our livelihood.'

'I appreciate that,' she returned coolly, 'but you must appreciate my position. I have advanced several hundred pounds of my own money to safeguard your livelihoods. Westfield's Men were quick enough to take it.'

'And gratefully, my lady.'

'I expect more than gratitude in return, Nicholas. I had thought that Sylvester's friendship would be reward enough but his death has changed that.' A mischievous gleam came into her eye. 'Arrange a meeting for me with Lawrence Firethorn.'

'You wish to reveal your identity to him?'

'No,' she stressed. 'He must not know my name or my connection with the company. Tell him that I am an ardent admirer. Give him a flattering description of me.'

'There is no such thing, my lady,' said Nicholas gallantly.

'Then say as much to him,' she said, acknowledging his compliment with a smile. 'I know his reputation. He will come running. When Lawrence Firethorn and I are alone together, I will be able to appraise him properly.'

Nicholas was stunned. Her request put him in an even more ambiguous position. It was an effort to conceal from his fellows the name of their benefactor but a more onerous charge was laid upon him now. He had to contrive a meeting between her and Firethorn by dint of lying to the actor. The Countess of Dartford would exploit the situation to her own advantage and Firethorn would hardly resist. Nicholas ran through them in his mind. Earl of Dartford, Viscount Havelock, Sylvester Pryde, the young man who owned the house and no doubt others besides. Now she had decided to add Lawrence Firethorn to her list of conquests, engaging Nicholas to act as her pandar.

Westfield's Men had looked upon their benefactor as a visitor from heaven. Nicholas alone knew the truth. The loan which helped them might also enslave them to the Countess of Dartford. They would be in the grasp of a wanton angel.

Chapter Twelve

As the hour of decision drew nearer, Westfield's Men grew increasingly nervous. It worried them that their whole future might turn on a single performance at Court and what should have been welcomed as a signal honour came to seem more like a trial. *The Italian Tragedy* was a popular choice of play but they secretly feared that Havelock's Men would have a clear advantage with a new work. If only one company were licensed south of the river, The Rose was the real threat to The Angel and the fact that Viscount Havelock's uncle sat on the Privy Council sent tremors running through Westfield's Men. Their patron was working strenuously to expand his faction at Court but he was up against some skilful politicians.

Notwithstanding their fears, Westfield's Men were resolved to give a good account of themselves. While keeping up their regular performances in the inn yard, they also found time to rehearse and refine *The Italian Tragedy*. Edmund Hoode was instructed to write a new prologue and to insert new speeches in certain scenes in order to freshen the play. Nor was The Angel neglected. A team of volunteers from the Queen's Head went there every day and Thomas Bradd employed them well. With the site cleared once more, timbers were delivered by barge and hauled up the muddy bank to the foundations. Bricks were laid, posts were sunk and the walls slowly began to rise.

Their work did not end at sunset. Nicholas Bracewell organised a team of men to guard the site until midnight when they were relieved by night watchmen from the company. He was eager to take his turn on patrol and spent a first night, armed and ready, sitting in the drizzle on the edge of the Thames. No attack was made on the site and no incidents of any kind were reported but it was a necessary safeguard, even if it did introduce more yawns into their afternoon performances than were set down in the play by the author.

Nicholas was proud of the way that the company was reacting to the challenge which confronted them but he was tormented by guilt at having to hold back information from them which would rapidly change their attitude. If they knew that their benefactor was really an ambitious countess who wished to take over the company, they might not work with such conviction, and if they realised that she had designs on their actor-manager into the bargain, they would have quailed. A patron was there to lend the protection and kudos of a name and not to exert control over their activities. The worst of it was that the company still thought of their benefactor as an example of divine intervention.

George Dart shared in the common illusion.

'Will he be able to come to The Angel?' he asked.

'Who?' said Nicholas.

'Our saviour.'

'I expect so, George.'

'He must come. He is our guardian angel and we named the playhouse after him. On our first day there, he must come to share in the excitement.'

'I agree,' said Nicholas evasively.

'It was one of the many good things Sylvester brought to this company. He had such loyal friends. Someone must have loved him dearly to advance so much money to us solely on his word.'

'Yes, George.'

'And will it be enough?' asked the assistant stagekeeper.

'Enough to help us survive? I do not know.'

'But they must take us more seriously if we have our own playhouse. That is the biggest single bar against us.' He saw Thomas Skillen coming into the inn yard. 'I must go before I get my ears boxed again. But please thank him on my behalf.'

'I will.'

'Tell our benefactor that we worship him.'

Nicholas gave a smile but his stomach was churning. He hated having to lie to his fellows. The simple faith of George Dart would be shattered when he learnt the truth

287

about the source of the loan and his trust in Nicholas would also be broken. It was morning at the Queen's Head and Dart went off to get his first orders of the day from the old stagekeeper. Actors were starting to arrive to rehearse some scenes for the afternoon's offering. Alexander Marwood drifted across the yard with his customary scowl. Leonard was filling wooden buckets from the well. A dark sky threatened rain.

Yet a sudden upsurge of affection seized Nicholas. With all its imperfections, he loved the Queen's Head. A playhouse of their own would offer untold benefits but only if they were free to enjoy those benefits. An inn yard theatre with a glowering landlord was preferable to a new playhouse under the domination of the Countess of Dartford. Nicholas could not bear to view the uncertain future. He threw himself into his work by way of distraction. Minutes later, he was hauled away from it as a stallion came prancing into the yard.

One glance at Lawrence Firethorn showed that he had heard.

'Nick!' he bellowed. 'Come here!'

'What is amiss?'

'This!' said Firethorn, pulling a letter from inside his doublet and handing it over. 'An act of treachery worthy of a Spaniard. Nay, a scheming Italian. We are lost, Nick.'

'I do not think so,' said the other calmly.

'Read the missive.'

'I do not need to. It is from Master Gill, I believe.'

'Yes!'

'Telling you that he wishes to leave the company.'

'Worse than that!' growled Firethorn. 'Leave us and go to them. To that pack of wolves in Shoreditch. Wolves? Foxes, I should say, for they have tricked him with their cunning. I cannot believe that Barnaby would do this to us. But two days before we play at Court!'

'Banbury's Men have worked on him for some time.'

'You *knew*?'

'Yes,' said Nicholas. 'I had him followed to Shoreditch. Owen saw him talking closely with Giles Randolph.'

'Why was I not told?'

'I favoured another strategy.'

'The only strategy Barnaby deserves is a foot of naked steel between the ribs. Sweet Jesus! I'll cut him into shreds and hang them up to dry! I'll boil him in oil! I'll turn him on a spit over a slow fire.' He dropped down from the saddle. 'This will be the death of us, Nick.'

'I do not think so.'

'How can you be so cool at such dreaded tidings?'

'Because I helped him to frame the letter.'

Firethorn quivered. '*You* were his confederate? You stood by and let him sell his miserable skin to Banbury's Men?'

'No,' said Nicholas, 'and if you hear me out, you will find that he is not the villain you take him for. And neither,' he added quickly, smothering Firethorn's retort with a raised palm, 'am I. The reason I helped with the letter was that he wished to show it to Giles Randolph before it was sent as proof that he was in earnest.'

'Then he is not?'

'Not since I talked to him of loyalty.'

'What does he know of the word?'

'A great deal. Do not despair of him. He will return.'

'My sword will be ready.'

'Were you a king, you would use it to knight him for his services to you.' Nicholas grinned. 'They wooed him hard to get him to Shoreditch and he has gone. But he may not fulfil their high expectations.'

Barnaby Gill arrived early at The Curtain to meet his new fellows and to rehearse the scenes in *Richard Crookback* in which his comic gifts would be given full rein. A beaming Giles Randolph gave him a formal welcome before introducing him to the others. Henry Quine was delighted to see him there, patting him like a favourite dog, and most of the sharers were honoured to have such a celebrated actor in their ranks but there were some who resented his promotion over their heads and who felt that his links with their rivals was a form of contamination. To bring him in at short notice for such an important performance was a risk but Randolph took it without a second thought. Gill learnt fast and had a tenacious memory. But the core of his art was inspired improvisation.

'Clear the stage!' said Randolph. 'We will begin.'

'I am ready,' said Gill.

'Are you happy with your role?'

'Very happy, Giles.'

'The play needed more comedy to brighten its darkness.

You will be the silver lining on a dark cloud, Barnaby.'

'I will strive to please you.'

'Stand by with the book!' called Randolph.

But nobody expected that a prompt would be needed by two such experienced players. Randolph had taken the title role many times in the past and could perform it without thinking. Gill had been given a few days to study the scenes in which he featured and would already have mastered his role. It was the first time that two outstanding actors had shared the stage and the rest of the company watched with interest, conscious that they might be witnessing a historic moment.

Richard Crookback began with the coronation of its central character, who had schemed his way to the throne and rejoiced in his villainy while doing so. It was in the second scene of the play that the jester made his appearance. Summoned to entertain the king and his entourage at their banquet, the jester amused the assembly with his antics before engaging with the king in a long argument. Like so many authors, the playwright put wise words into the mouth of a fool but they were disregarded by the impatient Richard who did not wish to be told that his reign would be short.

Trestle tables were set out for the banquet and a few cups placed on them. Richard III and his guests took their place at the banquet and indulged in witty badinage. Gill, lurking behind the arras, awaited his cue. When it came, he made a bold entrance but deliberately hooked his dagger in The Curtain so that he dragged part of it with him. Several of the actors onstage laughed involuntarily but their laughter changed to cries of surprise when Gill appeared to stumble and knocked their table to the ground, sending the wine cups rolling noisily across the boards. Executing a little dance, the jester bowed low before the king and broke wind with such rasping authority that he drowned out his master's first line and produced some more unscheduled hilarity.

Giles Randolph took his role too seriously to find any humour in the mishaps and quelled his company with a regal glare before repeating his line again.

'Where have you been, my mad Gurney?'

'Gurney?' queried Gill.

'That is your name.'

'It is a strange one for a clown.'

'No matter. Let us proceed.'

'But I do not like the name of Gurney.'

'We will talk of it later.'

'I would rather settle this argument now, Giles, for the name makes me uneasy. Must I Gurney myself for two whole hours in Court? It is a foul name for a fine character.'

'Nobody has complained before.'

'I do not complain. I ask merely as a favour.'

'It will be changed, Barnaby.'

'Now or later?'

'At the end of the scene.'

'But I have the name hurled at me a dozen times or more. Gurneys will come at me from every direction to offend my ears and distract me from my lines. Give me no Gurneys, sir.'

'What name would you prefer to be called?'

'Anything you wish, Giles,' said Gill with an ingratiating smile. 'I am happy to oblige you.'

'Morton?' suggested Randolph.

'Too upright a name for a clown.'

'Bernard?'

'Too French for the jester of an English king.'

'Call him Will,' said the other with exasperation, 'or Arthur, Tom or Robert. Call him what you choose, Barnaby, but let us get on with the rehearsal.'

'I am deeply sorry,' said Gill with a show of penitence.

'What, then, will the jester be called?'

'Gurney.'

'But that is the name which annoyed you.'

'It annoys me less than the others I was offered. Let me be Gurney until the end of the scene then we can baptise the jester afresh. Will that suit?'

'Yes,' said Randolph through gritted teeth.

'Shall we continue or start again?'

'We will start again, Barnaby.'

'I am Gurney now, remember.'

'Let us start again!'

Gill bowed apologetically and withdrew behind the arras again. Controlling his irritation, the king began the scene again with a speech to his subjects, only to be interrupted by the jester who popped his head around The Curtain and smirked.

'Give me instruction, please.'

'Well?' said Randolph, breaking off from his speech.

'When I bow in front of you?'

'Yes?'

'Would you prefer one fart or two, your Grace?'

The intensity of her anguish finally exhausted Rose Marwood and she fell into a deep sleep. Martin had deserted her. It was impossible to reach any other conclusion. The man she had loved so completely that she surrendered her heart, soul and body to him was not the kind and trustworthy person he had pretended to be. Instead of carrying the child of a man whom she adored, Rose was now saddled with the unwanted offspring of a hateful deceiver. A future which once looked so bright now seemed bleak and terrifying. The enormity of her misjudgement made her fear for her sanity.

It happened in the dark, so quickly and silently that she was not even aware of it at first. Nature, in its wisdom, took a decision which Sybil Marwood had tried to bring about by more inconsiderate means. A distant pain brought Rose awake to discover herself in a clammy and uncomfortable bed. When she learnt the reason for it, she shed her drowsiness at once and let out such a cry of fear that half-a-dozen people came running to her bedchamber.

Sybil got there first, holding a candle in one hand while beating away the servants with the flailing palm of the other. She ordered her husband to guard the door while she went in.

'Mother! Mother! Mother!' screamed Rose.

'What ails you, girl?'

'I am hurting so.'

'Where is the pain?'

As soon as the flame cast its flickering light on the bed, Sybil knew what had happened. Sympathy welled up in her and she enfolded the girl in her arms.

'Do not cry, Rose. It is God's will.'

'What has happened?' asked Rose in the panic of ignorance. 'Is it all over?'

'Alas, yes.'

'Has my child been born?'

'No, Rose,' said Sybil softly. 'It will never be born now.'

'What do you mean, mother?'

'You have miscarried.'

The girl went off into such a fit of sobbing that her father came bursting in to investigate. Wearing a nightshirt, Alexander Marwood padded barefoot across the boards.

'What is going on, Sybil?'

'Rose has lost the baby.'

Honesty betrayed him. 'But that is good news, surely?'

His daughter wept more bitterly and his wife looked with such rancour that her eyes seemed to glow in the dark. Her voice came out like a hiss of steam.

'Fetch the doctor at once, Alexander!'

'But that will be costly, my love.'

'Fetch him! Our daughter needs help!'

Rain which had been falling intermittently for two days came in earnest after midnight. It turned the site into a quagmire and made the night watchmen think of their beds.

'This is madness!' said Owen Elias. 'We will be nothing but three drowned rats by morning.'

'I am drowned already,' moaned Edmund Hoode.

'Someone must be on duty,' insisted Nicholas Bracewell. 'The task fell to us tonight.'

'Why not to someone else?' argued Elias, stifling a sneeze. 'Edmund and I play at Court tomorrow. We need sleep so that we may be fully refreshed for such an important event.'

'Nick will do his share,' Hoode reminded him. 'All three of us should be abed. Do we really need to stay? Only a lunatic would be out in this foul weather.'

Elias nodded. 'That is what we are. Three lunatics.'

They were huddled under a sheet of canvas which had been stretched over a few poles to form an impromptu tent. It kept out much of the rain but enough still dripped through to add to their discomfort in the darkness. Nicholas sought to cheer his companions up with a reminiscence.

'Think of Banbury's Men,' he said with a chuckle. 'Their plan to steal our clown went seriously awry.'

'That was your doing,' noted Elias.

'And yours, Owen. It was you who went to Shoreditch to get the proof we needed. Without that, I would not have dared to confront him.'

Hoode smiled. 'Barnaby must have jumped out of his breeches when you accosted him at The Curtain, Nick. But he made amends for his folly. Schooled by you, he turned their rehearsal into such a farrago of errors that they were glad to see him go.' He gave a laugh. '*Richard Crookback* collapsed in ruins about them.'

'Yes,' said Elias, 'and the beauty of it was that they did not realise Barnaby's mistakes were deliberate. They made so many allowances for him that a whole morning was wasted. He struck a shrewd blow for Westfield's Men.'

'And made his peace with us,' observed Nicholas. 'That was the important thing. We have him back in the fold.'

'Where he belongs,' said Elias. 'Lawrence was so pleased to see him return that he wanted to kill the fatted calf. He even forgave Nick for not telling him how we learnt of Barnaby's visit to Shoreditch.'

'It was right to keep Lawrence ignorant,' said Hoode. 'He would have assaulted Barnaby and sent him racing off to the arms of Banbury's Men. Nick's device was much more cunning. It won us back our clown and left a company in disarray at The Curtain. Trust in Nick,' he said, patting his friend. 'He always knows what to tell Lawrence and what to hold back.'

The book holder felt a pang of guilt at the compliment.

Though the rain eased, their misery continued. Elias wanted to abandon the vigil, Nicholas volunteered to stay alone and Hoode dozed off to sleep on his shoulder.

An hour passed before the intruders came. Nicholas saw them first, ghostly figures emerging out of the gloom. Alerting Elias with a squeeze on his arm, he woke Hoode gently but kept a hand over his mouth to muffle any words. All three of them were soon crouched for action. Nicholas and Hoode each wore a dagger. Elias favoured a short knobbly club and he fingered it with damp hands, thrilled at the promise of action. There were three of them and they had brought ropes to move the timbers. Nicholas waited until they looped a rope over the first post in the wall before giving the signal.

Surprise was everything. The sudden attack from behind took the men completely unawares. Elias felled his man with the club, knocking him senseless with a series of blows. Nicholas kicked his man to the ground and held a sword point at his neck to hold him pinned there. Hoode was less effective. Though he jumped on his adversary and pummelled him with a fist, the man was strong and elusive. Throwing Hoode off, he scrambled to his feet and ran off along the riverbank.

Nicholas was after him like a flash, abandoning his own captive to Elias who stood over him with a raised club. Hoode got up and came to help his friend.

'Get their rope!' ordered Elias.

'Shall we tie them up, Owen?'

'I'd sooner hang the rogues! Come on, Edmund. We'll truss the pair of them up like turkeys ready for market.'

'Then what? Shall I go and help Nick?'

'He will not need you.'

Anger was lending speed to Nicholas's feet. He felt certain that the three intruders had been those who attacked him and he was determined to get his revenge. He closed on his man until the latter suddenly swung round and swished at him with a dagger. Nicholas halted and dodged out of reach.

'I should have killed you when I had the chance!' said the man, lunging at him again. 'I should have sent you where I sent Sylvester Pryde.'

Nicholas recognised a voice he heard in Shoreditch. It served to sharpen his anger. He pulled out his own dagger and circled is adversary in search of the moment to strike.

'What shall I call you?' he said. 'Martin or Henry Quine?'

'Call me what you will for it will be the last word you speak.' His jab sent the point of the dagger through the arm of Nicholas's buff jerkin but the wound was slight. 'Say your prayers, Master Bracewell.'

'Is this how Giles Randolph instructs his players?'

'He knows nothing of this,' sneered Quine. 'He is too tame for violence. His way to wreck your chances was simply to poach Barnaby Gill but I wanted to make sure.'

'By murdering Sylvester and burning our timbers.'

'There is a surer way still. By killing you.'

He feinted to jab but slashed his dagger through the air instead in a vicious semi-circle. Nicholas ducked beneath it, grabbed his wrist and twisted the weapon from his grasp. As they wrestled on the slippery bank, they lost their footing and slithered along the ground. Nicholas had a firm grip on him but Quine fought back hard. They rolled over and over until they fell with a loud splash into the river. The shock made Quine release his man to thresh about wildly with both arms and beg for help because he could not swim.

Nicholas overpowered and rescued him within minutes. He grabbed him by the throat with one hand and used the other to pound his face until there was neither sound nor resistance coming from him. Pulling his adversary by the hair, Nicholas dragged him out of the water and onto the bank. He was still panting for breath when Elias came hurrying over.

'Did you get him, Nick?'

'I got him.'

'The other two are tied up with their own rope.'

'Here's a third that can be securely bound,' said Nicholas. 'His name is Henry Quine but we knew him as Martin. He is another actor who will not play at Court for Banbury's Men. The rogue murdered Sylvester and I fancy he blighted the life of Rose Marwood as well. Give me a hand, Owen. We'll lug him back to the others.'

'But how is she now?' asked Leonard with great concern.

'Better,' grunted the landlord. 'And so she should be. The doctor charged a large enough fee.'

'When we heard her cry out in the night, we thought that she was dying. What was wrong with poor Rose?'

'Nothing, Leonard. It is all past.'

Alexander Marwood shuttled between relief at the loss of the child and sympathy for his daughter. Now that Rose had been treated by a doctor, she had some understanding of what happened to her and was far less afraid. It would take time for her to come to terms with the tragedy but it had brought her mother closer to her and that was a blessing. Marwood, by contrast, had been thrust further away from her by his wife. Such was her hostility towards him that he began to think that the nocturnal kiss which Sybil planted upon his cheek was a cruel figment of his imagination.

Leonard knew little about the mystery of childbirth. Rose was in distress and that was all that troubled him. He had lumbered into the church at dawn to pray for her. As he stood with his employer in the taproom, he tried to find a trace of guilt in Marwood.

'You wronged them,' he said quietly.

'Who?'

'Westfield's Men. You swore that one of them had lain with Rose and tried to turn them out. It was not one of the players at all but Martin, who worked here for you.'

'He was an actor with Banbury's Men!' snarled Marwood.

'Not any more.'

'He filled Rose's head with tales of wonder.'

'I thank God that she is free from the villain now.'

'So am I.'

'What will happen to him?'

'He will dangle at the end of a rope, Leonard. And I will be there to cheer on the hangman.' He looked through the window at the empty inn yard. 'As to Westfield's Men, they are lost to me and soon may be to everyone else.'

'Alas, yes!' sighed Leonard.

'Today they play at Court,' said Marwood. 'Tomorrow there may not even *be* a Westfield's Men.'

'It is unjust!' said Lord Westfield angrily. 'The advantage has already been handed to Havelock's Men. They performed their play here yesterday in glorious isolation. We have to follow Banbury's Men and perform *The Italian Tragedy* today.'

'That may serve our purpose,' said the Countess.

'How?'

'Banbury's Men have been shaken to their roots by this news about Henry Quine. They did not know they harboured a killer in their midst. Giles Randolph will have difficulty holding his shattered company together,' she argued. '*Richard Crookback* will get a crookbacked performance at best.'

'I saw the noble earl even now,' said Sir Patrick Skelton. 'He fretted with discontent. When the Earl of Banbury has no confidence in Banbury's Men, we may take heart.'

'I take none,' said Lord Westfield.

'You must,' said the Countess. 'When your troupe follows Banbury's Men, they will look bright and fresh after the disarray which preceded them.'

The patron was still depressed. 'Two plays in one afternoon is too great a burden to place on any audience. They will be jaded by drama and boredom will set in when *The Italian Tragedy* is only half-done.'

'There'll be no danger of boredom when Lawrence Firethorn takes the stage,' she said. 'He'll wake the sleepers with a voice of doom and lead his company on to triumph.'

Lord Westfield was not convinced. He was standing in a corridor at the Palace of Whitehall, conferring with Sir Patrick Skelton and the Countess of Dartford. Now that the moment of truth was imminent, the patron was suffering a complete loss of faith. His discomfort increased when Viscount Havelock strolled past with his entourage and gave his rival a polite bow. Cordelia Bartram turned her back on her former lover but Lord Westfield looked him full in the face and saw the complacent smile.

'He is safe!' said Lord Westfield. 'The Viscount knows that his company is secure. *A Looking Glass for London* has already been approved by the Privy Council. I see it in his face. I feel it in my blood.'

'It was a sparkling comedy,' conceded Skelton.

'Played by a dull and unexciting company,' said the Countess. 'With such a romp in their hands, Westfield's Men would have made the whole palace ring with laughter.'

'But we do not have such a play!' moaned the patron.

'You have a better one,' she argued.

'Let me see what I can find out,' volunteered Skelton. 'I have a friend or two on the Privy Council. I'll see how warmly they received this looking glass from The Rose. They are judicious men. I'm sure that no verdict will be made until all the evidence has been considered.'

Skelton gave a slight bow and took his leave. Lord Westfield was not reassured. The last time that his troupe performed at Court, he was able to bask in the praise of the Queen herself. This time they might unwittingly be giving their farewell performance. Perspiration broke out on his face.

'Hold fast, my lord,' urged the Countess. 'Your troupe will want brave words and encouragement from you, not this portrait of defeat I see before me. You look as if you wish you did not have a theatre company at all.'

'Then I look as I feel, Cordelia,' he confessed. 'This anxiety is sickening. If I could trade Westfield's Men for money at this moment, I would take any offer and be happy.'

* * *

They were ready. Sylvester Pryde's murderer had been caught and the men who had assaulted Nicholas Bracewell before wreaking destruction at the site of The Angel were also fettered in a prison cell. Of more immediate importance to the company, Barnaby Gill was back among them once more, having caused confusion and disorder at a rehearsal with their rivals. Banbury's Men had now staged their play at Court and Giles Randolph had somehow wrested a creditable performance out of his troupe. *Richard Crookback* was a sound choice and there had been an ovation when the wicked usurper was crushed in battle by the Earl of Richmond, wearing a tunic that was emblazoned with the Tudor rose.

Lawrence Firethorn did not underestimate the challenge. Gathering his company around him, he spoke in quiet, persuasive tones to men more used to hearing his bawled abuse or rousing rhetoric. He surveyed each face in turn.

'Gentlemen,' he said, 'we are here. Her Grace, the Queen, and all the peers of the realm are your audience today. We are truly honoured and we must show that we are worthy of that honour. Forget our rivals. They are done. It is our turn now and we have a chance to wipe all memory of Havelock's Men and Banbury's Men and any other company from the minds of our spectators. Let them see us at our best. Show them what they would lose if Westfield's Men were to perish.' He paused to let his words sink in. 'Gentlemen,' he said at length in a coaxing whisper. 'We have come through dangers and setbacks which would have daunted any other company. But we are here. Let us give a royal performance before this royal assembly and show them that Westfield's Men are the finest troupe of actors in Christendom.'

George Dart was so moved that he started to clap his hands in spontaneous applause until cuffed into silence by Thomas Skillen. They were in their tiring-house, a room off the Great Chamber, where *The Italian Tragedy* would be performed. Scenery from their rivals' play had been removed and their own scenic devices were waiting to be carried out. Sharing the occasion with a rival company, they had little time to rehearse on the stage itself and that induced a general nervousness but it was largely dispelled by Firethorn's speech. Westfield's Men knew what was at stake. They had to act for their livelihoods.

Nicholas Bracewell moved among his fellows to check their costumes and issue reminders about cues to be taken and properties to be used. He paid particular attention to the apprentices, young boys who would profit most from his reassuring presence and whose dresses and farthingales, head-tire and fans would come under the intense scrutiny of the very court ladies whom the apprentices were counterfeiting. Every detail had to be right, every move and gesture so convincing that the audience would not even realise that they were looking at four boys in female attire.

They could hear the heavy murmur of anticipation in the Great Chamber. The room was filling up. Wooden tiers of seats covered in green baize had been erected against all four walls. A canopied throne was set for the Queen on a carpeted podium in front of a high stand at the head of the

Chamber. Red velvet cushions had been set out on the floor in readiness for selected ladies to lounge and pose. The stage itself was a rectangle in the middle of the hall, some twenty feet wide and not much above twenty-five feet long. Since the play would be viewed from all sides of the arena, scenery had to be used to decorate without obscuring any part of the action.

The floor was made of polished wood, ideal for dancing and much more solid than the quaking boards on which they acted at the Queen's Head. Instead of open sky above an inn yard, they would be acting beneath an ornamented and fretted ceiling of hard plaster. Instead of competing with the bells and street clamour of London, their voices would be clarified by the tapestried walls and the solid ceiling. Hundreds of branched candles, hung on wires, stretched across the room.

Most of the audience were in position but the throne and all the scaffolds in the upper part of the room were empty, guarded by yeoman with halberds. The Gentleman Usher sounded a warning, then twelve trumpets announced the approach of the Queen and her train. Everyone in the Chamber rose to their feet and the actors in the tiring-house felt a surge of pride which was tempered with a dryness in the mouth. They were almost there. Elizabeth I, Queen of England, had come to witness their performance.

They could hear the exact moment of her entry into the Great Chamber. It was a long procession. The trumpeters came first, then the heralds in their coats of arms, then the nobles and Knights of the Garter. Distinguished foreign visitors to the palace were also included, led by the Lord Chamberlain with a white staff which he used to marshal the fifty Gentlemen Pensioners, who acted as the Nearest Guard, and who, bearing gilt poleaxes, formed a hedge on either side. The Earl of Banbury was given the honour of bearing the crimson-sheathed Sword and the Lord Keeper carried the Great Seal. Then came the Queen herself, arrayed in all her finery, sweeping majestically into the Chamber with Ladies of Honour in her wake. Only when she was escorted to her throne by the Lord Chamberlain and lowered herself into it did anyone else dare to seat themselves.

To the waiting actors, it seemed like an eternity before they were given their signal. When it came, George Dart and the other assistants swiftly carried out the scenery and stage properties. After bowing to the Queen, they set them in position then bowed again and withdrew. There was a murmur of approval at the brightly painted scenic devices. The play opened in the Great Hall of a castle. At a glance, the audience could tell exactly where they were.

The Chamberlain used his staff to beat on the floor.

'Sound, trumpets!' he ordered. 'Sound out!'

The ringing fanfare was their cue. With Firethorn at their head, the company walked bravely into the Chamber and bowed three times before distributing themselves around the stage. Those who did not appear in the first scene sat on green rushes at the edge of the stage. Book in hand, Nicholas sat among them to watch and control. Peter Digby and his consort took up their positions to the side of the stage, their instruments tuned. The Lord Chamberlain raised his staff again and boomed over the hubbub.

'Peace! Ha' peace! Let the play commence.'

Silence slowly fell on the banked audience and the music started. Owen Elias stepped out to deliver the Prologue, bowing to the Queen, before declaiming the words which Edmund Hoode had penned during the long hours of the previous night.

> *'Good friends, for friendship is our constant aim,*
> *Y'are welcome to a play that will not maim*
> *A king with crookback vile and wicked tongue*
> *Nor let a merry looking glass be hung*
> *In front of London town. To Italy we go,*
> *And there, for your delight, we straightway show*
> *What history so often sadly finds,*
> *Upright men with dark and crooked minds*
> *That make King Richard seem a silver saint,*
> *For all those layers of black Banburian paint,*
> *Which you have seen this very afternoon*
> *Splashed thick upon a foul, misshapen loon.*
> *You will not have a lock of London's hair*
> *In Italy. Dear friends, we take you there*
> *To show you lust, deceit and civil strife,*
> *To hold our Westfield mirror up to Life!'*

The first burst of applause broke and the spirits of the whole company were lifted. Even their patron was encouraged. Angered at the sight of his hated rival, bearing in the Sword with such dignity, he smiled at the mention of Banburian paint and laughed aloud at the play on Viscount Havelock's name. He was also reminded what a fine, clear-voiced actor Owen Elias was. Seated beside him, the Countess of Dartford did not let her gaze linger on the Welshman. It was Lawrence Firethorn who commanded her full attention. Magnificently attired as the Duke of Milan, he moved around the stage with an authority and grace which was breathtaking.

The Italian Tragedy proved a happy choice. It was a brilliant study of political duplicity and, since it involved Court spies from France, Spain and Holland, it enabled the audience to laugh at four different nationalities while realising at the same time that they were watching eternal traits of human nature which they themselves possessed. Firethorn was inspired as the villainous Duke, plotting, seducing, betraying, stabbing and poisoning his way through five acts of heady drama. Richard Honeydew was so moving as his hapless victim that even the Queen herself had to brush away a tear. Edmund Hoode was elevated to papal status and reinforced the Protestant prejudices of his audience with a display of scheming and manipulation. Owen Elias was the valiant hero who finally vanquished the tyrannical Duke.

It was Barnaby Gill, however, who gleaned the most applause. Relieved to be back with the company and smarting at his folly in considering defection, he was determined to atone for his mistake and pushed himself to the outer limits of his art. His timing was perfect, his gestures vivid, his facial contortions a delight and his dances a source of pure joy. The comic songs which Hoode had inserted into the play for him were greeted with thunderous clapping and the Queen's hand patted the arm of her throne in acknowledgement. Those who had laughed at *A Looking Glass for London* discovered what real laughter was.

Nicholas was proud of them all. He could rely on the more experienced actors to rise to the occasion but the younger ones and the apprentices also distinguished themselves. Even the error-prone George Dart came through unscathed. When the company brought the play to its bloody climax, the ovation turned the Great Chamber into a cauldron of noise. Nicholas stole a glance at Lord Westfield, who was smiling with joy. When the book holder looked at their patron's companion, however, he was reminded of another threat which still hung over the company. Cordelia Bartram, Countess of Dartford, surveyed the players with a glint of ownership and it was on Firethorn that her gaze rested. Even if they survived one crisis, the company would soon be confronted by another and only Nicholas could see it coming.

Lucius Kindell walked up and down outside the Queen's Head and tried to pluck up enough courage to go in. An inn which had offered him so much joy and friendship now seemed to be sealed off from him by an invisible barrier. Guilt jostled with necessity. Ashamed to show himself, Kindell knew that he must do so if there was any hope of reconciliation. He licked his lips, bunched his fists, straightened his back and summoned up every ounce of resolution. Then he went in through the gate.

Westfield's Men had just broken off from their morning rehearsal. They were in a jovial mood. Their sense of unity was forbidding to the exile. He was afraid that they would shun him as one, if not drive him away with blows and harsh words. His steps became slower and more tentative. It was Edmund Hoode who saw him first and the young playwright could detect none of the apparent friendliness Hoode showed at their last meeting. Others glowered at him, a few turned away. When he collected a searing glare from Lawrence Firethorn, the newcomer lost all heart. He began to slink off.

Nicholas Bracewell went quickly after him.

'Wait, Lucius!' he called. 'I crave a word.'

'I fear that it will come with a blow,' said the other, pausing at the gate and raising a protective arm. 'You must think me the worst species of traitor.'

'No, Lucius. You were practised upon.'

'I was, I was. Master Kitely beguiled me.'

'If you have realised that, you are already halfway to redemption.' Nicholas smiled and gave him a pat on the arm. 'Have you heard the glad tidings?'

'It was the reason that I came.'

'The Privy Council has spoken. They were so impressed by all three companies who performed at Court that they will not debar any of them. Westfield's Men have been reprieved. And there is better news yet,' he said. 'We hear that they will also renounce their plan to close the inn yard theatres. The Queen's Head may yet resound to our pandemonium.'

'Until you move to The Angel,' noted Kindell. 'That is what vexes Havelock's Men. To have another playhouse so close to The Rose in Bankside. What will happen to this inn when Westfield's Men leave?'

Nicholas shook his head in doubt then looked shrewdly at the visitor. Kindell's arrival might yet be providential.

'Why did you come, Lucius?' he asked.

'To make my apologies.'

'It is too late for that.'

'I know,' said the other, 'but I am perplexed. I made a great mistake and I will pay dearly for it.'

'In what way?'

'When Master Kitely commissioned a new play from me, I was flattered. I thought it would take me from my fledgling role. In my vanity, I dreamt of being the Edmund Hoode of The Rose.' He gave a shrug. 'It will not come. Though I beat at my brains day and night, the new play will not come easily onto the page. What I have written only saddens me and it will appal Master Kitely when he reads it. The truth is . . . I am not yet ready to fly on my own. I need another's feathers to buoy me up in the air.'

'Honestly spoken, Lucius!'

'Do not mock me.'

'I pity you,' said Nicholas, 'but I also admire you for admitting the error of your ways and recognising that you still have limitations.'

'Hideous limitations! My play is doomed.'

'What does Rupert Kitely say?'

'If it will not suit, it will be rejected outright.'

'Has he not tried to help you?'

'Yes,' said Kindell, 'but only to shape his own role into prominence. He is no craftsman like Edmund Hoode. He does not work at the carpentry of the whole piece.'

Nicholas let him unburden his woes. He was struck by the other's candour and by his genuine remorse. Kindell had been naive rather than treacherous. His crime was forgivable.

'Would you like to come back to us, Lucius?' he said.

'I dream of nothing else.'

'It may take time.'

'I will wait patiently.'

'Then do the company a service as proof of your loyalty.'

'I will do *anything*!' vowed the boy.

'How often does their patron visit Havelock's Men?'

'The Viscount attends almost every performance.'

'Then deliver this to him,' said Nicholas, taking a letter from inside his jerkin. 'Be sure that you put it into his hands yourself.'

'What shall I tell him?' asked Kindell, holding the missive and staring at its large seal. 'That it was given to me by Nicholas Bracewell?'

'No,' said the book holder. 'Tell him the truth. That it comes from a beautiful lady who desired you to deliver it in person. I was there when the lady in question penned this letter so I can vouch for her. Say nothing more than that, Lucius. It is enough.'

'He will press for the lady's name.'

'If you do not know it, you cannot speak it.'

'How will I describe her?'

'As I have. Beautiful and gracious.'

He rehearsed Kindell in his role as messenger then sent him on his way. Firethorn came sauntering across to him.

'I hope that you chastised him roundly, Nick.'

'There was no need.'

'Lucius Kindell is a villain.'

'He is a foolish young man as we once were ourselves.'

Firethorn grinned. 'In some senses, I still am. But why were you so civil to that traitor?' he said, scowling again. 'He is in the pay of Havelock's Men now.'

'That is exactly why I courted him.'

'But Rupert Kitely is as base a man as Giles Randolph. Between the two of them, they do not amount to one complete actor. As for their patron at The Rose, he made my blood boil when I saw him at Court, smiling at us as if he already knew we would be disbanded. I loathe that devious Viscount, Nick. Do you know what I will do?'

'What?'

'Ask Edmund to put him in a play, to bring the whole city's ridicule upon his head. If it is done cunningly enough, he will not sue for libel. Yes,' he said warming to the notion. 'That is a role I long to play. Lawrence Firethorn in the guise of Viscount Havelock.'

Nicholas suppressed the urge to burst into laughter.

* * *

Persistent rain turned the streets of London into a sea of mud but Viscount Havelock was not deterred by inclement weather. The invitation had been so enticing that he would have kept the assignation if the city had been swept by a blizzard. His carriage squelched its way along a wide thoroughfare before turning into a street. The rain drummed ceaselessly above his head. When they reached the designated house, the Viscount took out the letter once more, inhaled its fragrance and read its honeyed words by the light of the lantern.

It had been delivered to him by Lucius Kindell who was patently ignorant of the identity of the sender. The lady's anonymity lent a piquance to the whole evening. Viscount Havelock could not wait to meet her and to solve a mystery which so intrigued him. Alighting from the coach, he picked his way through the mud and went in through the already open door of a large house. The maid who admitted him curtseyed but was too shy to raise her eyes to him. She conducted him upstairs and into an antechamber. The Viscount was left alone in a pleasant room with branched candelabra throwing a shadowy light. When he saw the wine in readiness on the table, he rubbed his hands in delight.

Noises from the adjoining bedchamber told him that she was there and he tried to construct her appearance in his mind. He was still adding the finishing touches to his portrait when he heard the door open. Keeping his back to it, he waited until she had time to enter the room then turned to survey his latest conquest. Her beauty was striking, her attire wondrous and her perfume alluring but Viscount Havelock was proof against all of her attractions.

'Cordelia!' he exclaimed.

'Charles!' she said. 'What are you doing here?'

'You invited me.'

'I did no such thing, sir,' she said, having expected Lawrence Firethorn instead. 'You are the last person in London I would wish to see. I would sooner seek the company of the meanest beggar than lower myself to your level.'

'You insult me, Cordelia.'

'Not as much as you once insulted me.'

'Still harping on that, are you?'

'Get out, sir! Get out of the house!'

The wrangling continued apace for a full hour.

Heavy during the day, the rain became torrential at night, working in league with a fierce wind to wash London like a tidal wave. Bankside bore the brunt of the downpour. Water streamed off thatched roofs and swelled the rivulets that ran through every street. Swollen and angry, the Thames itself started to test the strength and height of its banks. The site of The Angel theatre was especially vulnerable. Ground which was already sodden after a week of rain now became completely waterlogged. As the foundations were weakened, brick walls and wooden posts began to sway slightly in the howling wind.

But the real enemy were the huge timbers themselves. Delivered by barge, they had been dragged by rope up the incline and a deep trench had been gouged out of the mud. It was now a gushing waterfall, pouring into a river that was already lapping dangerously at the remains of the derelict wharf. Wind, rain and river had no respect for angels. As the night wore on, the wind reached gale force, the rain became a deluge and the River Thames, dark and unruly, burst its bank and sent its overflow surging up the trench to meet the waterfall. The whole site was soon flooded.

Timbers which lay in readiness were picked up and borne away, walls which had seemed solid were knocked over as if by a giant hand, and wooden posts were uprooted and tossed onto the flood. As more water poured irresistibly into the site, and as the wind reached a new pitch of hysteria, The Angel theatre was swept away in its entirety and the dreams of Westfield's Men went sailing away for ever downstream.

A week wrought substantial changes in the company's position. They lost their benefactor, abandoned the notion of building a playhouse, paid compensation to Thomas Bradd, allowed Lucius Kindell back into their ranks and elected to remain at the Queen's Head. Though forced upon them, it was a universally popular decision. The Angel theatre had fired their imaginations at first but Owen Elias was not the only one to see its inherent drawbacks. They were happy to be safely back in their own home.

Nicholas Bracewell looked around the taproom at the grinning faces with a mixture of relief and satisfaction. His deft stage management had rescued them from the threat of the Countess of Dartford and The Angel theatre had been destroyed by force of nature rather than by the depredations of any rival. He was content, especially as none of his fellows would ever know how close they came to being taken over by a new and dangerous patron. When Lawrence Firethorn had talked about portraying Viscount Havelock on stage, he had no idea that his book holder had arranged for the Viscount to take on the part of the actor for an evening.

Lucius Kindell came over to sit beside Nicholas.

'A thousand thanks,' he said. 'I never hoped that I would be invited back to Westfield's Men.'

'On sufferance,' warned Nicholas.

'I know it well.'

'Work with Edmund and make amends for what happened.'

'He tells me that it was your doing,' said the other. 'You persuaded them to have me back. The offer could not have been more timely. I was thrown out of Havelock's Men by their patron himself. The letter which I gave him seemed to delight him at first but he hurled it at me when we next met.'

'You were a good messenger, Lucius.'

'Viscount Havelock did not think so. Who wrote it?'

'I told you. A beautiful lady.'

'But what was her name?'

'That would betray a confidence,' said Nicholas, recalling how Anne Hendrik had penned the missive at his dictation, her elegant feminine hand ensnaring a viscount. 'A gentleman must always protect a lady's reputation, Lucius. And this one prefers to remain unknown.'

Kindell thanked him again and went to rejoin Hoode

over a drink. The two of them were soon deep in discussion over their next collaboration. Nicholas watched with pleasure then caught a glimpse of Rose Marwood as she tripped across the taproom, now recovered and regaining something of her bloom. Leonard, too, was there, thrilled that his friends would be staying at the inn after all. Lawrence Firethorn was engaged in a heated argument with Alexander Marwood, the one yelling and the other gesticulating wildly. When the landlord stumped angrily out, Firethorn came across to Nicholas with a huge grin.

'That is what I would have missed, Nick.'

'What is that?'

'My battles with that mangy cur of a landlord. I thrive on them. With all its virtues, a new playhouse could never compare with the Queen's Head. We have lost our guardian angel but we have also lost the huge debt which the loan incurred. No,' he said with philosophical calm, 'we are fortunate men.'

'We are!' said Nicholas with feeling.

'Alexander Marwood is a menace but remember this, Nick. Better the devil we know than The Angel we do not!'

If you liked *The Wanton Angel*,
try Edward Marston's other series . . .

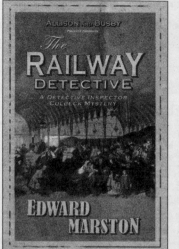

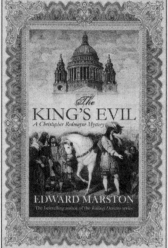

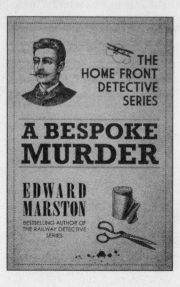